PRAISE FOR RELEASED

Released is one of the finest sequels I've had the pleasure of reading! The pacing, the characters, the heartache, the swoon—none of it is lacking in any way. A perfect second install-ment."

—AJ SKELLY, bestselling author of The Wolves of Rock Falls series and Magik Prep Academy series

"*Released* more than delivers in this action-packed sequel! Kirk-patrick skillfully draws us deeper into the lives of Fenris, Sara, Mar-cel and crew, expanding the world and adding depth to characters we already adore. With growing stakes and twists that keep you on the edge of your seat, this book will have you brewing an extra cup of coffee in solidarity and reading late into the night."

—KATEE STEIN, author of *Glass Helix*

"Sweetly sizzling, romantic, and intense, *Released* builds to the crescendo you want from a sequel. With the superhero vibes of X-Men and high-stakes you expect from an action movie, this book has everything needed to take you on a wild adventure. And don't forget that perfectly satisfying ending."

-E. A. HENDRYX, author of *Suspended in the Stars*

PRAISE FOR UNLEASHED

"Discovering who you are requires courage, and taking a chance on love risks more than just your heart. In *Unleashed*, Amber Kirkpatrick has crafted a superhero novel with romance, humor, tears, and (of course) Fen's ever-present coffee. More Fen and Sara, please?"

—CATHY MCCRUMB, bestselling author of The Children of the Consortium series

"*Unleashed* is a powerful novel penned with memorable prose and witty banter. With scenes of humor and heartbreak, Kirkpatrick delivers a story with relatable characters you'll want to remember for years to come."

—V. ROMAS BURTON, award-winning, bestselling author of the Heartmaker Trilogy

"I laughed so hard I snorted in parts. Then I nearly sobbed in others. For readers who love all the swoon, the super-human element, the heartbreak, the high stakes, the coffee, and echoes of heroism from a lost age, *Unleashed* delivers."

—AJ SKELLY, bestselling author of The Wolves of Rock Falls series and Magik Prep Academy series

"*Unleashed* is a fun, action-packed adventure story, about love lost and rekindled, hackers, killers, hidden powers, and discovering the power of true love to change even the coldest of hearts. *Unleashed* will have you fall in love with Sara and Fenris and rooting for them every step of the way, and Kirkpatrick's delightful cast of characters will stay with you long after you close the book!"
—CANDACE KADE, bestselling author of *Enhanced*

"With the perfect blend of snark and swoon, Kirkpatrick's take on the superhuman genre is refreshingly funny with a whopping shot of save-the-world and my goodness, never have sparks between characters been so seriously real. The off-the-charts romantic chemistry is beyond perfect, while realistic stakes in a near-future world seriously imagine the daunting impact of mutant abilities and how those with powers carve out their lives and protect each other. With a dose of dark roast sarcasm and signature notes of love that defies all the odds, Fen & Co. deserve their own coffee company and need to give desperate readers like me a sequel, like yesterday."
—BRITTANY EDEN, bestselling author of *Wishes* and *Hearts*

Quill & Flame
PUBLISHING HOUSE

Released

Cover design by EAHCreative

For those who fear their Gifts have been lost—
Be still, and you may hear them whisper to you once more.

PROLOGUE

A young man walked down an endless hallway lit by sickly fluorescent bulbs. He rubbed his tired eyes and scratched at the stubble emerging on his face. Shaving had not been a priority the last few weeks.

Stopping at a room he knew all too well, he hesitated before plastering on a smile and pushing the door open. Beeps and the potent smell of chemicals greeted him. They waged war against the delicious scent coming from the paper bag he carried. He stepped into the room and froze, his heart jittering. The figure lying on the hospital bed was so still, so pale. But the patient's bleary eyes opened, and his face brightened as he focused on the sight of his son standing there.

"Fen." Robert Trygg heaved a breath, fighting for the oxygen that ran up a tube into his nose.

"Hey, Dad," the younger man said. Fen crossed the remaining distance to the bed and sat beside his father, careful not to disturb any wires or tubes. "Brought some contraband. Mama Aguilar sent you some fresh tortillas."

"She is ... so kind." Robert poked a weak finger at the bag. "Tell her ... thank you."

"Hard to breathe today?"

"Harder … every day."

"I hate this place, but at least you can get oxygen here. Durgan told me you might be the last Gifted allowed in a city hospital. We're banned after this."

"Probably the healthier for it." Robert wheezed a laugh, surprising Fen. His father's laughter was his favorite sound in the world, and there had been far too little of it lately.

Fen chuckled along while he opened the bag. "You want one?"

"Not … right now."

"You sure?" Fen's voice cracked with worry, and he worked to cover the sound. "You wouldn't believe the effort it took to sneak this in. They're still warm. You need to eat more."

"I'm sure. Fen … I need to talk to you. The doctors—"

"Are idiots. How many times have I told you this? I don't know why you even listen to them."

Robert waved a hand. "You're going to have to let me speak. I can't … argue you down … anymore."

"You never could," Fen said with a grin.

"True. Just like your mother. God rest her soul." Robert shifted in the bed with a groan. "Please, Fen."

"Okay," Fen whispered, his smile fading. "Talk to me."

Robert gazed at his son with deep love and reached for him. Fen grasped his father's hand, frightened, though he didn't know why.

"I'm … sorry about baseball. And Teresa."

Whatever Fen had expected his father to say, this was not it. His throat closed up, a hot lump building at the mention of his dead fiancée.

"Teresa gone … and now your old man. Not fair."

"You're *not* going anywhere," Fen insisted.

"Yes. I am. You know it. The doctors certainly do."

"Dad, I—" He was silenced by his father giving his hand a weak squeeze.

"Durgan says he'll watch out for you. And Alicia Aguilar. Couldn't keep that woman away if I wanted to. Which I don't. She's good for you. Papers are in order for the house. You'll ... do more with it than I have. I never touched the insurance money from your mother. It's all yours. Everything else is set. You'll be fine."

Fen swallowed thickly. "I won't. Not without you. How—how am I supposed to keep going if you leave me, too?"

"Who's leaving?" chirped a voice. Marcel Aguilar sauntered through the doorway, as though he hadn't a care in the world. "Hey, Mr. T! Looking good today!"

Robert wheezed a chuckle as Marcel clapped Fen on the back and pulled up a chair. Fen scrubbed his face, struggling to maintain his composure. Robert gave him an understanding glance and sighed. "Fen ... why don't you take a break and ... get us some coffee."

"You know I hate coffee, Dad."

"I would *love* some coffee," Marcel said. "Bet we could stick some in an IV for you, Mr. Trygg. How about that?"

Robert huffed another laugh. Exasperated with both of them, Fen stood while rolling his eyes. He hesitated, then leaned over to kiss his father's forehead before grumping out of the room, digging dollars and change out of his pockets. At the vending machine, he jammed at the buttons with unnecessary violence. Regular coffee was bad enough, but this hospital stuff was the worst.

Marcel's infectious laughter drifted down the hallway and despite everything, Fen smiled. His dad was depressed about being in the hospital again, that was all. His best friend's cheery nature would snap him out of it, and they could talk about getting his dad out of here. For Fen desperately needed his father home. The ramshackle old bungalow was too quiet without him.

Lost in his thoughts, he didn't see the nurses rushing past but came to life at the sound of Marcel shouting his name. Bolting back to the room, he skidded inside. His father's eyes were wide open and staring while the alarms blared. Marcel had been pushed to a corner, a frightened expression on his face. Fen forced his way past the nurses and grabbed hold of his father's hand as he fell to his knees beside the bed.

"Dad! Dad, listen to me. You need to breathe. We've talked about this. You can't let it—can someone turn off those blasted alarms?"

"Fen ..." his father whispered. "Whatever comes. I know ... you'll always make me proud."

"Yeah, I'll believe that the next time I threaten to ditch college for the Red Sox. C'mon Dad, deep breaths. You can—you can do this. Dad, *please*," Fen pleaded.

Robert's eyes glazed over, unseeing as he gasped for air.

The alarms continued, and a doctor strode in. He motioned for the nurses to leave and clicked a few buttons on the machines. Silence fell over the room. The doctor put a hand to Fen's shoulders. "He's almost gone."

Fen willed himself not to strike the man and growled through clenched teeth. "No, he's not. I won't let him."

"It's time you accepted—"

"You think you're helping?" demanded Marcel. "Get out of here."

The doctor shrugged and left the room, muttering. Marcel turned to Fen, tears forming in his eyes. "Fen—"

"No. Not going to happen. I will *not* allow it." Fen shook his head even as his own tears began to fall. "Please ..."

Robert released one more gasping breath. When the hand Fen held went limp, he leapt to his feet. He stared at his father, comprehension settling upon him in slow waves. Turning on Marcel, he lashed out, "You! All this time, with all your healing powers, and you let this happen?"

"Fen—"

"How could you let him die?" Fen shouted.

"I can't stop death! Not everything can be healed!"

Fen spun, breathing hard, shaking. He couldn't be dead ... *Dad* ... he bent over, heaving.

Marcel reached out to his friend, but Fen shoved him back, wild-eyed. Barreling from the room, he shot down the hallway—faster and faster, until he was running, blasting doors open without touching them. More corridors, more doors before he burst outside into the cold night.

Fen fell against the exterior wall and vomited onto the concrete. Clutching his head, he moaned incoherent pleadings and accusations. Wracking sobs strangled him until his voice broke free at last.

"You couldn't have left him alone? Why did you take him too? WHY?"

There was no answer.

He fell to his knees and screamed into the silence.

BACK TO THE END

T he birds woke him first, a sweet spring clamor rejoicing in the sun rising once more.

Fenris attempted to drag the pillow over his head to muffle the sound, but intense aches and pains assaulted his entire body. He groaned and rolled over to his side.

Then he saw her.

Red hair fanned out, Sara was curled up in his bed and asleep, facing him. Grimacing in his pain, he held out one hand to stroke her cheek. Sara's green eyes opened at his touch, and she gazed at him with a drowsy warmth.

When he opened his mouth to speak, all that came out was a rusty croak. Fenris coughed and tried again. "Are you really here? Please be real."

"I think I'm real," she mused. "Why do you ask?"

"Because while we were—captured—I kept dreaming of this moment, except I would wake up and it would be—" Fear began to lace his voice as he remembered the last twenty-four hours. The torture he had undergone by that horrible woman, Josephine. Those electric guns ...

"No dreams. We're both here and safe. Together." Sara took his hand. "*This* is real."

"You stayed all night?"

"Yes."

"The scandal of it all, Red."

"I don't care. I'm not leaving you again."

Fenris's breath caught, and his throat clogged. "Promise?"

"I promise," she whispered.

He nuzzled her, dropping a kiss into her hair. "I love you."

Sara kissed him on the lips in answer. Brushing black hair away from his face, she traced her fingers along his jawline before kissing him once more. She snuggled against him, tucking her head under his chin.

He held her as tightly as he could. Despite his aches, a wave of contentment swept over him, knowing she was there. Before Fenris could begin to count his blessings, he was asleep once more.

⌒∾⁕∾⌒

The smell of coffee tickled his nose before he was fully awake, and a tired smile crossed over his face. Winking one eye open, he saw Sara sitting in bed with a steaming mug and a book.

"What'cha reading, Red?"

"Rilke. All this time, I had no idea you liked poetry."

"*Letters to a Young Poet* isn't poetry," he said, a trifle embarrassed.

"I disagree. This is the most poetic prose I've ever read."

"That ... doesn't make sense." Fenris gasped. Sudden vertigo hit him, and he couldn't breathe. Sara set her mug and book aside and crawled across the bed to him.

"Fen?"

He shook his head, trying to dash away the fuzziness that had taken over. The room blurred and spun around him. She spoke his name again sharply, and he held up a shaky hand. "Give me a minute."

"No. I want you to sit. Come on."

"Hurts." He winced as she tugged at him.

"I don't care. Sit up."

With an immense effort, he pushed himself upright while she propped pillows behind him. Immediately, the mental fog diminished.

"Better?" she asked.

"Yup," he growled, clenching his teeth against the pain.

"Hold on."

Sara was gone for a few moments before returning with another mug and a glass of water in her hands, and a bottle under her arm. Setting down the drinks, she opened the bottle and tipped out two pills. "Take these," she ordered, holding them out to Fenris with the water. He obeyed without question. Despite the worry in her eyes, she smiled as she exchanged the glass for the mug. "I added cream and sugar because I thought you could use a treat."

Fenris inhaled the aroma before taking a sip. He sighed with pleasure. "This is good. Thank you." Thinking, he scowled at the coffee, his face scrunched up. Fenris gave a huff of frustration as he took another drink. "I still can't sense them. Any of my Gifts."

Sara frowned from her perch on the edge of the bed. "It's been one day. Marcel said to give it time."

"Marcel doesn't know—"

"Perhaps not. But he is our Healer, so we need to trust he understands what is happening to you better than the rest of us."

"How much time? What if they don't come back? What if—" His mouth snapped shut as panic began to take over. Sara took his mug and placed it on the side table near the bed, and Fenris reached for her hand. "How bad is it? What they did to me?"

"Marcel and Durgan are hashing that out. As far as we know, no other Gifted has dealt with what you experienced—specialized weapons designed to decimate our Gifts? It's unprecedented. Not to mention horrific."

"Tell me something I don't know," grumbled Fenris.

"Marcel said he may need more healing sessions to catch everything. Your heart rate has been incredibly erratic. That's why I wanted you to sit up. He said the pressure from lying down could cause problems, and you were losing oxygen. It's been—" She choked on her words, eyes glimmering.

"Hey, come here." Fenris held out his arms, and with a quiet sob she fell against him. He dipped his head to kiss her cheek, but soon her lips were on his. For a moment, his pain melted away as the sweet taste of her took over his senses. She pulled back far too soon.

"Don't stop," he said. "Things were just starting to get good!"

She laughed, and the sound warmed his heart even more than her kisses. "I think that is about as much excitement as you can handle."

Fenris let out a rueful chuckle, knowing she was right. He was already exhausted. He rubbed his eyes and groaned.

"Well, this is fantastic. I'm a physical wreck and have no working Gifts."

"Fen ..." Sara whispered, squeezing his hand.

"It's weird. All these years, I've resented what happened. Every-thing being Changed took away from me." Fenris punched his pillow. "Now ... my whole identity is wrapped up in my Gifts. What if they never come back, and I can't fight Hunters? What if I can't protect you? Can you love me if I'm—"

"Stop it." Sara took his face in her hands. "You listen to me. You are Fenris Robert Trygg. You are my champion, my knight. You have the sweetest, most loving heart I've ever known, despite your best efforts to hide it. I love you for that heart of yours, not for your Gifts."

Tears filled his own eyes, and he kissed her. He hungered for the reassurance of her lips on his. Fenris was aching all over, weary to the bone, and frightened for his future, yet Sara's warmth and sweetness enveloped him in a delicious tide. He wanted to protest when she drew away, but found he hadn't the strength. All he could do was hold on to her, keeping her as close as he could.

A mischievous grin broke past his weariness. "You know, once I feel better, I don't think you can stay in my bed, or things will start to become quite awkward. We're going to have to figure out something if you meant it when you said you aren't leaving."

She sat back with a funny smirk. Fenris thought she looked as though she was hiding some secret.

"What is it, Sara?"

"I've been thinking about that."

"About what?"

"I think we should get married."

"What?"

"You heard me."

"I'm sorry, did I miss something?"

"Do you love me?"

"You know I do, but we haven't—"

Sara waved him off with her hand. "We've worked side by side for a year and know each other better than most couples who have dated for far longer. We've been through hell and back together, and we both know this isn't over. I love you, and I want to be with you for whatever comes next."

"Can't we wait—"

"No!" Tears rushed to her eyes again, this time spilling down.

"Don't you think—"

"I will not let you—let you—"

It dawned on Fenris her seemingly calm appearance since their horrific ordeal was her usual coping method, bottling things up until they exploded. Distraught, he cradled her to his chest as she sobbed against him. He let her cry, holding her and stroking her hair. After a few minutes, her weeping slowed, and he smiled when he heard a hiccup.

"Sara," he whispered. "I love you so very much. All I was trying to say was ... will you give me some time, and maybe let *me* do the asking?"

She jerked back and studied his face. "What are you saying?"

"Well, I'm kind of a traditional guy, if you've never picked up on that before. I thought I might do the proposing."

She sat there stunned and his lopsided grin broke free. So often he was the one spiraling while she remained calm. It felt good to catch her by surprise for once.

"You mean you—"

"I mean, I've known you were the one for me since the day you broke my nose. How could any man resist?"

She flung herself at him, kissing him with delight. Fenris fell back against the pillows, laughter bubbling up at her response. This one time she could overthrow him, and he didn't mind at all. But when he groaned through his chuckles, she settled down. They lay there for some time, and Fenris began to relax into sleep.

"Fen?" Sara whispered.

"Mmm-hmmm ..."

Fenris felt her tucking the blanket around him and easing away. He shifted around enough to wrap his arms around her.

"Stay."

"Always."

⸎

A loud banging on the door shattered his sleep. The room held the dusky, golden light of late afternoon.

"Go away," Fenris muttered, keenly aware of waking with Sara in his embrace. At the sound of her laughter, he drew her close for a gentle kiss and longed for more.

The bang on the door reverberated through the house again.

"I think that's Marcel," said Sara. "He said he'd come this afternoon to check on you."

Fenris sighed and planted one more kiss on the tip of Sara's nose. Sitting, he grabbed the mug of cold coffee off the bedside table and took a gulp, grimacing at the muddy taste. "What time is it? I haven't kept track of the hours."

"Give me that." Sara snatched the mug away over his weak protests. "Don't be such a baby. I'll make you some fresh coffee. It's around five, I think. I'm going to let Marcel in."

"Don't bother. He has a key—"

A tiny blonde head popped around the doorframe. Before anyone could stop her, Sophie jumped onto the bed and hugged Fenris. Sara made a move to pull her foster daughter away, but a grinning Fenris stopped her. He held Sophie and let her babble nonsense into his ear.

Marcel appeared in the doorway. "Sorry, Sara. She's been a handful, and I thought maybe coming over for a while might help. She misses you."

"Me? Fen is the one she wants! She couldn't care less about seeing me."

Despite his enthusiasm at seeing Sophie, when she began bouncing on his lap, Fenris's face went pale. "I'm okay. She's a bit ... rambunctious," he stammered, trying to hide the pain as Sara removed Sophie.

"All right. I'm going to make you boys some coffee and take this wild child outside." Sara took Sophie by the hand and led her into the kitchen. The minute they were out of sight, Fenris stopped pretending and slumped into his pillows with a moan.

Marcel studied his friend. "Well, I can lie and say I've seen you look worse ..."

"I know. Let's wait until they go outside. Grab that chair and sit down."

"Hey, you want some good news for once?" Marcel dragged the chair over and sat with a happy expression on his face. "Frances and I—well, technically her, I guess—we got another one coming."

"Another what?"

"Sheesh, Fen."

Fenris sat straighter. "Another baby?"

"Well, yeah."

"That's fantastic! Congratulations."

"Thanks—whoa, you okay?" Marcel eyed Fenris, who had gripped the edge of the bed in pain.

"Don't worry about me."

"That'll be the day. You know, Mama wanted to come today."

"Please don't let her. She'll fuss away what life is left in me. I'm thrilled about the baby. And tell Frances I said that, okay?"

Marcel chuckled, but Fenris could see worry lurking in his eyes. They sat talking until Sara returned with two mugs of coffee. Before she could hand one to Marcel, he snapped his fingers and reached into his pocket for a phone. "We found your car—it's totaled by the way—"

"I figured," said Fenris.

"At least your phone survived. Sorry, Sara. Yours was smashed up."

She shrugged. "It's just a phone."

"I know. We'll replace it as soon as we can."

"It doesn't matter," she said as she handed the other coffee to Marcel and bent to kiss Fenris on his cheek. "I have the few things I care about right here with me. Now, Sophie and I will be outside if you need us."

Feeling lit up inside, Fenris watched as she left the room.

"You've got it bad, don't you?" Marcel asked.

Fenris nodded and whispered, "You want to see something? Go look in the top drawer of the nightstand, back right corner."

Amused with the air of secrecy, Marcel poked his hand around in the drawer until he found a small box. He flicked it open and stared. "Fen—this is a—are you serious? How long have you had this?"

"Not long. A few weeks." He could see Marcel thinking hard, trying to put the timeline together. "I'll tell you everything but keep it to yourself. Not even Frances, okay? Put that away before she comes back."

Marcel tucked the sparkling engagement ring into the drawer and settled down to hear the story he had been hoping for.

⚬⚬❋⚬⚬

"Wait, she proposed to you, when all along you were planning on doing it?" Marcel cackled. "I love that woman!"

Fenris tried to laugh along with his best friend. Instead, it came out as a wheeze, and he bent over trying to get some air into his lungs.

Marcel's laughter fell away. "I'm sorry, here we've been talking while you're barely functioning. Lie back and let me see if I can find the problem." Marcel's voice dropped to his healing murmur, and Fenris relaxed into the familiar cadence. "Shut your eyes, Fen. You know the rules. I can't have you staring at me while I'm searching for the hot spots. It's too weird."

Fenris closed his eyes, weary to the bone. "You can't do anything about my Gifts, can you?"

His friend remained silent.

"Marcel—" Fenris pleaded. They had always been honest with one another.

"We rescued you from that rubble heap yesterday. I told you it could take a while. The body and mind are connected. If I can take care of one, I think the other will follow."

"I'm not the patient type," Fenris said.

"No? Really?" Marcel rolled his eyes. "Never would have guessed that. For the record, I don't think they are all going to come back at once. Although ..."

"What?"

"Nothing."

"Marcel," Fenris growled.

"Okay, but don't freak out on me. You're an Assimilator, remember? Most of your Gifts you've stolen—"

"Borrowed!"

"—*stolen* from other Gifted over the years. I do wonder if maybe ..."

Fenris opened his eyes to glare at Marcel, who sighed.

"They may not all come back." At his friend's horrified expression, Marcel rushed on. "Listen, you have powers that make you look like a comic book superhero on steroids. Even not getting them all back, you'll still be the most powerful Gifted I know."

Fenris swore to himself.

"What does Sara say?"

"She ..." Fenris smiled reluctantly. "Well, you know Sara."

"Indeed I do," Marcel said. He flinched as he found a hot, inflamed area. "You know, she might enjoy being the one with the powers for once. What she did to that building was pretty impressive."

"Wasn't it?" Fenris said with pride. "I love her."

"I know. I'm thrilled for you, buddy."

"I can't wait to—" Fenris inhaled and sat upright, a bolt of pain shooting through him. Pain and something more. Something ... dark. He clutched at Marcel's arm, panting.

"Whoa, sorry. What was that?"

"You—tell me—"

"What *did* they do to you?" Marcel said, trying to source the pain. "Can you lie back down? Fen?"

Fenris began to shake and a cold sweat broke out over his skin. His only thought was to clutch the blanket as a shield against the frigid darkness that threatened to overwhelm him. He was drowning, and there was no bringing him back ...

A warm hand was on his face, her sweet voice pulling him out of the cold. Sara gathered him into her arms. "I leave you for a few minutes and look at you. Scaring us all half to death."

"Sorry." He shivered in her embrace.

"Sara," said Marcel. "I need to finish. Keep him with us."

"Don't—" breathed Fenris, frightened of drowning once more.

"I won't let you go, my sweet Fen. Please, let's end this."

Fenris nuzzled into her neck and felt Marcel's hands on him again; Marcel's voice muttering prayers, humming, dredging the depths for whatever poison ran through him, whatever damage had been done. Fenris fell in and out of the darkness as time slipped past. Words tumbled out of his mouth without thought. He continued to shake, but Sara held him fast, whispering reassurances. Fenris heard a cry without realizing it was his own voice and—warmth flooded through him. Healing light.

One deep breath. And another.

Sara's lips were on his cheek, kissing him. Marcel's kind voice murmured, "I think it's done. Let him rest, and we'll see."

When Fenris managed to open his eyes, Sara was still holding him. Reassured by her presence, he slept.

SETTLING IN

F enris sat upright in bed, startled by a dream. He had been cold, terribly cold. Alone in the dark ...

"How are you feeling?"

He leaned into Sara's embrace, thankful for the light she brought to his heart.

"Weird. I was having this horrible dream and—" Fenris stopped, confused. He grasped the bridge of his nose between thumb and forefinger, rubbing hard. It all began to rush back to him in a flood. "That wasn't a dream, though, was it? It was real. What happened? Where's Marcel?"

"Fen, that was hours ago. You slept through the night."

"I did?"

"Yes. What *do* you remember?"

"Everything was cold, and dark. It felt like I was drowning in the darkness. Then I heard your voice ... Please tell me what happened."

"I was outside with Sophie, and Marcel began yelling for me. During his healing session, you had a seizure of some sort, like what you had before, but worse. You were screaming and ..." Sara's face went pale. Fenris tugged at her hand to continue, anxious to hear the rest. "I don't know, Fen. It was terrible. Marcel needed me to help hold you so he could keep working."

Fenris furrowed his brow, thinking. "Where was Sophie during all of this?"

"She was in your library, playing with a toy she brought with her. Whatever was going on, it didn't bother her at all. Maybe she knew you'd be okay?"

He sighed and hugged her. "I'm sorry for putting you through all this. I feel better than I did though. Stronger."

"How's your head?"

Knowing what she meant, Fenris closed his eyes and reached into his mind, afraid to find the same emptiness. But now there was something there. Something familiar, although very faint. He looked around the room before spotting a pen on his bureau. Fenris bent his will into the small object.

The pen remained motionless.

"Move," he whispered, beyond frustrated with himself.

"You're trying too hard," she said.

"I know." He sat straighter and tried to ease into it, not forcing the Gift. He closed his eyes and shivered as he felt Sara's breath on his neck.

"Relax."

"Okay. Although how I'm supposed to relax with you doing that ..." he said, staring hard at the pen. Asking, not demanding. Fenris inhaled as the pen trembled and shook. Another breath, and it lifted an inch or two before dropping with a click.

"Told you." Sara kissed him on the cheek.

"I don't know if I should be happy to have done that much, or discouraged that was all I could do," Fenris said. Despite the words, a slow grin spread across his face as he flexed his muscles, pleased to discover they no longer ached. In fact, physically, he felt good. Maybe *too* good. He glanced at Sara, who put her arms around his neck.

"Choose happy," she said.

While Fenris wasn't sure of Sara's intentions, he knew precisely what he wanted. He rolled over to pin her down, and she squealed with laughter before she fell silent at the intense look in his eyes.

"Be still," he whispered. He brushed his lips against hers but didn't let her kiss him. Rather, he dropped kisses along her jawline up to her ear with tantalizing slowness. She held her breath as he nibbled on her earlobe.

"You *are* feeling better."

"I'm hungry," he growled.

"I'll make you food."

"That's not what I'm hungry for." Fenris took another bite at her ear. Dipping his head an inch, he tickled his nose along her delicate skin before placing an open-mouth kiss on her neck. He traveled down until his teeth grazed her collarbone, causing her to gasp aloud.

Her reaction sent molten lava through his veins, his breath ragged as he brought his mouth to hers. They hadn't kissed like this in so long ... not since that rainy night weeks ago ...

"I've missed this."

"Don't talk," she murmured.

The air crackled with their energy as they kissed more deeply. His neurons spiked in ways that had nothing to do with his Gifts. Sara trembled in his arms, and he wanted nothing more than to bring her heart into his own.

But when tiny sparks burst out between them, Fenris reared back in surprise, chest heaving. "What the—what was that?"

"Fireworks—we made actual *fireworks* together," whispered Sara. She laughed in wonder. "Have you ever heard of that happening?"

"Never, although who would tell? No one would believe it."

"I'm going to ask Marcel."

"Don't you dare!" said Fenris, horrified at the idea until he caught her teasing smile. He sighed and brushed his fingers across her face. "How can I resist you?"

"You don't have to," she said.

"You're such a flirt."

"Do you mind?"

"What do you think?" Fenris chuckled. "Maybe it's better not to play with fire."

"Is that what this is?"

"When I'm with you? Definitely." He lay back against the headboard, and she rested her head on his chest. They sat holding hands, their fingers entwined. "How are we going to do this, Red? You know you can't actually stay here, not until—But I'm not going to feel good about you and Sophie alone at your place."

"You have a spare bedroom."

"I'm not sure I can trust myself with you in the house."

"Is it that bad?"

Fenris grinned. "You have no idea."

"Well, my lease comes up for renewal in a couple of weeks."

"I don't want to rush things because of a lease. That's not the way I want to do this."

"Stop worrying about getting everything perfect, Fen. You know I don't care about that."

"I do! Imagine telling our kids in twenty years that we got married at city hall because your lease was up."

"You are such a romantic," Sara said with a laugh.

"Maybe. But I only plan on doing this once, and I want to get it right. We'll figure out something, I promise." He kissed her, careful to keep a firm rein on the still burning embers of desire. "Meanwhile, I *am* hungry for food. I can't remember the last time I ate."

"I'll make you some cheese toast."

"Cheese what?"

"It's delicious, trust me."

"All right. If it's okay, I'm going to take a shower. A very cold shower."

Sara laughed, and Fenris swung his legs over the edge of the bed, standing cautiously. He was weak, but there was no pain. Whatever Marcel battled the night before had worked wonders on his body as well as his mind. At the bathroom door, he turned around to see Sara smoothing down her hair.

"Sara?" he said, as she was about to leave the room. She paused and gave him a smile that lit up his heart. "I love you."

Her eyes misted, and she came back to him, cupping his face and kissing him until he was breathless once more.

"Love you too, Fen. With all my heart."

☙❊❧

Sara hummed as she worked in the kitchen, admiring how spacious and bright the space was compared to the one in her apartment. Fenris had done a wonderful job transforming the dilapidated old house into a charming, revitalized bungalow. Not a single detail had escaped his eye, and Sara knew he had poured himself into the project.

The song on her lips died as she remembered the previous night. She shivered, wondering if she dared tell Fenris what had happened. How he had screamed and sobbed in her arms while Marcel worked over him. He had started talking in delirium, things that made no sense at first, but as they became clear, she and Marcel had stared at each other in horror. They were the dark confessions of a soul held back far too long from the light. A life lived in shadows. And then—a black mist filled the room as Marcel wrenched free whatever malignancy lay deep inside his friend. Marcel himself had cried out in surprise, babbling something about the mist and a Gift working in reverse. Sara had paid no attention to him. Instead, she had focused on her sweet Fenris, kissing and murmuring to him as he clung to her, weeping about the cold and the dark.

No, she wouldn't tell him. Fear for his life had wrung her dry the last few days, and she prayed he was past all danger. She made a choice she had made many times throughout her young life—to move forward and not look back. Sara frowned, knowing Fenris wouldn't like her locking her feelings down, but she had never seen the point of dwelling on dark things.

She started as his arms wrapped around her from behind, his warm lips on her neck a stark contrast to the cold droplets falling from his hair onto her skin. Her body relaxed into his embrace, the tension dissolving.

"Are you all right?" he whispered, snuggling her closer. "You seemed lost in thought."

She turned to face him. Despite his usual stubbled beard, he appeared almost boyish, with his wet hair falling over his forehead, tangled and messy. His gold eyes were bright behind his hair, shining with love and tenderness. "I'm fine. The last few days have been a lot to handle."

Understanding flashed across his face. "Anything we need to talk about?"

"I'm not sure. What if I said I needed to process it on my own first?"

His worried eyes searched hers before he gave a little nod, but his voice was strained when he whispered, "Just don't get scared and run away from me. I couldn't bear losing you again."

"Oh, Fen," she choked, pulling him close as his arms tightened around her. "I'll never forgive myself for hurting you the way I did. No more running away in fear," she said. "I promise."

The oven timer beeped, breaking them apart. Sara shooed him to a stool at the island, and after a few minutes, set a plate before him.

"This is cheese toast? It smells amazing."

"Yes, and here's some fresh coffee."

Fenris took one bite and groaned. Talking with his mouth full, he mumbled, "This is good."

"Well, it's one of the few things I can cook, so get used to it."

"I could live on this!"

Sara rolled her eyes. "I suppose it's no worse than subsisting on coffee for five years."

They sat in companionable silence for a few minutes, munching. While they ate, Sara debated with herself about bringing up something that had been weighing upon her heart. She took a deep breath.

"Fen? What about Sophie?"

"What about her?"

"What were you thinking would become of her after, if we ...?"

His chewing slowed, and he swallowed. She gave him space to think, as he wiped his hands on a napkin. A smile tugged up one corner of his mouth. "Did I ever tell you I was there when Sophie was born? Well, there at the house with Ted and the rest of the kids."

"What? No, you never told me that."

"It was after the Gifted were banned from hospitals. Women were scrambling to have babies at homes and midwives were slammed. Ted called because Mary was having some complications, and he wanted Marcel there in case anything went wrong. I went with him. Funny, I don't remember why. Anyway, I was right there, right outside the door when Sophie cried for the first time. Ted brought her out and ... well, I had never held a baby before. I was a mess back then, but I remember thinking how holding her was nice. Ted ... he ..."

His voice trailed off. Sara knew he was remembering that horrible night when all of Sophie's family had been killed. She reached for his hand. Fenris cleared his throat, and a wobbly smile appeared. "I'm sorry. It's still hard to think about."

"I know."

"Anyway, I always felt like I had this special connection with Sophie."

Sara made the leap. "I think we should adopt her. Together."

He sat still as her words sunk in, and then his eyes lit up. "We can do that?"

"I think so. I'm her legal guardian already. You wouldn't mind?"

"Seriously? Aside from being with you, nothing would make me happier, didn't you—"

He never got a chance to finish, for Sara had launched herself into his lap, kissing him. She could feel laughter rumbling up through his chest as his lips met hers.

"Hmm... You taste like butter and cheese," he whispered. But he eased her off his lap and stood, pacing around the kitchen. "I keep losing track of time. How long have we been away from the office?"

"The database was compromised on Thursday, and we were captured—"

"And picked up Friday morning. Marcel was here again yesterday. That makes today—"

His phone rang.

"Sunday." They finished together.

"How much you want to bet?" Fenris asked a roll of his eyes.

"Mama?"

He went to the bedroom to find his phone. A wry smile came onto his face when he picked it up.

"Hello, Mama! ... Yes, I'm doing much better. Marcel was great ..." Fenris wandered into the library, chatting away, waving for Sara to follow him. They settled down together on the sofa, Sara leaning against him with his arm around her shoulders.

"Yes, she's here. She's not left my side since—yes, we've straightened things out—I love her very much ...."

His arm squeezed her tight at those words, and she snuggled even closer.

"What? Well, you know, I have a spare bedroom—um ... well ... Mama! You gave me an idea, hold on a sec." He put the phone on mute and shifted to look at Sara. "What if you and Sophie stayed at the Aguilars? Their place is huge, and they won't mind. And I would feel much better knowing you were with other people after what happened."

"That's an idea!" Sara brightened. "For how long?"

"Not long, I promise," he said with a wink. He turned back to the phone, and they resumed their original position while he continued to talk. Sara loved hearing how light and happy his voice was as he and Mrs. Aguilar made plans. But as the conversation continued, the usual edge began to creep into his voice.

"No, I didn't go to Mass this morning. I was almost dead, if you recall—no, I'm not sassing you! Really, Mama, you have to stop—yes ma'am—no ma'am, we do not want to be raising little heathens ... Mama! Yes, next Sunday. I promise."

Sara giggled to herself as the Spanish started, knowing what was coming. Hanging up, Fenris tossed the phone onto the coffee table, breathing hard. "That woman!"

"Was she inferring our future children would be heathens?" Fenris chuckled.

"You love her."

"I do, but sometimes ..."

"Did I hear you lie to her?"

"What?"

Sara narrowed her eyes at him. "The spare bedroom?"

"You notice I never said you *slept* in the spare bedroom." Fenris grinned. Sara arched an eyebrow and he hurried on. "Listen, we've done nothing inappropriate, but I'm not sure she would understand—what—"

"You're blushing!" she teased.

"I am not," he growled. "Anyway, I'm changing the subject now. This will work out great. Until my Gifts come back you will be safer there than anywhere else."

"Why do you always say that?"

"What?"

"You've always emphasized how safe their place is. You even compared it to the office once."

"Well ..." Fenris hedged. At her exasperated sound, he fidgeted. "For one thing, some of the family have powerful Gifts."

"I've never heard of any of their Gifts other than Marcel."

Fenris remained silent.

"Fen?"

"Yeah, well, like I said. They have some rather ... interesting ones. That's all I can say, Red! You know how it goes. Until someone chooses to tell you, or you see it for yourself, it's a private thing. Anyway, there are other reasons why their house is safer. Some security measures they've put in place."

"Ugh. Way to tease me."

Fenris pulled her onto his lap and bent his forehead to hers. "If it's teasing you want ..." One long kiss, and he began to chuckle.

"What is it?"

"I was thinking, why do the movies and books always end once the couple get together?"

"Maybe because all the tension is gone, and they think no one wants to know what happens next?"

"They're missing out," he mumbled while kissing her neck. "This is definitely the best part."

"I thought we weren't doing this?"

"Well ... for a minute ..."

～❋～

The rest of the day was spent moving the most pressing items from Sara's apartment to the Aguilars. Fenris was still weak, and he chafed at his slow progress.

"If my Gifts were working, I could do this twice as fast!"

Sara hushed him with a kiss. "You're here. We're together. It's enough."

"Fine," he grumbled, but his eyes were shining.

When they arrived at the Aguilar home, Sophie rushed out to Fenris and he scooped her up, grateful he had that much strength. With one arm holding her and the other around Sara, he couldn't stop himself from grinning. The future had never looked so bright.

FRUSTRATED FENRIS

G etting to the office was more complicated than Fenris had anticipated since he no longer had a working vehicle. After some heated debate, it was decided he would drive Sara's car to the office, while she returned to her motorcycle or could borrow a car from the Aguilars when needed. Fenris disliked any arrangement that involved Sara getting back on her motorcycle, but there were few options until he could find a new car.

This issue, along with his impatience at the slow return of his Gifts and his longing for Sara, had him in a roaring state by the time he pushed in his various passcodes to enter the office.

It didn't help that the first thing he saw was the empty coffee pot.

Fenris groaned. Although he had known Sara had always been the best about keeping the coffee flowing, he hadn't realized until that moment she was the *only* person who had ever bothered. Determined not to yell at the office, he set about making a new pot.

In the midst of dumping the old coffee grounds, he slumped. He missed her. Fenris acknowledged it was ridiculous, and she would be at the office soon, but he missed her. The previous night had been miserable without her sweet warmth beside him, even if the scent of strawberries still lingered on that side of the bed. Despite his insistence on courting her before proposing, he knew he couldn't live without her one day longer than necessary.

"Hey, buddy. How you feeling?"

Startled out of his reverie, Fenris jumped to Marcel's obvious enjoyment.

"Not often I catch you by surprise. Feeling okay? Any relapses?" Fenris grunted.

"Oh, they forgot the coffee again. You know, I was trying to stay on top of it, but with you gone—"

"It's Monday morning. I've been gone since what, Thursday? How does the world fall apart in that short amount of time?" Fenris erupted. "Look at this! Chaos! The kitchen is a mess. I don't even want to think about the bathrooms. I can't leave you people for three days without—" His face softened. Marcel followed his gaze to the office doorway where Sara had just entered. She glanced around and lit up with a glowing smile when she saw Fenris.

A mug shot off from the counter and sped like a ceramic bullet for the wall, crashing into pieces. Fenris flinched. "Oops."

"Sheesh, Fen ..." Marcel muttered before brightening. "But hey, your Gifts are coming back!"

Ignoring Marcel, Fenris trotted from the kitchen to meet Sara halfway.

"Hi," he whispered. Fenris bent his head to kiss her but stopped short. They had never officially dated while working together, and he was unsure of the protocol or her expectations. He felt fifteen again, with a girlfriend for the first time and clueless how to proceed. At her bemused expression, he waffled a moment, overthinking various scenarios until settling for a light peck on the cheek. "I've missed you."

"Me too," she responded, and pulled his head down for a proper kiss. He didn't mind one bit. A light cough interrupted them, and they broke apart to see Durgan standing off to the side.

"Fen, my office. In five minutes," he said before walking away.

With a chuckle, Fenris intertwined his fingers with Sara's as they strolled to the kitchen.

"How did you sleep?" she asked.

"Terrible. Your side of the bed was empty."

"I have a side already?"

He squeezed her hand. "Absolutely."

"What if I want the other side?"

"I'm open to negotiation."

They reached the kitchen and Fenris managed to float an apple from a fruit bowl into his hands. Pleased, he took a bite while Sara made herself a cup of tea. "How's Sophie?"

"She's fine, but ..."

Fenris paused in his chewing, concerned. "What is it?"

"It's nothing. I guess I hate feeling unsettled, all the back and forth. She's had no stability."

"I know. I'm sorry about that. It won't be long, sweetheart. I promise."

With another kiss on the cheek, he left her, heading to Durgan's office. Before opening the door, he turned around.

"Love you."

"Love you more."

Fenris took a bite of apple and almost closed the door before poking out his head and calling back. "Not possible."

Some of his pleasure over having had the last word dissipated at the sight of Durgan. His boss looked terrible sitting behind his desk. Haggard, bloodshot eyes, thinner than usual. But Durgan's strained smile was the biggest sign something was wrong. Fenris sat in the one spare chair.

"You all right?"

Durgan waved him off, ignoring the question and opting for one of his own. "It looks as though you and Sara have patched things up?"

Fenris allowed himself a cautious smile. Durgan didn't return it. Disapproval almost radiated from him.

"Are you sure that's the wisest thing to be considering at this time?"

Prickles of apprehension running down his spine, Fenris straightened in his chair. "What are you saying?"

"I'm merely suggesting that perhaps hooking up with a coworker isn't the best idea at the moment."

Fenris winced at the implied vulgarity. "We are not *hooking up*."

"Look, Fen. She's a pretty girl. I wouldn't blame you—"

"We're getting married."

Durgan blanched. "When?"

"As soon as I can work everything out."

"It's that serious already?"

"Yes. I thought you would be happy for me."

"I knew you two had been sweet on each other, but this—"

"Sheesh, Durgan! A couple months ago you were practically pushing me at her. Now you're warning me against it? What's the problem?"

"You are *distracted,* Fenris!" Durgan spat out. "All the mess with that Josephine woman! If you hadn't been so caught up with Sara, you wouldn't have been trapped like you were. You would have seen it coming!"

"What's your excuse?" Fenris asked, his voice shifting into a low growl.

"I beg your pardon?"

"*You* sent me on a wild goose chase for Sophie, knowing full well Hunters don't kidnap children. They kill, plain and simple. I'll admit, I might be distracted, but let's not pretend I'm the only one."

Durgan remained silent, and Fenris fought his frustration, wishing he could access his Gift of Telepathy. Yanking his simmering temper into submission, he tried another tack, forcing a smile.

"You look tired, boss. Maybe you should work shorter hours for a few weeks. Need you feeling good for the wedding—"

"Fenris, I really don't think this is—"

Fenris jumped to his feet and angled his tall frame over Durgan's desk, causing the older man to lean back in surprise.

"Okay, you listen to me. There is no official policy on coworkers not being allowed to date, much less get married. You know I go by the rules, and I checked. If that's something you want to change, you have the authority to do so. But ask yourself first who you're willing to do without, me or your cyber security expert. Because my gut tells me you would prefer to keep us both around."

"If I didn't?"

"I'm gone."

"After all these years, all you've put into this, you would leave the Guild for her?"

"In a heartbeat," Fenris snapped.

Durgan stood and licked his lips. "Fine. I think it's a mistake, having you work side by side like that, but you're right. I can't stop you. And I can't afford to lose either of you." He walked around the desk to put a hand on his protégé's shoulders. "The news caught me by surprise, that's all. Please, sit."

Fenris remained standing, nonplussed by the sudden mood shift.

"This isn't even what I brought you in here to discuss. I'm sorry. As long as you are happy."

With a curt nod, Fenris sat once more. Durgan leaned back against his desk.

"How you are you doing? After all this mess?"

Fenris recoiled at the false friendliness of Durgan's tone but kept his face a mask. "Physically, much better."

"Are your Gifts back?"

"Some," Fenris hedged.

"You still can't hear me, though, can you?"

There was a long, empty silence. Too late, Fenris realized Durgan must have thrown something at him telepathically, and he had not heard. He grimaced. "As I said, some are better than others."

"I hate what Josephine did to you."

"You and me both."

"How painful was it? What she did?" Durgan whispered.

Fenris shuddered and turned away to look through the glass wall. He watched Sara at her desk, chatting with Marcel. "You don't want to know."

Durgan grunted and shifted back around his desk to sit in his chair. He indicated for Fenris to bring his own chair closer.

"We need to talk about what happened."

"Sara and I told you all we—"

"No, I don't mean that. I meant leading up to it. The bug in the computer. While we can thank Sara for stopping it when she did, we need more information. How did it get there? We need to figure out who planted it and when."

Fenris took a deep breath, feeling like they were arriving at more familiar territory for them both. Perhaps Durgan truly had been caught by surprise. "Didn't Sara say it had been planted when we were both gone? That would make it within two weeks after the Hollings family was killed."

"Did she clarify where it came from?"

Fenris thought a moment, his brain foggy. He had trouble remembering the hours before the electric guns had blown his memory and Gifts to bits. "I—I'm not sure. We can ask her."

Durgan drummed his fingers on his desk.

"What are you thinking?" asked Fenris.

"Erin."

"Erin, what?"

"What if she planted it while Sara was out?"

"Don't be ridiculous. Erin would never—"

"How do you know?"

"I know because ... I know the minute we start pointing fingers at each other, this whole thing is over. We've got to have faith in each other. I've spent years building this trust, and I'm not going to give up on it now."

"Your fighters, I can see. Erin has never been under your jurisdiction—"

"*Everyone* in this office is under my jurisdiction."

"You know what I mean. You don't know computers any better than I do. Do you have any idea what she does each day? Especially since Derek's death, she's entirely alone over there."

"Sara would know."

"Talk to her. See what she thinks. Well, that's all I wanted to talk about for today. Let's do lunch soon, okay?" Fenris stood to leave, but Durgan called him back. "I am happy for you, Fen. As long as you're sure."

Fenris gave him a tight smile. "I am. Thanks."

⸙

Fenris walked to his desk, deep in thought. He heard Sara's voice, but it didn't register as he slammed into his chair with a thump.

"Fen? Are you okay?" she asked again.

"I'm fine," he snapped.

Sara pulled back in surprise at his tone. Regretting his reaction, he reached for her hand. "I'm sorry—" He stopped short when he saw Erin walk past. Fenris grabbed his phone to shoot out a quick text and then bent his head down close enough to whisper into Sara's ear. "Can you come with me for a little while?"

"We just got here!"

"Please, Sara," he pleaded, throwing as much urgency into his voice as possible and hoping she heard it. Her green eyes widened, and she nodded. The two slipped out of the office, and Fenris guided her down the street, his arm hooked into hers.

"Where are we going?"

"The coffeehouse. Marcel will be meeting us in a few minutes."

"Since when can you communicate with him without speaking?"

Fenris smiled and held up his phone.

"That's who you were texting?"

"Yeah."

Nothing more was said until they arrived, and after scanning the space for any danger, Fenris relaxed. "Can I get you anything?"

"Coffee is fine."

"I love that you're drinking coffee." He hesitated, and his lopsided grin broke forth. "Can I get you something different? Get you to branch out a bit?"

Fenris felt the tension in his chest ease when Sara laughed and stood on her tiptoes to kiss him.

"Surprise me," she said with a wink, and she left his side to grab a table in a quiet corner. A few minutes later, he joined her with an exasperated huff.

"Is he late?"

"Not yet. I told him to come a few minutes after we left. I didn't want us all leaving the office at once."

"What's going on?"

"Hmm, tell you in a bit. Here." Fenris shoved a drink at her unceremoniously. "I hope you like it."

Sara took a whiff, and her eyes lit up. "Chocolate in coffee?"

"You've missed out on so much, Red." She took a sip and moaned. His breath caught. "You have some whipped cream on your nose ..."

He brushed his thumb over her nose and leaned in for a chocolaty kiss. For the second time that day, a cough interrupted them.

"Sorry to intrude." Marcel drew up another chair with a grin.

Fenris sighed as he sat back. Gathering his thoughts, he waved at Marcel to scoot closer while he took a good look around the coffee shop. With his more advanced Gifts shut down, he fought the frustration that he couldn't ensure security as well as he was used to. "Keep your voices down. No telling who could be here."

"Getting paranoid, are we?"

"You would be too if you had been tortured by Josephine. Now listen. We need to talk about that computer hack job from last week. Sara, can you give me anything that might help?"

"There's nothing you don't already know."

"Except my memory is completely shot. You need to help me out."

"I can tell you it was planted weeks ago."

"Do you think it was on a timer, or did someone pull the trigger that day?"

"It was set to go off at a precise time. The virus was slow moving, thank heavens. Don't you remember how we wondered if maybe getting into the database wasn't even the goal? It might have been bait to get you out of the office."

"Why am I here?" Marcel grumbled.

"Wait a minute," said Fenris. "Durgan wanted to know where the virus came from."

"How it got in our system, you mean? I have no idea, but I will be checking into it."

Fenris turned to Marcel. "Durgan suggested it might have been an inside job."

"You're joking."

"I wish I were. What does your gut say? Anyone in the office?"

Marcel sat back, considering the matter for several minutes. Fenris was patient, trusting in his friend's intuition. Marcel knew the staff better than anyone, given his enjoyment of chitchat and gossip. Finally, he shook his head. "No way."

Sara narrowed her eyes at Fenris. "You aren't saying everything. What are you holding back?"

"You know me too well," he said with a wry smile. "What would you say—based on computer proficiency—could Erin have done this?"

"What?"

"Durgan wondered. Since she works alone with the database and computers."

Sara scoffed. "That's ridiculous. Durgan can think what he wants, but she doesn't work alone. I work with Erin every day. In fact, I would say we are a team. She would never betray us."

"You've had your run-ins with her."

"Sure. And while I love you, you aren't always a joy to be around either, Fen."

Marcel guffawed until a look from Fenris shut him up.

"My point is," Sara continued, "We all have our moments. Being annoying doesn't make a person a traitor."

"Fair enough."

"Also, Erin doesn't have the computer literacy for that degree of hacking. She's good but not *that* good."

"You sure she couldn't hide it?"

"Not possible."

"Even if she could," Marcel inserted. "Why now? She could have done it anytime over the last few years. It makes no sense."

"No, it doesn't. Even if Erin's never been a favorite of mine, I would trust her with my life. Especially after what happened with Derek." Fenris rubbed at his temple, which was starting to ache. He caught both Sara and Marcel watching him with concern and dropped his hand. "I'm fine, just—tired. Let's leave it at this today. Both of you keep your eyes and ears open, okay? Can I buy you a coffee, Marcel?"

༄

Fenris watched Marcel until he was out of the door before whipping his head back to Sara. "Am I really that much of a pain to be around?"

"What?"

"You said, and I quote, 'You aren't always a joy to be around either.'"

Sara laughed. "At the office, this is true. Sometimes. But alone with you ..."

She brushed her hand over his cheek, her green eyes sparkling. Fenris swallowed hard. He sidled closer to her, whispering in her ear. "You know, there's a park around the corner. With benches. There's one hidden away behind an oak tree—"

"Fenris! We have work to do!"

"Ten minutes," he pleaded. "Give me ten minutes of kissing you without interruption, and I promise, I'll behave the rest of the day."

"Let's go."

ROBERT'S PIER

Marcel had been searching for Fenris for a good fifteen minutes when Sara suggested he check the practice room. He trotted up the stairs and found his friend crouched down on his knees with his hands resting on the floor. Fenris was gasping for breath.

"You okay?"

"Yeah."

"You don't look like it."

In a fit of frustration, Fenris slammed his fist onto the mat and swore.

"Better not let Sara hear you talk like that," Marcel chided, unphased by his temper. He strode to a stack of folding chairs leaning against the wall. Taking a chair and kicking it open, he sat while Fenris struggled to his feet.

Fenris shot Marcel a withering glare. "Don't tell her about this."

"What's going on?"

"I was trying to work with my Gifts—*any* Gifts—and ..."

"I thought some of them were back?"

"I can float a few little things. Nothing that matters in a fight."

"You need more time."

"It's been weeks!"

"Two weeks. We have zero experience with those weapons. I have no idea how long it will take for them to come back—"

"Or if they will come back at all. Right?"

Marcel sighed. "Right."

Fenris groaned and ran his hand through his sweaty hair. Marcel cautiously ventured to another topic. "I'm sure Durgan told you we've had a team going through the debris of that warehouse, where you and Sara were—"

"And?"

"They've found some bodies in the rubble. Two men."

"There were three guards. Josephine?"

"Nothing yet."

Fenris began pacing the room, muttering to himself.

"Fen, I think you need to cut yourself some slack. Take a break." Fenris's face went a shade redder, and Marcel rushed on. "I mean, you may need to decompress a bit. You've been going at it pretty hard. I bet you haven't even given yourself a chance to think about proposing to Sara."

Fenris yanked a second chair away from the wall, unfolded it, and sat down across from Marcel. It was true. They had gone on their long-delayed date, and it had been everything he had hoped it would be. But since that night, he had spent almost no time with Sara outside of the office. "How can I think of proposing, when I can't even ..." he held his hands out and glowered at them, before slumping.

"You know she doesn't care about that."

"*I* do."

"You're a mess. You have this beautiful woman who wants nothing more than to marry you, and here you are dithering because of a few minor details."

"Minor—details!" Fenris spluttered.

"Come over this weekend. Sunday lunch. Or dinner if you want. Let's all hang out, have a few beers, and relax."

Fenris took a deep breath. "Okay."

"Yeah? That's a yes?"

"Yes, I'll come. You're right. I've been so busy I haven't even spent much time with Sara and Sophie. This will be good."

Marcel brightened and clapped his friend on the back.

"But Marcel, I mean it. Don't tell Sara about this. About how pathetic I am."

"You should have more faith in her. She doesn't love you for all that."

Fenris shrugged and headed for the showers.

꩜

Despite his dislike of summer, Fenris had to acknowledge that Sunday afternoon was a beautiful day. At least the lush landscape surrounding the Aguilar patio made the heat bearable. He regretted not bringing his swimming trunks and wondered how Sara would look in a bikini. Pushing aside the vision that danced through his head, Fenris spent some time playing with Sophie, tossing her into the pool as she shrieked with delight. Eventually, he left her to fill his plate with some delicious *barbacoa*.

"What seasoning did you use for this, Pops?" he asked Mr. Aguilar, who had been in charge of watching the meat since the evening before.

"A bit of this, a bit of that," said the older man with a smile.

"Someday, you're going to have to let me in on your secrets. I want to be able to cook this for Sara."

"The day you propose marriage like a man, that is when I will start to teach you."

Fenris rolled his eyes. "I have proposed before, if you recall."

"Bah. You were a big, lanky kid proposing to a child. Not like our Sara."

"Oh, she's *our Sara* now?"

Mr. Aguilar winked and turned the meat over. Fenris knew he would get nothing further out of the man and wandered off to the courtyard closer where the ladies were chatting in a cluster. He came in behind Sara and leaned over her shoulder to kiss her cheek, but Frances pushed him away.

"Girl talk! Go away, Fen."

"I want to see Sara."

"You can have her later. We're talking about things that cannot be discussed with a man around."

"Don't be ridiculous," Fenris fumed. "I came here to spend time with my—girlfriend—" He fumbled over the word. It seemed a shallow expression for what she meant to him.

"Ha! Make her your wife, and I will listen to you."

"Frances, I swear—"

"Are you actually thinking you can tell me what to do, Fenris Trygg?"

"I—" He broke off. As a bachelor, Fenris had a healthy fear of pregnant women and their moods, and Frances seemed more riled than typical. He decided discretion might be the better part of valor. Still, he fisted his hands in frustration.

Sara broke away from the ladies and took his hand in hers, leading him away. After giving Frances a smirk of victory, Fenris kissed her with a sigh of relief. "Alone at last."

"Come with me," she said. "I want to show you something."

She led him from the courtyard, past the pool. Reaching the quiet expanse of yard, Fenris saw Mrs. Aguilar waiting for them and felt his patience sorely tested. He had hoped for some time alone with Sara.

She saw his scowl and laughed. "Don't worry, you'll like this."

"Not as much as ..." He kissed her once more. When she pulled back, her face was flushed.

"Stop. I need to concentrate."

"On what?"

"You'll see."

They reached Mrs. Aguilar, who beamed at them both. "Such light between you two! Are you ready, Sara?"

"Yes."

"What's going on?" asked Fenris, his curiosity getting the better of him.

"Mama's been working with me on my Gift. Helping me learn to control it better. We thought you might like to see it."

Fenris fell into a state of anxious conflict. Mrs. Aguilar was powerfully Gifted, far more than anyone would ever assume looking at her. Few people knew the full extent of her various Gifts. Fenris had often imagined she would have made a good street fighter had she been younger. But her most valuable Gift was the ability to enhance and train younger Gifted. Given what he had heard about Sara's Gift, this would be worth seeing. Yet it tore his heart that he had nothing left in himself. So in the face of Sara's enthusiasm, he merely grunted his assent.

"Show him, *mija*."

Sara took a deep breath, and as she exhaled, a golden bubble emerged from her hands, growing until it formed a dome-like shape before them.

"Watch the melon, Fenris," Mrs. Aguilar said, pointing to a large watermelon set up on the garden wall. A burst of light shot from the sphere to the melon, the impact causing the hapless fruit to explode it into a mess of red and green juices.

"Wow," Fenris whispered, and he marveled at Sara's Gift. "An offensive Shield. I've never seen that before. Can you move it?"

"Yes. Wait ..."

Fenris could see how much using her Gift was costing her. The golden bubble simmered in a liquid state until they were enclosed within its protection. Fenris took a step forward and placed his hand on the Shield wall, and it repelled him. No escape then; it blocked from both directions. He touched it again and closed his eyes, feeling it out, wishing ...

With a sudden whoosh, the Shield collapsed, and Sara cried out. Fenris ran to catch her in his arms. "That was amazing, sweetheart."

"I feel like I should be able to hold it longer," she groaned.

She was trembling all over with the exertion. He kissed her forehead. "No. I'm so proud of you. Thank you for showing me."

"I'm curious, Fenris," said Mrs. Aguilar. "Why did you never bring Sara to me before?"

Fenris stiffened, and Sara glanced between the two before asking, "What do you mean?"

"When your Gift first appeared, Fenris should have brought you to me at once. I might have been able to bring it out much sooner."

They both looked at Fenris. He almost squirmed.

"I—okay, I wanted to do it myself. To teach her. To be the one to—I should have—"

Sara placed a hand over his mouth. "It's okay."

"I'm sorry," he whispered, kissing her fingertips.

"Let's discuss you, Fenris," said Mrs. Aguilar.

"What about me?" he asked, startled.

"Marcel has told me of your troubles. Your Gifts have still not returned?"

Fenris sensed Sara's gaze piercing into him. Feeling strangely trapped and betrayed, he backed away a few feet. The sound of the family laughing in the courtyard caught his attention and he began to stalk toward them, making a beeline for Marcel.

"Marcel!" he yelled. "I told you to keep it quiet."

At the sight of his friend blossoming into an outraged temper, Marcel held his hands up. "You told me not to tell *Sara*! You never said anything about Mama. I thought she could help."

"Fen, stop," Sara pleaded. "I already knew."

Fenris halted with a jerk. He moaned in protest but didn't resist when Sara put her arms around him. She kissed his cheek. "My sweet Fen, did you really think I didn't know?"

"I had hoped you didn't." He swallowed hard.

She put both hands around his face and forced his eyes to meet hers. "I've told you that doesn't matter. Do you have so little faith in me?"

"I have little faith in life. It's not you."

"You have to trust me. Trust our love."

"I know," he muttered.

She entwined her fingers with his and turned to Mrs. Aguilar, who was standing apace, watching them both. "Not today, Mama."

"As you wish, *mija*." To Fenris's surprise, Mrs. Aguilar inclined her head to Sara. "He's yours to manage now."

"Or will be, if Fen ever works up the courage to propose," Marcel yelled from the safety of the courtyard, grinning.

Fenris swore explosively. Frances gasped. Mrs. Aguilar crossed herself and smacked Fenris across the head. He might have been in a rage, but she was a petite fury herself. "You will not use that word in this house!"

"And I won't be harassed and bullied into proposing to my future wife before I'm ready!" Fenris bellowed back.

"Fen ..." Sara murmured, blushing.

A rush of desire flooded over him with such strength he staggered back a step. Without analyzing his actions, he grabbed her hand and began hauling her to the garden gate.

"Uh, where are you going?" Marcel asked, confused.

Sophie ran to Fenris and tugged at his hand. He raised his eyebrows questioningly before sinking into a crouch before her. She whispered into his ear. Fenris grinned and whispered something back. A wide smile came over her face. Satisfied, he rose and took Sara's hand again.

"Come on, Red."

"What—"

He kissed her before breaking away breathless. "This time, trust *me.*"

Eyes sparkling, she waved farewell to the Aguilars.

⸙

Once driving down the road, Fenris let out a deep breath.

"Are you really that mad?" Sara asked.

"I was a little bit. Not now."

"Where are we going?"

"I'm going to take you to—well, you'll see." He smiled and gave her hand a gentle squeeze.

"So, it's a surprise?"

"I guess. You might not understand at first, but it's a special place to me, okay? It will be easier to explain when we get there."

"What was up between you and Sophie?"

"That's between Sophie and myself, thank you very much."

"That's not fair!"

"All will be revealed soon enough. Relax. We'll be there in about twenty minutes."

"I'm dying of curiosity!"

He chuckled. "You'll survive."

It was a beautiful day for a drive. They were easy in each other's company, chatting. Fenris did his best to push down the anxiety always threatening to coil up inside. Sophie had erased most of the doubt that lurked in his heart, and for once he wanted to embrace the future with open arms.

They came to a fishing shack with a long pier extending over the river. Fenris drove into the small parking lot with several old, banged-up cars and a few trucks.

"We're not going fishing, are we?" asked Sara.

"Have you ever fished?"

"I have not."

"Well, I suppose it's time to fix that."

"No! Are we really?"

Fenris broke down laughing. "Don't worry. I didn't bring you here to fish. Besides, I don't have my gear with me. Someday I'll have to taking you fishing though. It would be fun."

He took her hand, and they walked down the pier. Men, mostly seniors, were scattered along the rail with fishing poles. Quite a few acknowledged the young pair with smiles, and others called out to Fenris by name. He came to a stop at a low, wooden bench along the far end of the pier. After checking it for any fishy remains, he sat and pulled her down to sit alongside him. The familiar slap of the waves on the pier was relaxing. Fenris kept his gaze on the river until he was ready to break the silence.

"This was my father's pier," he said. "Well, not *his*, of course. It's where we always went fishing. If I wasn't playing ball, this was our weekend place. A lot of the guys you see here were his cronies. Some of them have known me since I was ten or eleven. After he was gone, I kept coming back. Sometimes to fish, sometimes to remember or talk to him. He feels more real to me here than standing over a cold stone in a cemetery."

"You miss him terribly, don't you? Even now." Sara squeezed his hand.

Unable to speak for a moment, Fenris nodded, fighting to control his emotions. He had wept many tears on this bench over the years. Today, he wanted to be happy.

"Can I tell you a story?" he asked.

"Is it a happy one?"

"I hope so."

"You hope?"

"You'll have to help me with the end," he said with a smile. Then he sobered. "It does begin sad, though."

"As long as it ends happy, I can take a sad beginning."

"Okay." Fenris took a deep breath. "It begins the night the Hollings family was killed."

Sara flinched.

"I told you it began sad."

"I know."

"When you sent me away the next morning—"

"Fen, I—"

Fenris brushed a feather-light kiss on her lips. "It's okay. Let me finish."

She sighed and shifted to be closer to him.

"I was hurt. I felt … betrayed. I had been falling in love with you for months but was too scared to admit it. It was stupid. Then you sent me away, so I shot off for San Francisco in a fit of temper. I was miserable there—wandering the streets, at a loss for what to do next. That's when I found this."

Fenris took a small black box from his pocket. It was covered with cracked, ancient leather, with a tiny metal hook looping through a clasp.

"All I could think about was how much I wanted to buy this for you. It seemed ridiculous. We had grown close, yet we had never actually dated. I knew I loved you, that you were the one for me ... Anyway, I stomped off in a tantrum, angrier than ever. Except I couldn't stop thinking about it, or the idea it represented. To be with you, to love you, to take care of you.

"I went to see the Red Sox play the Giants, and that's when you called me in the middle of the game. It lasted what, a minute? Still, that call changed everything. My heart beat again. As soon as the game was over, I ran back to the shop and bought this. For you."

He turned to look her in the eyes, which were sparkling with tears.

"I took a little more time and came back. Afterward," he smiled ruefully, "You put me through a few miserable weeks. Despite that, I never stopped believing it would happen for us. I wasn't sure when or how it would work out, but I knew it would."

He bent his head to hers, heart pounding, voice hoarse. "Sara, I'm not a man who has lived with a great deal of hope for a happy life. I don't deserve you. I never did. Especially now, without—but I trust our love. With you, I have hope." He flicked open the box, and the sunshine struck the ring, sending tiny darts of light dancing from the oval sapphire set with small diamonds.

"Can I—see if it fits?" Fenris knelt and slid the ring onto her finger while his own hands trembled. His eyes flashed up. "It fits. *We* fit."

"Fenris ..." she choked out.

He clasped her hand and placed it over his pounding heart. "Sara Rachel Gardien, protector of my heart and keeper of my soul. I can't promise it will be easy, not with the world we've been given. I *can* promise to always love you. Will you marry me?"

Sara sat there, silent. Tears fell down her face.

"Why are you crying?" he demanded, flustered and anxious. "Is that a yes?"

"Yes!"

His own eyes filling with tears, Fenris gathered her into his arms as an unfamiliar sensation bubbled up inside his heart, better than any Gift he had ever known.

It could only be joy.

WHEN SPARKS FLY

F enris released a yell before falling to his knees in frustration.

Mrs. Aguilar placed a hand on his shoulder. He flinched at her touch and she jerked her hand away. "Fenris, *mijo*, you are trying too hard."

For days, the tension had been building up in Fenris. While he had recovered physically, his Gifts still lagged behind, and he found himself back in training with Mrs. Aguilar. She had been the one to help him process the Changing years ago, when he was assaulted with a new Gift every few weeks before anyone understood what was happening to him. Now, she worked with him to recover what he had lost. It was exhausting, and he despaired of ever regaining anything more than the most trivial of his powers.

The irony wasn't lost on Fenris. For years, he had resented being one of the Changed, to have his previous life stolen from him, and here he was struggling to get them back. He was ready to snap.

"Of course I'm trying too hard!" He jumped to his feet. "How can I marry Sara if—if I can't protect—"

"Fenris," murmured Mrs. Aguilar. "Be *still*. Your restless nature is not allowing you to focus."

"I am focused," he said through gritted teeth.

"Not on the right things. Listen to me." The woman took his face in her hands and jerked his head down to hers. "Love. Focus on love."

"What do you mean?" he asked. He was ashamed to hear his voice quivering.

"You are thinking of your Gifts with anger, with vengeance, even rage. Call them forth with love. Focus on your desire to protect those around you."

Fenris stood straighter, considering her words. It was true that since his encounter with Josephine and losing his Gifts, a relentless anger had been gnawing at his heart without mercy.

"Okay," he said. "Show me."

"Think of Sara. Sophie. Marcel ... Any of those you would give your life to protect. Think of them. Protect them."

Fenris stared at the large watermelon twenty feet away. It was ridiculous trying to imagine it could cause any harm. "This is stupid," he muttered.

Mrs. Aguilar smacked him across the head. "Do it."

After a glare at her, he focused on the melon. Shutting his eyes, he called up the memory of that horrible night, when a man had held Sara with a knife to her throat. The fear of losing her—

Inhaling sharply, he opened his eyes and drilled his powers at the hapless melon. A satisfied grin came over his face as it exploded into a hundred pieces. He glanced at Mrs. Aguilar and she nodded.

"It's a start, *mijo*. Again."

⸎

The next few weeks were some of the happiest Fenris could remember. As he continued to work with Mrs. Aguilar, his Gifts
began to return in rapid succession. While some took longer to
reach full strength, he was pleased to find others returning even
stronger than they had been before.

Every spare moment he had was spent with Sara and Sophie,
building up a family dynamic as much as possible, given the circumstances. Even though Fenris longed for more time alone with
Sara, it was important to them both that Sophie feel safe and
secure.

Mrs. Aguilar watched and prayed over the fledgling family, her
joy tempered with the knowledge that life in their world was frag-
ile.

༄

Sara had been relieved her relationship with Fenris had not gar-
nered much attention at the office. Indeed, Erin merely snarked
to Sara one day, "I thought you guys had been dating for months
already."

Sara laughed, watching Fenris on the phone across the room. "It
was complicated in the beginning."

"I can imagine. Well, you can have him. I don't go for the broody
types."

"He's not like that, not when we're alone," Sara said. She
thought a moment. "Well, at least not as much."

"I bet," Erin snorted. Dropping her voice, she asked, "How's the
kissing?"

"*So* amazing."

"Huh." Erin studied Fenris as he continued to talk on the phone. He saw both women gazing at him and raised a suspicious eyebrow. Erin laughed. "Yes, I can see that. He has a lot of fire, that's for sure."

"What about you?"

"Me? I'm not most men's type."

Sara heard a wistful note in Erin's voice and took a moment to scrutinize her colleague. Erin was short and a little on plumpish side, but not unattractive. Sara suspected it was her sharp tongue more than her looks that drove men away. Still, some men liked that. Sara considered the few single men she knew, determining which among them might enjoy Erin's razor wit instead of being threatened by it. The list was short, and she doubted any of them—a lightbulb lit up in her head.

"What about Toby? He's sweet."

"Adonis? He's gorgeous and a lawyer. He could have any woman he wanted."

Despite the dismissal, Sara caught the sparkle in Erin's eye. Her thoughts were broken by the sudden appearance of Fenris.

"Should I be afraid to ask what you two are talking about?"

"Only how wonderful you are, my sweet Fen." Sara laughed, pecking his cheek.

"Don't be ridiculous," he muttered, but a reluctant smile emerged.

A sudden shout made all three jump, and Sara peered in the direction of Durgan's office. Through the glass windows they could see him gesticulating while on the phone, his voice raised in anger.

"He's getting worse," she whispered to Fenris.

"I know ..."

Durgan slammed the phone down and saw the others staring at him through the window. He stalked out of the office and toward the building's exit, yelling, "Don't you have anything else to do?"

He almost ran over Marcel, who was coming in late, as usual. Marcel dodged his boss and made a beeline for Fenris. "What now?"

Fenris shook his head. "I wish I knew."

Sara slipped her hand into his. Despite the sweet look he gave her, she could see the concern in his eyes. "What are you thinking?"

"I don't know. Maybe Durgan was right when he said I was distracted. I feel like there is something—something obvious I'm missing. It's frustrating." He shrugged and groaned at the movement, putting his hand to his waist. Both Marcel and Sara looked at each other in surprise.

"What's up?" asked Marcel.

"Nothing, just a little ache from—" Fenris stopped and turned his attention to Erin. "Were you ever able to figure out that gun Josephine used on me?"

Erin lit up like someone had handed her an early Christmas present. "Yes! It's the most fascinating thing I've ever seen. I've broken it down and drawn up some schematics."

She waved at them to follow her to one of the conference rooms on the opposite end of the building. The unused room was a perfect place for her to spread out all the drawings and pieces of the gun as she broke it down bit by bit. Marcel gave a low whistle at the sight.

"This is impressive, Erin," Fenris said, looking over the display. "What can you tell me about it?"

Erin fiddled with a small contraption on the table. Sparks flew and a crackle of electricity filled the air. Fenris jumped back, swearing.

"Stop it!" Sara snapped, putting her arm around Fenris.

"Sorry, it's a taser," said Erin, abashed. "I was using it for comparison and research."

A cold sweat broke out over Fenris. "Just … tell me what I need to know."

"Right. What Josephine's crew used in their guns was not pure electricity. I knew it couldn't be based on what you told me. I don't care who you are, you should have been long dead with what you described. When I took what remained in your body, it didn't feel normal. I mean, electricity is kinda my thing. I should know. It's some new variation, an altered electrical current that affects the overall body less while frying the electrodes in the brain."

"That makes sense, given what I had to deal with later," said Marcel. "His heart was affected like all muscles from the stimulation, but it was his brain that suffered the most."

"What I can give and take with my Gift—I'm going to demonstrate, Fen, don't freak out." Erin held her hands up, facing away from the rest, and shot out a current of electricity. Despite the warning, Fenris flinched. "That's your regular, garden variety electricity. Now this" —Erin fondled the gun and almost crooned— "We are talking about something else. An entirely new creation. I mean, enough current will stop your heart and kill you—"

"Erin," Sara hissed. There was no mistaking the ice in her voice. Erin faltered for a second.

"Well, it would kill you if you used enough on the highest setting. My guess is they used the lower settings, for the most part. Maybe a burst or two of the higher end."

"I need to sit," Sara said. Fenris knelt at her side and took both her hands into his. "I'm all right," she reassured him. "I was remembering when they turned all three of those guns on you. You slamming into the wall. The blood. It was—"

"Hey, we got out of it. We're both okay, right?"

Marcel raised his hand. "Question? Who was behind these? Does anyone know?"

"No," Erin answered. "This is a highly exclusive branch of technology. I used to keep up with who was at the top of the field, but I've lost track in the last year or two. My guess is there are only a handful of people in the world who have the background and intellect to invent something like this."

"Anyone Gifted come to mind?" Fenris asked, still kneeling before Sara.

"Not here in the U.S. or Europe. I'm not familiar enough with those in Asia. Whoever it is, I would love to meet him. Or her." She brushed her hands over the pieces of weaponry, almost a caress.

Fenris shuddered. "All right. Enough fun for today," he said, standing and pulling Sara up with him. "How are you?"

She gave him a weak smile. "I hate that thing."

"Me too."

"I can't shake this feeling it's not over, Fen."

He cuddled her close. "I know. Talking about all this doesn't help. Let's get out of here."

Erin had gone ahead, allowing Marcel to whisper, "It's freaky, how much she admires that thing."

"Yeah, I wish she wasn't quite so enthused about it," Fenris said.

Sara scoffed. "Her entire Gift is centered around electricity. Do you expect her *not* to be interested?"

"I guess not. How about lunch, Red? I need something to settle my stomach."

⚜

"Fen!" A voice boomed in the cavernous office space as Hugo made his way to the kitchen.

Fenris swallowed the last of his sandwich and stood to clap him on the back. "What are you doing here?"

"I wanted to see Durgan. You know where he is?"

"No. He left a while ago. Not sure when he'll be back."

"No biggie. Hey, have you recovered from the other night?"

Fenris grinned and opened his mouth to answer before choking back the words when he remembered Sara was sitting beside him. He cringed when she asked, "Recovered from what?"

"Ah, it's nothing—"

Hugo laughed. *Loudly.* "'Nothing', the man says. Nothing more than an epic showdown the other night with a pack of Hunters. They should make movies about us."

"Oh, should they?" Sara asked, exhibiting nothing but sweetness and curiosity. Fenris knew better. He would pay for whatever was coming. With a smile, Sara urged Hugo to continue. "You know, Fen never wants to tell me these stories."

"And we definitely don't need to be telling this one," Fenris rushed to add.

"Why? This is a good one! There were what, eight, nine Hunters? Way more than we should have been dealing with, just the two of us, but there's no stopping this man when he gets his temper riled. After one of them swiped that dagger at him, he was in a rage. A *rage*, I tell you!"

Fenris buried his head in his hands and mumbled something unintelligible. Hugo proceeded to tell a grandiose tale involving Hunters, many guns, one dagger, narrow escapes, bloodshed, and mayhem, all encouraged by Sara's reactions. Hugo wound up the story with their midnight trip to Marcel for their wounds. At last he left, a happy man who lived for telling a good yarn.

Silence fell. Sara sat motionless, staring off into the distance.

Fenris shifted uneasily. "Do you want to go out for dinner tonight?"

Her eyes flashed over to his. "A little ache."

"Wha—what?"

"You said earlier you had a little ache. Was that the residual effects of this adventure two nights ago?"

"Sara, listen—"

"Was this why you were avoiding me yesterday after work? So I wouldn't know you were injured?"

"I never avoided you. I was going to—well, yes, I *was* avoiding you. But only because you fuss over things."

"I *fuss*?"

Fenris clammed up, for Sara had a dangerous glint her eye that meant trouble.

"Show me."

"Sara—"

"Now."

He groaned and yanked up his shirt, revealing a long scar that was red and healing. She studied it a moment before meeting his gaze.

"If we are to be married, Fenris"—He shivered at the emphasis on *if* and her use of his full name— "You need to be honest with me. Honesty is more than telling the truth. It also means you don't keep things away from me. I know you don't want me to worry, but I'm going to do that anyway. It won't help if I think you are holding things back."

"I'm sorry," he whispered, wanting to kiss her. As soon as he was sure that she was safe.

She kissed him on the forehead. "Dinner sounds nice."

✳

As summer progressed, the workload increased with Anniversary Day approaching. There wasn't a person in the office who didn't dread the day that marked the Changing, when the Gifts were bestowed upon people with no rhyme or reason. After the mad chaos of the previous year, tensions were higher than ever and Durgan's continued rages did nothing to help.

Because of this, Fenris treasured what time he had with Sara and Sophie away from work. He took them out for walks or excursions to the park, affording them the privacy they could never have with family hovering about the Aguilar home. It wasn't until late June before he joined up with everyone for another pool day. Pops once again manned the grill, and much of the extended Aguilar family was present.

Fenris was standing around the pit, laughing with Marcel and several of the Aguilar cousins when the ladies came out of the house. He did a double take at the lovely redhead who walked past in a dark blue one-piece. Her coy glance in his direction sent his blood rushing, and like a man heeding a siren's call, he left the men and came straight to her.

"Wow," he murmured. "I've never seen you in a swimsuit."

Sara opened her mouth to respond when Sophie came running. "Throw me into the water, Fenwis!"

"Sophie. We've talked about this." Fenris knelt down and tweaked her nose.

Sophie scrunched her face in concentration. "Fen-*ris*."

"Good job. Now hold on. I want to talk to Sara." A long-suffering sigh from the little girl made him chuckle.

"She's getting much better saying her R's!" Sara beamed.

"She is, although I'll miss the cuteness once she gets it down for good."

"Me too. Now go play with her. We'll be here all day. There's plenty of time."

"I know." Fenris leaned close to whisper, "You really do look beautiful, Red."

"What, this old thing? I only wear this when I don't care how I look ..." She sauntered away.

Fenris groaned. Already irresistible, her ease at quoting a favorite classic movie almost sent him over the edge. He had no time to mull over it, for Sophie was tugging at his hand. With one last look of yearning, he followed her to the pool.

⁓❋⁓

From the first day Sara had laid eyes on Fenris, she had thought he was too handsome for his own good. How could she not, with his tousled black hair and gorgeous eyes. Then he opened his mouth, bound and determined to be the youngest grouchy old man that ever existed. But even in those early days, she couldn't help being drawn to him. He was a classic Darcy—tall, dark, brooding. Once his kind heart and dry humor had revealed itself, she was sunk. Sara didn't think he could do anything to make himself more attractive until seeing his sweet affection and patience with Sophie.

He sat at the edge of the pool, feet dangling in the water, tossing Sophie in every time she came to him. Eventually, more people got in the pool, including some roughhousing cousins. Fenris pulled the child out and led her to the kiddie pool at the far end, where Mrs. Aguilar watched over the smaller children like a hawk. Sara giggled as he dodged an attempt by Marcel to shove him into the pool, resulting in Fenris pushing Marcel into the pool instead. Laughing, he took off his shirt before following with a leap.

Sara sucked in her breath. Fenris might have made much of her swimsuit, but she had never seen *him* in his trunks before. As he pulled himself up out of the pool, wet hair hanging in his face, always a touch too long and unkempt, she almost swooned.

"Sara!"

Sara jumped. Frances watched her with amusement. "You were in la-la land. What are you doing, checking Fen out? He looks good, doesn't he?"

"He—don't be ridiculous," Sara mumbled.

"Ah, look at you! All starry-eyed. Hey, Fen! Come get your woman."

"Frances, my word ..." Sara could feel the rush of blood staining her cheeks. Fenris approached them both.

"Take Sara and run away with her!" Frances laughed and pushed Sara at him.

Confused, Fenris shrugged and led her to the pool. "You getting in? It feels great."

"Mhmm."

"You okay?"

"Yes, I'm just thinking."

"About what?"

Sara shook her head and slipped into the water, heading to a shadowed corner. He followed her there, putting his hands around her waist as he backed her up against the edge. "You mad at me?"

Again, she shook her head. Exasperation showed in his face, but he bent to kiss her.

Sara loved the way he kissed her. Slow. Deep. Like he had all the time in the world, and he was there for the sole purpose of loving her. Sara ran her hands up his back, encouraging him. They sank deeper into the water, neither wanting to break apart.

A wolf whistle came from the other end of the pool. Embarrassed, Sara dropped her head and looked away. There were a few titters from the crowd, and someone called out, "Get a room!"

Fenris rolled his eyes but stayed focused on her.

"You're scaring me, Red. What's going on? You getting cold feet? Because we can always—"

Sara burst out laughing. She was the polar opposite of cold. "Set a date, Fen."

"A date? For what?"

"Fenris."

"What, the wedding? Today—this minute?"

"Yes."

"I think we should wait until after—"

Sara pressed against him, wrapping her arms around him, and his eyes went wide. She pushed herself up on her toes to whisper in his ear. "I want you, Fen. All of you. I can't wait any longer."

He groaned. Sara melted at the emotions in his eyes, shy and burning all at once.

"How soon can you be ready?" he asked.

"Today."

Fenris choked out a laugh. They gazed at each other, and without breaking eye contact, he called out to the crowd behind him. "Hey, Marcel! What are you doing on Friday?"

"Work, I guess. I mean, it all depends on—"

"Take off early."

"Okay." Marcel considered it longer and moved in the water toward them, obviously confused. "Um, why?"

Never taking his eyes away from Sara's, Fenris grinned. "Because I'm getting married on Friday, and I need my best man there."

It took a moment for Marcel to connect all the dots. When he did, everyone jumped at his yell. "Yes!"

Sara's eyes sparkled with joy. "You mean it? Are we doing this?"

"Too late to back out now, Red."

"Fen!" She squealed and threw her arms around his neck. "I do love you!"

"Love you more," he whispered.

"Not possible."

A COTTAGE BY THE SEA

O nce they determined the day, Fenris set forth with a zeal that impressed Sara. It took both him and Mrs. Aguilar to convince the priest to rush the wedding, and only Sara's good standing at the neighboring St. Michael's allowed them to move forward. At least, Sara hoped that was how they managed it. She secretly wondered if poor Fr. Stephens may have been bullied into performing the vows by those two formidable personalities. Fenris later joked that Mrs. Aguilar should have been a Jesuit; her arguments for bypassing the usual six-month wait were so convincing.

While it bothered Sara that neither she nor Fenris had any true family to attend, her heart swelled at the presence of the Aguilars' extended family and as many from the office as could be spared. She was especially thankful when Durgan showed up, though he sat in the back, separated from the rest. Sara knew his attendance was important to Fenris and given his recent attitude, they had been unsure if he would show. After the ceremony, he hugged them both, and Sara saw Fenris start in surprise when Durgan whispered into his ear.

"What did he tell you?"

Fenris didn't answer right away, watching his boss go out the tall wooden doors of the church. She saw him swallow hard. "He said he was happy for us, and—that Dad would have been proud."

"He *is* proud. I'm sure of it, Fen," she said, kissing his cheek.

"I hope so," he whispered.

⚜

Fenris and Sara had agreed to keep the honeymoon abbreviated. They were eager to begin life as a family with Sophie, but also wanted to be back home before Anniversary Day rolled around. The small wedding reception at the Aguilar home was brief and soon they were on their way to their destination—a tiny, isolated cottage near Bodega Bay with views spanning the Pacific. The miles flew by with conversation and laughter.

"Did you choose Bodega Bay because of *The Birds*, Fen?"

"No, but now I wish I had. You know how much I love Hitchcock."

"I do. Let's hope we aren't assaulted by any feathered creatures." Sara giggled at the idea. "How are you liking your new car?"

"It's nice, although I still miss my old one."

"I don't know why. That was a grandpa car. This one has a little more pizzaz at least."

"That's what getting married to a beautiful woman will do to you."

"Speaking of which, how do you feel about being a married man now?"

"Incredible. Although ..." Fenris hesitated and cocked his head, spiking her curiosity.

"What?"

He shrugged.

"Fen?"

"Well." He gave her a sidelong look. "I'm thinking by this time tomorrow, I may say it's even better."

"Why, Fenris Trygg! You rake!"

He snorted and without taking his eyes off the road, took hold of her hand and lifted it to his lips for a quick kiss on her palm. "You know, you might want to rest on the drive, because there's no telling how much sleep you'll get tonight."

"Fen!" Sara squealed, jerking her hand away to smack him on the arm.

"Hey, none of that," he said, laughing.

Sara settled into her seat, gazing at him. "I do love you."

He glanced at her, gold eyes brighter than she had ever seen them. "And I love you. I meant it, by the way. You can rest if you want. About another hour to go."

◦◦✳◦◦

She hadn't meant to fall asleep, so Sara was surprised to feel a gentle nudge on her shoulder and his rich, deep voice near her ear.

"Sweetheart, wake up. We're here."

"I'm sorry." Sara yawned. "What lousy company I've been!"

His expression was warm and soft. "It's fine. Your snore kept me company."

"What? I don't snore!"

"Sara—"

"I just breathe heavy!"

Fenris rolled his eyes and left to take their bags into the house while Sara took in their surroundings. A sweet cottage overlooking the Pacific stood before her. The sun hung low in the sky, sending diamond sparkles across the ocean. Sara remained lost in a reverie until Fenris came up behind her and pulled her close, her back against his chest. "I'm sorry for teasing you about snoring."

Sara giggled. "That's okay. So are you admitting I don't snore?"

"No, you definitely do. But it's adorable. I'm glad you got some rest. It's been a crazy few days."

"I suppose I should be thankful I don't talk in my sleep. Do you snore or anything? I don't remember."

"Not that I know of. I suppose you'll find out soon enough and can tattle on me." He bent to kiss her cheek. He remained in that position, his head on her shoulder. "Are you all right? You seem tense."

After a second's hesitation, she dug up the courage to reply. "I guess I'm a little nervous."

His arms tightened around her, and he nuzzled his face into her neck.

"Me too," he whispered.

They were both silent for a time, gazing out at the ocean until Fenris cleared his throat. "Hey, it's about an hour until sunset, and the cottage has a porch swing facing the ocean. How about we settle in, then we can sit and watch the sunset from the porch."

"That sounds lovely. I'll make hot chocolate."

"Now we're talking. Come on." Fenris picked up a cardboard box he had set on the ground. He adjusted his grip so he could carry it with one arm and rested his free hand on the small of her back.

"Our bags?"

"Already inside." Sara loved how he took her arm to guide her along the rocky path. "Be careful here."

It was a tiny cottage; long and narrow, with a porch barely large enough for the swing and the doorway. Inside was a delightful open floorplan with many windows, allowing the natural light to flow in. The whole space was designed for comfort. Soft chairs and a sofa were placed at one end of the rectangular room, with warm, muted rugs on the floor. A small wood burning stove stood in the corner with a basket of driftwood nearby. On the opposite end was a kitchen with barstools up against an island. For Sara, with her artist's eye, most captivating of all were the plate glass windows that ran the length of the place and looked out upon the ocean. Directly across the window wall was another door leading to what Sara assumed to be the bedroom.

"What do you think?" Fenris asked, his voice anxious as he set the box on the table.

"It's perfect."

He let out a sigh of relief. "I thought it was nice, but it's what you think that matters."

"Where did you put our bags?"

"They're in the bedro—ah, the other room."

Sara smothered a smile at the faint flush on his face as he fumbled over the word while poking into the box.

"What's in the box?"

"A few groceries and sundries. That way we don't have to go back out right away. We can even cook something here in the kitchen."

"That was smart, Fen!"

"Yeah, well, I have my moments. Or wait—I never asked. Did you want to go out tonight?"

"Not at all."

"Whew. I'm happy you dislike people almost as much as I do."

"That isn't how I would put it—" Sara's sudden laughter was cut short as he took out a larger item. "Fen! You didn't—is that your coffeemaker?"

"*Our* coffeemaker now, and yes."

"Fenris. You brought a whole coffeemaker. To a fully-equipped cottage. Did you think they wouldn't have one?"

He pursed his lips. "Well, you know how these places are, Red! Most of them have either those weird pod things or a tiny coffee pot. I may drink less than I used to, but I'm *still* a coffee man. Besides, I need the proper equipment to make the best coffee for you. Which reminds me ..." He pulled out a manual coffee grinder.

Sara broke down into peals of laughter, which grew at the mock scowl he threw in her direction. Wiping tears away from her eyes, she pointed to a door. "Are the bags in this room?"

His answer was a grunt as he sorted through an array of coffee bags before looking up, concerned. "I hope you didn't forget anything. I saw one bag of yours, and it was a small duffel."

"I normally pack light."

"What a relief," he smiled, digging into the box once more.

"Besides, I was under the impression I wouldn't need too many clothes the next few days."

Fenris froze, and his eyes flashed up at her. Sara gave him a wink as she sashayed into the bedroom. After closing the door, however, she leaned against it, trying to tame her racing heart and the blush heating her cheeks.

"Pull yourself together. You can do this," she whispered.

As soon as the door to the bedroom closed, Fenris sank into a near-by chair, stunned. He buried his face into his hands and groaned. He was a wreck.

"Be a man and pull yourself together," he muttered to himself. He got up and sorted out the rest of the groceries. Despite his current mood, he chuckled at all the coffee. Perhaps he had gone a touch overboard. He blamed it on the need to distract his mind from other things.

Fenris had nearly put away the last of the groceries when he heard Sara say his name. He turned and staggered back against the counter. She was posing against the doorframe of the bedroom, wearing a Red Sox shirt. It was large enough to fall mid-thigh, and her legs were bare. He wasn't sure what stunned him more, the intimacy of her apparel, or that his New York Yankees-loving wife was wearing anything with the Red Sox name. Fenris wanted to speak but discovered he had no air left in his lungs.

"Please say something, Fen."

"Wh-where did you get that?" he choked out, gripping the edge of the counter until his knuckles popped.

"It's yours. I found it in your drawer before we left." Sara's face fell. "Oh, Fen, I'm sorry. I guess most women get something slinky for their honeymoon ..."

Fenris blinked. "Come here."

"What's wrong?"

"Nothing, but you've made my knees so weak, if I step away from this counter, I'm going to fall over."

Eyes twinkling, she sidled across the room. Watching her hips sway beneath that oversized shirt made his heart thunder in his chest. Steadying himself against the counter, he placed his hands on either side of her face.

"You look amazing," he whispered. "This is better than any slinky thing you could have worn."

Hungry for the taste of her, Fenris brought her close. He had considered stoking the fire cautiously until her eager response threw out all thoughts of keeping it slow. His hands roamed lower and lower down her back, delighting in the newfound freedom. Grasping at her hips, he slumped further against the counter at the feel of her skin on his fingertips. The familiar scent of strawberries floated past his nose.

"I love how you smell," he murmured, without thinking. She laughed and whatever anxieties had remained fled, leaving behind smoldering desire. Her lips traveled along his neck. Fenris was torn between wanting her mouth back on his versus the surprise of whatever she planned to do next. Tension thrummed through him, building up to a crescendo.

"You know, I've never been with anyone before. Not ... like this."

"Neither have I," she murmured.

"I'm probably not going to get this right the first few times."

"Practice makes perfect," she countered, breathing into his ear.

He gasped out a laugh before shifting his position and meeting her lips once more. His hands were beneath the shirt now, sliding up her back. He tipped his forehead to hers, speaking hoarsely. "It's not going to be magical."

"I don't care about magic, Fen. I never did. I care about you. I want you."

He tried to calm his galloping heart, wanting to capture this moment in his memory forever. "Sara, unless you tell me not to, in about three seconds, I'm going to swoop you up into my arms and carry you to the bed."

"Please ..." she whispered.

So, he did.

꙳✳꙳

They both forgot about the sunset.

And if there had been a passerby in the area at twilight, they would have seen an effervescent glow spill out of the cottage windows and sparks fly upward.

꙳✳꙳

Later, they lay together, caught up in the beautiful madness of marital intimacy. They were locked in each other's arms, partaking in slow, deep kisses.

"Look at me, Fen."

Gold eyes opened, bright behind the sweaty, dark hair that spilled over his forehead. Sara brushed the hair aside, and he tipped his head into her touch, with a kiss to her hand. She caught her breath at the rapt adoration in his eyes when they met hers.

"Tell me a secret," she whispered.

"A secret?"

"Yes. Something just between us, something no one else will ever know."

Fenris thought a moment and smiled. He stretched the full length of his body out next to hers and propped himself up on an elbow. His other arm remained wrapped around her waist.

"I hated my name when I was younger."

"That's it? I knew that already and I was hoping for something—"

"Hold on. You know Dad named me, and my mom went along with it, although I don't know why. When she died and we moved to Sacramento, I had a chance to start over and get people to call me Fen. It didn't take long before even Dad picked it up. I still use Fenris for introductions or formal things, but I've always preferred Fen, until ..." He dropped his head back to the pillow and with both arms, clutched her closer. His voice dipped into a husky murmur. "The way you said my name, my full name, a little while ago ... I *really* liked it. Please, do that again. When we're alone, like this."

"Okay," she whispered before kissing him again. Mid-kiss, she giggled. At his surprise, Sara said, "You were wrong about one thing though."

"What?"

"You said it wouldn't be magical. If that wasn't magic, I don't know what is."

Fenris laughed and rolled over to his back. Sara saw some color flood his face. "It was magical, wasn't it?"

"You know, I've decided something about you." She poked him playfully. "Now that your soft underbelly is all exposed."

"My *what*?"

"Your underbelly." Sara stroked her hand along his stomach. He stopped laughing, and his eyes slid shut at her touch. "You're a sweet, warm cinnamon roll at heart, aren't you?"

"Please don't tell anyone."

"Sorry, but I think everyone knows by now."

"Shoot."

"Would it help if I said you were a bit burnt around the edges?"

"Maybe."

She continued to stroke along his chest and stomach, and he shivered. Swallowing hard, he whispered her name. "Sara."

"Hmm?"

"I don't suppose—do you perhaps feel like making more magic?"

Her answer was a kiss.

⸙

Sara awoke to grey light and the distant sound of waves crashing. She attempted to stretch but found it difficult with the strong arm of her new husband holding her close to his body. She tried to wiggle free, and Fenris woke with a huff of breath. He yanked a pillow over his eyes.

"What time is it?" she asked with a yawn.

"I don't know," Fenris mumbled. "Whatever time it is, it must include coffee."

"Didn't sleep well, my love?"

He chuckled under the pillow and turned back over, once again pulling her close. "How could I possibly sleep with you beside me, like this ..."

Sara allowed one kiss before pushing him away. "Bathroom."

"Oh, sorry."

"It's okay."

"Take as long as you want. I'll go start the coffee."

Sara shimmied into a robe and took her time freshening up. When she ventured out, the coffee was ready. Fenris was sipping a cup, elbows on the kitchen counter and gazing out at the ocean. He had put on his sweatpants and T-shirt, and his hair was tousled, but he was still far more handsome than anyone had a right to look after getting out of bed.

Sara slipped up behind him and wrapped her arms around his waist. Fenris placed his mug down on the counter and turned in the circle of her arms. He rested his chin on her head.

"Happy?" she asked.

"Happy? Oh, sweetheart." He kissed her forehead. "Happy isn't the word for what I'm feeling. I never knew such joy even existed. My heart aches with it. You?"

She nuzzled her face into his neck. "So happy. But I keep smelling that coffee. After all the trouble you've gone to for my special honeymoon coffee experience, can I get a cup?"

"Absolutely." Fenris took a container of cream from the fridge. "You want me to fix it up, or do you want to?"

"You can do it."

He was so eager and happy to get her coffee, Sara's heart glowed. She cozied up on the sofa with a blanket onto her lap and saw that he had lit a fire in the stove. "This is so nice. Where did you find this place?"

"I called some of our people in San Francisco and asked them if they knew of anything. This was on the list."

He brought her coffee and eased in beside her, snuggling her close. The light in the cottage was dim and grey, and through the windows a fog could be seen swirling around the landscape. Despite it being summer, it was chilly this far north and the small fire offered the right amount of pleasant warmth.

"This coffee is delicious, Fen. You put chocolate in it, didn't you?"

"And some spices." His gaze drifted over to the window. "It's earlier than I guessed. I'm sorry we missed the sunset last night. I know you looked forward to it."

"I'm not sorry in the least." Sara laughed before kissing him. "We'll see it tonight."

"Well, in that case ..." Fenris kissed her back and couldn't pull himself away.

After a few moments, Sara whispered, "Could we maybe take the coffee with us to the bedroom?"

"Thought you would never ask," he muttered, his breath ragged.

Those two cups of coffee never stood a chance.

⸙

Neither Fenris nor Sara ever talked much to others about their honeymoon—they considered it a time both sacred and secret between the two of them. Brief though it was, they enjoyed it to the utmost, with hikes down to the beach and slow, delicious hours indoors.

They were both sad to leave the cottage but were determined to hold on to the precious memories as sustenance for whatever challenges life might bring them in the future. They left more deeply in love than ever and eager to start life as a family with Sophie.

WHAT THE MOON SAW

*T*hree months later ...

The glow of the moon reflected off the wet pavement. For the young woman dodging recent puddles, it was quiet on the college campus. Far too quiet. And far too dark, with the moon slipping in and out from behind clouds. The soft sound of footsteps behind her made the darkness and silence all the more foreboding.

The footsteps were steady, not rushing, and some distance away. The woman picked up her pace. Her father had drilled her incessantly on the methods the Hunters used to entrap their prey. She didn't want to make a rash decision and make things worse. Maybe it was another student on their way back home after a late night at the lab.

It was subtle, but the woman knew the person behind her had sped up as well, keeping pace with her. She fought down the panic and yanked her phone out of her bag, pulling up a number without looking at the screen. No one answered. She rolled her eyes. Her father had warned her Fenris was hard to get in touch with since his recent marriage. With a groan, she dialed her father. She hated to worry him; he had been so stressed the last few months. Still, it was better to risk his temper than to be taken by Hunters.

She switched paths, heading for a plaza she knew would be better lit. The phone rang twice before being picked up. "Dad?"

"What is it?"

Yes, calling him was a mistake. He sounded annoyed already.

"I'm sorry to bug you, Dad. I'm alone on campus, trying to get back to my apartment and ..."

His tone sharpened. "Where *exactly* are you?"

"Um, nearing the plaza on the north end of campus."

"Is there any public place nearby that's open?"

"If there were, I'd be there already."

"A dorm?"

"There's a—"

Silence fell.

"What is it, Laurel? Laurel!"

He called for her several times, but strong arms were holding her tight. She managed one scream before a gag was tied over her mouth and her head covered with a black cloth. A screech of tires announced a dark van running up along the sidewalk. It didn't matter how much she struggled—the four burly men had no problem dragging her into the van. The engine gunned and the van left the scene.

A smaller, petite figure lingered behind and picked up Laurel's dropped phone. She spoke in a cool, silky voice.

"Hello, Durgan. Your daughter, of all people, should know better than to be walking across campus alone in the dark. Dangerous people about. Hunters, you know."

Durgan let out a feral growl and Josephine smiled. "I think it would be a good idea for me to keep an eye on Laurel for a while.

Don't worry, I'll keep her *quite* safe. I'll be in touch soon, dear Durgan."

He screamed profanities over the line. Josephine dropped the phone back to the ground, and with a crush from her boot heel, his curses were silenced.

LATE NIGHT CALLERS

The door lock made a soft click as a gloved hand turned the key. A tall figure stumbled across the threshold, fighting off the wind and rain that whipped around him. He tried to shut the door quietly, but the draft sucked it closed with a bang, and he flinched.

It was a dark and stormy night, Fenris mused with a rueful chuckle as he kicked his wet shoes aside and peeled off his gloves and socks. It was unusual for Sacramento to get such a powerful front this time of the year, and he wondered what game the weather was playing. He shrugged out of his wet jacket and hung it on the doorknob before padding to the kitchen in his bare feet. Once there, Fenris ducked into the pantry.

Though he had long since given up his habit of coffee at the midnight hour, he thought a hot drink would be nice to take the chill out of his bones. Sara had stocked their pantry with a startling array of teas, though he had not found many he liked. Tonight, he was on the hunt for one very particular blend, his wife's own concoction she had made for him to drink when it was late and his anxieties were keeping him awake.

He grumbled at the tea canisters as he sniffed and poked his finger into a few. There was no telling which held that particular tea. With an exasperated grunt, he decided the best thing to do was take a hot shower and get to sleep. He smiled at the idea, thankful he no longer had to climb into bed alone. Instead, the sweet warmth of his wife waited for him.

Rounding the corner, the sight of the bedroom made him stop and pause a moment, his heart full. The bedside lamp was glowing. A book had slid to the floor, and Sara was asleep half sitting up in bed. He wondered how long she had waited before falling asleep.

Fenris sighed. It had been such a good night before things went haywire ...

࿊

After roughhousing on the floor with Sophie, the little girl had not wanted to go to bed. Fenris didn't mind in the least, happy for an excuse to sit with her and read story after story from his father's collection of Norwegian myths.

"She can't understand all that!" Sara said amid peals of laughter.

"Perhaps not," Fenris stated haughtily. "You know they say exposure at an early age is crucial."

"You'll be reading her Shakespeare next."

"There's a thought! I think I have a copy of Lamb's *Tales of Shakespeare* for children somewhere ... We'll start that next, okay, Soph?"

Sara raised her hands in a gesture of surrender, leaving them to it. Fenris read for a long time before Sophie fell asleep. Leaving the room, he found Sara on the sofa with a bowl of popcorn and watching baseball on TV. Fenris snuggled down next to her, pulling her into his lap while reaching around for some popcorn.

However, the Red Sox had a solid lead over the Cardinals, which made for an unexciting game, and Fenris became increasingly distracted by Sara.

Everything about her distracted him, all the time. Her hair tickled his chin, and he started kissing along her neck. Her giggles and playful slapping away his hands didn't do much to dissuade his efforts.

"Settle down, you!" she laughed, breathless after a long kiss. "I'm trying to watch the game."

"It's the Red Sox. Not appropriate behavior for a Yankees fan. Besides, this is a boring game and it's raining."

"What does rain have to do with anything?"

"It's ... cozy." He made a grab for the bowl and placed it on the coffee table. Without the worry of popcorn spilling everywhere, he shifted Sara about in his arms and focused all his attention on her.

That's when the phone rang.

Fenris had known he was on call that night, but it took him until the third ring before he managed to answer. He listened for several minutes, grunting in response as Sara continued to nibble his free ear, and hung up with an exasperated snort.

"You have to go out?" Sara asked, disappointment on her face.

"Yes, sorry. You know I don't want to leave, right?"

"I know."

He added a few warmer layers to his clothing and kissed her once more before leaving. "Don't wait up."

"You know I will. Please be careful. Love you."

"Love you, sweetheart. Lock up behind me, okay?"

With those final words, he was out in the storm.

⁓✳⁓

Fenris tiptoed over to the bed and knelt down beside it, watching her. Sara was a light sleeper, and he was surprised she hadn't woken upon his return. She had commented earlier in the evening about being more tired than usual. Thinking it might be safe, he brushed the lightest of kisses into her hair. He immediately regretted risking the kiss as she stirred.

"Fen?" she mumbled.

"Hey. I didn't mean to wake you."

"Come to bed."

"Let me jump in the shower first. I'm a mess."

Sara's eyes opened, and she grimaced at his appearance. "Is that blood?"

"I don't know, maybe? I think it's mud." He swiped his face and glanced down at his hand. "Oh. Yeah, it is. Don't worry about it. Let me get this shower done, and I'll be out pronto."

After a quick shower he left the bathroom to see that Sara was no longer in bed. Thinking Sophie might have woken up, he began to make his way to her room but saw the kitchen light burning. Sara was puttering about with a saucepan and mugs.

"You made me hot chocolate?" Fenris asked, his heart melting. "Come here."

He gathered her to him, the chill and aches from the night becoming a distant memory. She was tense in his arms however, and he gave her a gentle squeeze.

"You okay?" he whispered.

"Yes. I'll always worry."

"I know. I'm sorry about that." When she shrugged in his embrace, he knew it wasn't a good sign. "You know the rules, Red. Talk to me."

Sara stepped away and put the saucepan in the sink. "Drink up first."

"Yes ma'am." He grinned, taking a swallow. "I wanted a hot drink and rummaged through your teas, but this is so much better."

"I thought it looked like the dwarves going through Bilbo's pantry in there."

"I was trying to find that one tea you have that settles me down."

"Fenris Trygg! It was right here on the counter. I left it out for you in case you wanted some when you got back."

"Oh. I must have walked right past it." Fenris settled onto a stool and yawned, resting his chin on one hand. "What's up?"

Sara brushed her fingers over the fresh cut on his temple. Satisfied it wasn't anything serious, she sat down with a sigh. "I don't know. I feel ... restless. I guess I'm wondering how long you intend to do the fighter stuff—I'm not saying to quit today," she added hastily. "I just wish I had some idea about what you might be planning for down the road. How long will I wake up to you coming home with blood on your face?"

There was no mistaking the edge in her voice, even though it was clear she was trying to hide it. Fenris took another sip of his drink. He had known this was coming and wanted to tread the topic carefully. He held out his hand, palm up, in invitation. She placed her hand in his and waited.

"It's funny," he mused. "I've been thinking about this quite a lot the last few weeks, and I have some ideas. Keep in mind it may take some time to work through them though."

"What? You never said anything about this before."

"I didn't want to get you excited in case things didn't work out, but I've been feeling more optimistic about it the last few weeks. We have some new recruits coming in, which will help."

Her eyes began to sparkle. "Tell me more."

"Well, for the short term, I'm hoping to get off the regular rotation. I would still be on call in emergencies. My long-range goal is to oversee the fighter crew, much like Durgan does. Keep my direct involvement limited to the most extreme situations."

"I guess it's too much to hope you would ever stop completely."

"I'll admit it wouldn't feel right to abandon the team outright." Fenris paused to consider his words. "I would if that's what you needed me to do. I'll always choose you, Sara. I want you to know that. But I'm also going to trust that you won't force me to be anything other than I am. I'm a fighter, that's what I do. For our people."

"I understand." She squeezed his hand. "Let's go back to bed. I want to finish what we started earlier. If you aren't too tired."

"I'm *never* too tired for that." Fenris grinned. "Just let me—"

He hurled an oath when his phone rang again. Sara slumped in her seat.

"This had better be something you absolutely can't do on your own, Hugo," Fenris growled into the phone. He sat and listened, murmuring a few responses before hanging up the phone.

"Hugo and Raven are coming over."

"It's two in the morning!"

"I guess I should have asked you first."

"That would have been nice," she replied testily.

"I'm sorry. I didn't think. I'm not used to ..." He leaned over to kiss her before whispering, "Forgive me?"

Sara relented with a rueful smile. "Was this a common occurrence before we were married?"

"Well." He shrugged. "Sometimes. That's why I didn't think it through."

"Have they been working all night?"

"I would assume."

Sara turned to the fridge, removing lunchmeat and other items. "What are you doing?"

"Making some sandwiches. I'm sure they'll be hungry."

Fenris tugged her to him, her back against his chest as they faced the open fridge. "That's very kind. Thank you."

"It's no big deal."

"Yes, it is. I love you."

"Love you more," she whispered.

"Not possible."

She disengaged herself from his embrace. "Let me get to work on these. And Fen, make sure you get to the door before they knock, and tell them they need to be quiet. I don't want Sophie waking up if we can help it."

"Got it. We'll see them from here. They're coming the back way, and the porch light is on."

"Will they want coffee?"

"What do you think?"

"Don't drink any," she warned.

"I won't, don't worry."

The coffee and sandwiches were ready when a large shadow crossed the porch light. Sara jumped at the sight.

"It's okay," Fenris reassured her, crossing over to open the door. With a gust of wind and rain, Hugo and Raven blew in. Before Hugo could bellow out his usual enthusiastic greeting, Fenris raised his hand. "Keep your voices low, guys. Sophie is asleep."

"We're sorry about this," Raven whispered. "We weren't sure it could wait."

Sara poured out some coffee and indicated to the large plate of sandwiches. Hugo grabbed one appreciatively.

"Wow, thanks! We'll come over more often if this is the reception we get."

"Please don't," said Fenris. "Come on, it's late. Out with it."

Hugo and Raven exchanged a look, as though debating who should speak. After Fenris growled with impatience, Raven set down her mug of coffee. "We were over on the east side of town, out by Folsom Lake and—"

"Who do we know living out there?"

Hugo gave a low chuckle. "We don't. Sometimes after Raven and I have tangled with Hunters, we like to give chase for fun."

"Really?" Sara laughed.

"Not always, but it does liven things up if it's a slow night." Hugo shrugged. "Anyway, we were tailing some jerks and ran into a whole pack of Hunters camped out there."

"Whoa, wait a minute," said Fenris. "Hunters grouped together? Organized?"

"Yeah. Weird, don't you think?"

Fenris looked at the calendar on the wall. It was two months past Anniversary Day; the one time each year that Hunters were known to work together in packs.

"That's not all," Raven inserted. "There were Gifted with them."

"What? That's not—"

"I know," said Hugo. "Raven did her disappearing thing and snuck around to get a handle on what they were doing, all bunched up like that. There was this woman talking to them. She and some others were demonstrating their Gifts. She had this golden whip—"

"Excuse me?" Fenris stiffened. "What did she look like, Raven?"

"Short with black hair, had a stick or something on her back. Small, petite woman. Couldn't tell you much else from where I was."

"No," Sara whispered.

Fenris stood and paced the floor. "Is that it?"

For once, Hugo's eternal good humor failed him. He looked over to Raven and shrugged. She took a deep breath and shimmered in the air, as if even her Gift was reacting to the news.

"I could hear some of the conversation. Not all of it, with the wind gusting about. I managed to catch things about us, the Shadow Guild. That if the Hunters help her destroy us, she would give them run of this territory once she was done and moving on. She said, well, based on what I could gather, that someone in the Guild was helping her. Giving her inside information on all of us."

Silence fell among them.

"A traitor. You're telling me she claimed there's a traitor among us in the Shadow Guild." Fenris sat down and buried his face into his hands with a groan. The other three remained quiet. When Fenris raised his head to speak, his voice was cold and steely.

"Right. Not a word of this to anyone else. You hear me?" he snapped. "If I find out you spread this around—"

"We won't, Fen. Promise," said Hugo.

"Do you believe what she said?" asked Raven.

"I don't know." Fenris drummed his fingers on the counter a few times. "But we won't figure this out if the whole office knows. I need to work on this, and if it's true, figure out who the traitor is."

"We should go." Raven nudged Hugo.

"Okay. Thanks a lot for the sandwiches and coffee, Sara. We appreciate it."

"My pleasure," said Sara, but her eyes were on her husband. Taking his cue, Fenris came out of his reverie long enough to bid them farewell.

☙❈❧

As soon as their guests had departed, Fenris went on a tour of the house, checking every window and door to ensure they were all locked and secure. Sara watched him warily. Although his demeanor was businesslike, she detected a simmering anger beneath the surface.

"What will you do when you find out who did this?" she asked. Fenris met her gaze and she shivered when he said nothing. In the warmth of their marriage, it was easy to forget this aspect of his personality. The part of him that would do whatever was necessary to protect those he cared about.

He continued his inspection of the house. After dashing in and out of Sophie's room, he whispered, "Is she okay in there? Maybe she should sleep with us."

"No, we're not starting that," Sara said. He stood with his back against the wall, stiff and anxious. Sara realized anger alone wasn't motivating his actions—there was fear as well. "She's fine. Let's go to bed."

He didn't respond. She eased up against him, her arms encircling his waist.

"I never really believed she was dead," he muttered. "But at least it was easy to pretend even though we never found her body in the rubble. Now I don't even have that."

"I know."

"She's going to come after us, Sara."

Sara clung to him a little tighter.

"She'll pit us against each other. Everyone at the office. You, me. She'll do whatever she can, even if it means using our love for each other against us."

"We won't let her," Sara said. "Do you think if we go to bed, you'll be able to sleep?"

"I don't know."

"Well, let's try. It's late, and we're both exhausted."

Sara led him to the bed and tucked him in as though he were a child. He rolled over and spooned against her back, an arm around her waist holding her close. With a yawn, he murmured, "I guess I was wrong, Red. I can be too tired."

"I'm sorry the evening wasn't what you wanted."

Already almost asleep, his words came out in a tired mumble. "It's okay. I have you here. Sophie in the next room. If I can just hold on to that, I'm happy."

"You sure there isn't anything else you would wish for?"

But Fenris was asleep. Sara smiled to herself before thinking back over the evening. Her smile faded away, and she shivered.

LOCKDOWN

Before their marriage, Fenris had managed to remain somewhat restrained in his affection for Sara while at the office, limiting his actions to dropping a kiss on her head in passing, or holding her hand. However, now that they were married he saw no reason to restrain himself, so Sara was forced to establish some new rules concerning their behavior.

"You have no proper social filters," she exclaimed one day, when she had to fight him off from kissing her outside the bathrooms.

"I never have, and yet, you love me anyway," he stated between kisses.

"We can't be doing this. Not here." Sara hated, *hated* hearing herself giggle even as she spoke, and that she wanted to let him do whatever his fancy desired. But she knew all too well where that would lead.

All this led to the rule of no kissing at the office. Fenris despised the rule and often tried to circumvent it. This led to a frequent game of cat and mouse between them.

Fenris was always the cat.

⋆

She knew he was stalking her.

Fenris had wandered over to Erin's desk to ask a question about some security detail. Sara could see him glancing in her direction, his fingers twiddling a pen the whole time. They had only arrived at the office a short time ago, and if he was already in this much of a state, it was going to be a long day. Both aggravated and amused, Sara sighed. No woman whose husband looked at her the way Fenris did could be angry with him, but sometimes she did wish he was a *little* less intense about it all.

Sure enough, when he passed behind her, his hands fell upon her shoulders. The lingering touch made her want to whip around and kiss him. Instead, she lasered her focus on the long strings of computer code in front of her. He dropped a chaste kiss on her hair before moving to his own desk.

"Where's Marcel?" Sara asked. The office was always quieter when he was missing. "Late night for him?"

"He called and said he would be in around noon. Tudor and Cal were out, and one of them needed some help."

"Any word on Project Midnight?" Sara asked, using the designated code name for their attempt to locate a possible traitor within the office. It had been ten days since the visit from Hugo and Raven.

"Not yet." He dragged the desk phone closer, a sour frown on his face. Sara glanced at the date.

"Rotation time?"

"Yeah."

Every three months, Fenris spent several days on the phone, touching base with all the families in their database. Sara knew he preferred to do this in person, but time didn't always permit personal visits to everyone. That he managed to see as many people as he did throughout the year showed his dedication.

For the next hour, they worked alongside each other. Sara focused on the coding, lulled by the familiar murmur of Fenris talking on the phone. Late in the morning, she heard him swear a mild oath.

"Fen," she warned.

"Sorry," he said. "Mrs. Clancy is next."

Sara stifled a laugh. Mrs. Clancy was a lonely widow who had long ago taken a fancy to the handsome young Fenris, and he always dreaded calling her.

"Tell her you're married now. Maybe that will get her off your back."

"If anything, it will make her extra determined."

Sara could see him watching her out of the corner of her eye. Before she had a chance to stop him, he had rolled his chair over to hers.

"Maybe some … inspiration first? To help me emphasize how completely unavailable I am?" he whispered, nuzzling her.

"No."

"Sara …" he entreated.

She shivered, loving how he said her name in these moments. She stiffened her resolve. "We. Are. Working."

"*You* are working. I'm thinking about—"

Fenris fell back in shock as her Shield flared up, blasting him several feet away. Abashed, Sara giggled. "I'm sorry! It just happened—"

"Fine. I get the message," Fenris muttered, not quite meeting her eyes. He began to walk away.

"Fen?"

"Bathroom. Be back in a few."

She bit her lip, watching him march to the bathrooms. Sara hadn't meant to direct her Shield at him, but it had certainly been effective. The expression on his face ... She giggled again and turned back to her computer.

Sara lost herself in her work for the next half hour. She finished a batch of coding before she realized Fenris had never returned to his desk. She half-rose in her chair to get a better view. His height always made him easy to spot when he was nearby, but he was nowhere to be seen. Had she hurt his feelings that much? Sara stood completely and spun around. Not in Durgan's office or the kitchen. Maybe he had gone upstairs.

She headed toward the open staircase, seeing nothing along the way. Sara wasn't used to Fenris disappearing like this. Now she understood why he panicked whenever *she* wandered off for too long. Sara reached the staircase, and there came a slight noise from the dark shadows beneath and behind the metal stairs. She paused with one foot on the first step. Another rustle. Sara brought her foot down and eased around the staircase, peering into the gloom.

A long arm snaked out, pulling her under the staircase and covering her mouth. She fought back before the arm loosened, and his lips were on hers. For a second, she let him kiss her before yanking away and punching him in the arm.

"You jerk!" she gasped. "Scaring me half to death!"

Fenris laughed and stood over her, both hands braced against the wall. Sara wasn't entirely trapped, but close enough. He bent to kiss her again and she turned her head away. Still, she couldn't help smiling.

"Fine. There are many other places to kiss you," he murmured. Sara shivered as he placed an open-mouthed kiss on her neck, and she struggled to find the will to protest.

"Fen. Stop."

He took a step back with an exasperated expression on his face. "You have no idea what's it like to sit next to you all day, every day. Nothing until we get home, and even then, I have to wait for Sophie to go to bed. It drives me crazy to not at least kiss you."

"I suppose it *is* asking a lot of a newly married man," she conceded.

Taking that as permission, he grinned. This time, when his mouth covered hers, she reciprocated. He made a happy, soft humming sound, and their arms went around each other. For several long minutes, they remained hidden. Fenris was the one to break away, breathing hard.

"Okay. You were right. This isn't such a good idea," he groaned. "Because now all I can think about is—"

A yell and a crash interrupted him, and they both jumped. Instinctively, he swung around, blocking her from whatever danger might be nearby. He emerged from under the stairs, grasping Sara's hand. Another yell erupted, and this time it was easy to pinpoint the source of the sound. Durgan was on the phone, screaming.

"Fen ..." Sara whispered.

"I know."

They both jumped again when Durgan threw his phone against the glass wall of his office. The impact sent cracks scattering, but the glass held. Their boss sank into his chair, head in his hands.

"Okay. That's enough," said Fenris. "Go back to your desk. It's time to get to the bottom of this."

Sara wouldn't release his hand. Some intuition flared that she would lose him forever if she let him go. "Fen, don't. Stay with me."

He must have sensed her panic, for he pulled her close and held her, stroking her hair and covering her face with sweet, tender kisses. "I'll be fine, sweetheart. Durgan needs help. This has been going on far too long. I should have stepped in before now. You'll see me the whole time, right?"

Sara reluctantly allowed him to leave her. She made her way to the kitchen to grab a mug and pour herself some coffee. The central location afforded an excellent view of Durgan's office, and she took her time, watching.

Fenris strode in, purposeful but not aggressive. He dragged the one extra chair over and sat in front of Durgan, close enough for their heads to be almost touching. Their lips moved as they talked in low voices. Was Durgan weeping? Her heart went out to him. Whatever was troubling him must be—she caught her breath as Fenris shot to his feet, shoving the chair back with an explosive, "How could you?"

The whole office froze. A warm tingle passed through Sara with her Shield wanting to burst forth, to protect her love. Durgan had risen to his feet as well, his hands held out in a submissive gesture. Fenris swore violently and left the office, slamming the door behind him, causing the glass walls to tremble. He almost ran to her, jerking the coffee cup out of her hand. She started to speak, but he overrode her.

"I don't have time. Listen to me. Get anything you need out of the office. Anything you would miss if you never came back."

"What—"

"Don't interrupt. Anything you need, you hear me? Be quick about it."

"Fen! I don't understand." He spun around, and she could see him fighting his temper. She pressed on. "Do I need to transfer anything from the computers? If we aren't coming back?"

His face relaxed a fraction. "No. They've been copied. Always are. You'll have everything you need."

"Why—" Sara stopped, remembering how often she had demanded him to trust her. He deserved the same trust. "Okay."

Fenris took a deep breath. "I'm sorry for yelling. Go do what I said, please."

Sara trotted to her desk and rummaged around. She didn't keep many personal items there, but she removed a precious dried carnation she kept in her top drawer. She watched Fenris out of the corner of her eye as she searched. He'd gone straight to Erin and was whispering with her. Erin rolled her eyes once, and Sara hoped Fenris didn't outright assault her, given his current mood. He grabbed her wrist and continued talking. Erin blanched and stopped arguing, staring at Fenris in disbelief. After a brief stand-off, she began to feverishly type on her computer.

Fenris came back around to Sara. "Get Marcel on the phone. He might be on the way. Tell him I'm starting Lockdown and to turn around. He needs to pass that on to his parents. Ask him what we need to get from his desk."

Sara swallowed down all the questions and did as she was told. Marcel's initially happy-go-lucky apology for being late was cut short by her message, and his response offered no help in decoding the situation. He went silent for a long moment before responding with a much more serious tone. "Okay, tell Fen I'm on it. Grab the pictures on my desk, please."

Sara added his things to the bundle she had gathered and proceeded to rummage through Fenris's desk, taking care to remember the photo of him and his father. Finished, she stood ready, waiting on her husband as he dashed about—texting various people, running upstairs to catch anyone there. Wrapping up one final call on the phone, he came to her.

"Ready?"

"Yes."

"Marcel?"

"He knows."

"Okay. Let's go."

They reached the exterior office door when a voice called out to them. Durgan was standing in the doorway to his own office, his face worn and haggard.

"Lockdown?"

"Yes."

"And I'm out?"

"What do you think?"

Durgan slumped against the doorframe. "I'm sorry, Fen. For everything."

"Not sorry enough." Fenris snarled as he left the office, taking Sara with him.

⁓❊⁓

Fenris fought back the panic bubbling in his chest as he swung the car out of the parking lot for what might be the last time. Sara remained quiet in her seat, and he was thankful she wasn't asking questions yet. Suddenly, he tensed, gripping the wheel and fighting the urge to turn the car back around.

"Fen?"

"I forgot to go through my desk. I—"

"I got the picture of your dad, and a few personals from your drawer."

"Thank you." Fenris relaxed until another thought made him stiffen again. "What else did you get?"

"If you're asking about the picture of Teresa hidden away in the top drawer, yes, I got that as well."

Fenris raised his eyes heavenward and groaned. "Sara ..."

"It's okay, Fen. I'm not mad you that still had her picture."

He let his breath out with a whoosh and reached over the seat to grasp her hand. She didn't *seem* to be mad, but he was determined to repair whatever possible damage had been done by him holding onto the photo of his dead fiancée. "I had forgotten it was there."

"You didn't have to hide it. She was a part of your life."

"I didn't mean to hide it exactly. It was, well—remember the day you met Sophie?"

"What do you think?"

"Right. Do you remember the conversation we had later that day?"

"You told me about Teresa for the first time."

"Leave it to you not to forget a thing. Okay. What if I said that was the day I realized I was falling in love with you?" He took his eyes off the road long enough to glance at her. She was gazing at him, her eyes wide. "I mean, I had been thinking a lot about you, about our friendship. I had considered asking you out before. How *much* I cared though—that was the day I knew."

"You never told me before," she whispered.

"I put her picture away that night after you left. It wasn't a denial of anything, she'll always—but I knew then I was ready."

"Took you long enough to make a move afterward."

"Yes, well ..." Fenris shrugged. "Nobody's perfect."

"I always wondered if it might have been the Seeker, when you ..."

He chuckled, remembering his first kiss with Sara. "That was fun. One of my favorite memories but far too shocking for me to process at the time."

Fenris took a turn down a street Sara wasn't expecting. She looked at him, alert. "Aren't we getting Sophie?"

He clenched his jaw in concentration. Talking about Teresa had been a distraction and her question brought him back to the present. All the possibilities were running loose in his mind, and he was desperate to catch at least one and focus on it. Sara was saying something, the words were a jumble in his ears.

"Fen!"

"Sorry. No, we're going straight to the house. Picking up some things. We'll go to the Aguilars from there. We'll stay with them a while."

"After that?"

"I don't know."

"How long will we be there?"

"I don't know," he repeated. "Depends on if the house is still standing when all this is over."

"If the house—what's happening?"

He gritted his teeth on the words. "Our world is falling apart."

"Fen ..." Her voice shook, and Fenris squeezed her hand. "What happened with Durgan?"

He didn't reply right away, and when he did his words were barely more than a whisper. "He's the one. The mole. All along it was... Everything that happened to us ..."

She didn't respond. He could almost see her processing, working through everything. As everything fell into place, she whispered, "He's the one who called about Sophie."

Fenris struck his palm against the steering wheel. "I'm a fool, Sara. All along, it was right there in front of me. You even challenged him about that, and I brushed it off."

"You couldn't have ever—" Sara began, but something about his expression made her change the subject. "Why the Aguilars?"

"Lockdown."

"Don't say that like I'm supposed to know what you are talking about."

"We have—how do I put this? A back-up office. At the Aguilars. It's quite impressive."

"A back-up office?"

"Yes."

"With a full complement of computers recording everything going on at the main office."

"I can see where you are going with this, so let me—."

"That no one ever thought to tell me."

"Well—"

"And something called Lockdown, shutting down everything, alerting everyone, that again, nobody ever told me about."

"Sweetheart—"

Sara swore and jerked her hand away. Fenris stiffened.

"Oops," he whispered.

"*Oops* is right, Fenris," Sara hissed.

Fenris flinched at her use of his full name, in a decidedly non-loving way. "Okay. Don't—"

"Tell me everything. Now."

"We're in Lockdown. It's what we call our default emergency mode. We always knew there was a possibility of being compromised at our headquarters, so we had this ghost office set up. Every twenty-four hours at midnight, the system there uploads anything that took place at the office during the day. You and Erin will have everything we need to keep functioning at your fingertips, I promise."

"This is all at the Aguilars?"

"Yes."

"Don't be ridiculous. How have I never seen it?"

"It's well-hidden."

"Fen, I've *lived* there. Don't tell me that I don't—"

"Are you saying I'm making this up?" Fenris asked incredulously.

"You've got to admit this is a lot to take in." Sara paused. "I guess this is why you always said the Aguilars were safe. They have special protections."

"That's an understatement."

"Who else knew?"

"Marcel had to know. Everyone … well, *almost* everyone, has been briefed about the idea of Lockdown, but the location has always been kept secret. Protocol demands that once it's set in motion, necessary information will be passed down the chain of command."

"Did it ever occur to you that I knew nothing of this? What if we weren't already married? Would I have been left out in the dust?"

Fenris flushed. "You know I would never—"

"Is that why you were talking to Erin?"

"Yes. Certain ... well, I always call them keys, but they're computer codes. They start Lockdown protocol and inform everyone. In this case, it was more complicated than we planned."

"Why?"

"Durgan. I had to cut him out of the chain of command."

"He must know where we're going?"

"Yes, and that's a risk. But Erin redid some security things—" Fenris snorted. "Look, I don't know all the terminology for this stuff. Anyway, the short version is he no longer has access to anything, and he won't know the new codes or passwords."

"That's what he meant when we were leaving, asking if he was out?"

"Yes." His voice broke over the word, and he swallowed hard, struggling to master his emotions. She took his hand again and held it tightly.

"I'm sorry," she whispered.

"Me too."

"It just really hurts, Fen. That you never told me."

Fenris sighed. He had hoped he would never have to tell her.

THE BASEMENT

They reached the house without mishap, and after a terse command for Sara to wait, Fenris shot out of the car. He looked all around as he opened her door and almost dragged her to the house. Pushing Sara inside, he ignored her exclamation of surprise.

"Stay here," he ordered.

Closing his eyes, Fenris sensed the rest of the house, room by room, until he was convinced no one had broken in. He slumped against the wall. Scrubbing at his face, he peeked at Sara between his fingers, half expecting her to be angry or frightened. She closed the space between them and put her arms around him. Fenris clung to her, struggling to control his anxieties.

"We'll be okay," she said.

"If anything happens to you, or Soph ..." he choked out.

"Nothing will happen," Sara said firmly. "Tell me what to do."

He took a shaking breath and kissed her forehead. "Clothes, shoes, anything you and Sophie need. Any personal items. Anything you would rescue from the house if it was on fire."

Sara stared at her husband. "Is that what you think will happen?"

"I don't know. But you know what? It's just a house. Let it burn. I need to make sure you and Sophie are safe. That is all that matters to me."

With those words, he turned and made his way to the library.

⁓❀⁓

Sara watched him disappear around the corner and made an effort to pull herself together. She gathered up a few duffel bags and began filling them with clothes and other small items. The pictures of her parents and Chloe. A wedding photograph of her and Fenris. The one family picture with all three of them, taken right after their honeymoon.

She was not especially sentimental about material things, but as Sara walked around the house, her throat ached. Fenris had worked on it for years, planning every detail. It had been an act of faith for him, even when everything in his life had been shrouded in darkness—to create a safe, warm nest with the dim hope of sharing it with a family someday. It had become a place dear to her own heart, sanctified by their love for each other. Despite his words, she knew this wasn't just a house to Fenris. It was *home*.

As she looked for special toys in Sophie's room, Sara couldn't find the child's stuffed rabbit, the one they had given Sophie for her fifth birthday. She stood in the doorway and called out, "Fen, have you seen Bun?"

"Yes, I have Bun. Grabbed him first thing."

Sara smiled to herself. Fenris had taken to fatherhood with astonishing alacrity for a man who hated all disruption to his routine and patterns. She wasn't surprised he had grabbed Sophie's favorite stuffed animal before anything else.

There was a sunroom in the house, and with its abundance of natural light, Fenris had insisted it should be her art studio. Here, Sara went next. There were some pieces that would crush her if they were lost. She grabbed her portfolio case and tucked in a few paintings, pausing at a portrait of Fenris. She had painted it months ago, long before they were together but when she was already falling in love with him. It wasn't her best work, yet somehow she'd managed to capture his lopsided smile. She stuffed it into the portfolio and left the room without a backward glance.

ᴄᴇ﹒✳﹒ᴏᴏ

Fenris ran his fingers over the spines of his father's books, gulping down the panic. He paused and massaged the back of his neck. What was the matter with him? He had been through far worse and barely turned a hair.

Those times had been different. His home had never been threatened, his family ...

Family.

He felt in his pocket, reassured that Bun was still there. More than anything, he wanted to hold Sara and Sophie in his arms. Fenris focused his thoughts on the books before him, his father's treasures.

"I can't take you all," he whispered. He began sorting out the most important volumes in an organized fashion. All the books his father had written. One made him smile, *Fenrir and The Ragnarök*. He didn't have to open it to remember the dedication—*For my son, Fenris.* He slipped it in his bag. His father's treasured first edition of *The Hobbit.* The family Bible.

He refused to think about his piano. Or the restored window casings—those had taken him months to get right. He kept his eyes on the shelves as he searched for books or photographs. Whenever he hesitated, the soft weight of Bun reminded him he had a family now—he couldn't afford to fall apart.

⸎⁂⸎

They met at the door with battered hearts.

"Got everything?" he asked.

"I think so. You still have Bun?"

He patted his pocket. "Yup. Let's go."

After locking the door behind them, they hurried down to the car and loaded everything up.

Fenris got behind the wheel and took a long look at the house, praying it wouldn't be the last. Sara caught his eye and smiled. His heart lightened. Sara was with him; that's what mattered. He only needed one thing more.

"Let's get our girl."

⸎⁂⸎

Sara could almost feel the tension pouring out of Fenris, and she longed to help. She did nothing to distract him while he drove from the house, knowing the faster they got to the Aguilars, the better for his stress levels. She had to bite her tongue several times at his constant checking of the rearview mirror. Once they turned down the Aguilar's street, his anxiety appeared to lessen. Instead of parking in the front as usual, he swung around the corner, turning onto an old, grassy track.

The Aguilar place was located on a vast lot of multiple acres and tucked away in an isolated neighborhood. Even though Sara wasn't surprised there was another entrance to the property, it caught her off-guard that she didn't know it existed until now. She said nothing, for Fenris was obviously confident about where he was going. He swung up behind the house, near the walled-in courtyard and pool. After turning off the car, he sighed with relief.

"It's okay. We're going to be safe here."

Sara stepped out of the car and Fenris put his arm around her waist. "We'll get our things later. I need to see Sophie first."

Most days, Sara would have laughed to see his concern, but she was equally anxious to be with the small child. They passed through a gate near the shack that held all the things for the pool's upkeep and aimed straight for the house. It was bolted. Undeterred, Fenris pulled out a set of keys and unlocked the door. Stepping inside, the first person they saw was Marcel.

"There you are! Mama thought you would be here ages ago. She's been stressing me out."

"I wanted to get some things from the house."

Marcel nodded with understanding. "Everyone's down in the basement."

"Who's here?" asked Fenris.

"Family and people from the office are dribbling in but I've not heard from any of the fighters yet."

"You won't hear from them, it's protocol. They'll arrive when they can."

Marcel gave Sara a nudge. "You okay?"

"Just another day, right?" She managed a weak smile.

"Crazy, isn't it? Everything happening today."

"Not as crazy as not knowing about it."

"Yeah, let's not get back into that," Fenris said, giving Marcel a warning look.

Fenris strode down the hallway into a spare bedroom with Marcel and Sara. He opened the closet door and Sara saw nothing unusual. With the flick of a switch, a keypad came out of the wall. Fenris tapped in several passcodes, and Sara gasped as the back of the closet opened. "I'm not going to encounter snow and a lamppost, am I?"

Fenris huffed a laugh. "I wish. After you ..."

After a brief hesitation, Sara passed through with Fenris following. Her breath caught when the door shut behind them, enclosing them in darkness for a second. Weak overhead lights flickered on, dimly lighting their way. Fenris took her hand, lacing his fingers with hers.

"It will be all right. Come on."

They turned a corner and went down a narrow, metal staircase. It opened into a large space, and Sara came to a dead stop. The light was less than she was used to, and it took her eyes a moment to adjust to the darkness. Computers hummed in the background.

Marcel flicked a light switch and Sara was stunned at the sight. If she didn't know better, she would have thought she was in a smallish, industrial warehouse. It was a cavernous space for a house basement—smaller than their office downtown but a substantial size nonetheless. She did a quick headcount of the desks and computers. If the entire office was going to be camped out here, it would be a tight squeeze.

Fenris gestured to the computers. "They're as good as what you had at the other office." He tugged her hand, and they walked through the building. Fenris pointed out different parts of the office as they passed until they came to a door that opened into a conference room. Several people sat at the table, talking, and then Sara's vision was dominated by a tiny rush of blonde hair.

"Mommy!" Sophie shrieked, running toward them. Despite her exclamation, she went straight to Fenris, and he scooped her up into a tight hug, relieved to be holding the little girl once more.

Marcel gave Sara an amused look.

"Mommy?"

Sara shrugged. "She started calling me that a few days ago."

"I love how she yells out 'Mommy' but goes to Fen. Is he Daddy now?" He smirked.

"No. For some reason, she still calls him Fen. I think it hurts his feelings."

"Well, she was so young when her mother died, it was probably an easier adjustment. Ted hasn't been gone long."

"He knows that."

Fenris had walked away from them, whispering with Sophie. He pulled Bun out of his pocket, and Sophie laughed with delight at the sight of her favorite toy. No matter what she called him, there was no denying they had a special bond. Sara smiled at the two of them and turned to the others in the room.

It was a mix of a few office people—she spotted Erin and Vanessa—as well as most of the Aguilar family. She caught Mrs. Aguilar's eye, and they crossed the room to each other, meeting with a warm embrace.

"He never told you," Mrs. Aguilar said. It wasn't a question.

"Never," Sara said, the anger once again bubbling up.

The older woman sighed. "He didn't want to frighten you that there was even a need for such a thing."

"As if things were already so normal for us," Sara fussed.

"I know, *mija*, but he has always been determined to protect you. Especially from your own fears after ..."

Realization hit Sara. Fenris was scared she would run from her fears again. Run from *him* again. A warm hand landed on the small of her back, and she turned to see Fenris beside her. His eyes were searching and worried. She gave him her first true, warm smile since that morning. He drew her close, kissing the top of her head.

"I'm sorry," he whispered. "For everything. Not telling you. Having to drag you out of our home ..."

"As long as we're together. Is this it, then? We're going to be living in the basement?"

Fenris barked a laugh. "No, we have a bedroom all to ourselves upstairs."

"Thank heavens," Sara said. "I was worried this was our new home."

"What, you don't like it?" asked Marcel. "Maybe after some new rugs, and a few curtains ..."

"Windows first," Sara laughed.

Fenris rolled his eyes at the two of them and jerked his chin toward the door. "Let's all go back upstairs. We can keep track of everyone as they come in. It's already been a long day, and I have a feeling I'll be up all night. I'm going to need some coffee."

Mrs. Aguilar and Frances took over guiding the office people to places where they could stay for at least the next night or two, while Sara remained with Marcel and Fenris in the kitchen. Sophie continued to stay near Fenris, refusing to let him go far. Sara wondered if the child had Seen something that frightened her enough to not let him out of her sight, and her heart squeezed at the idea.

Fenris brought Marcel up to speed with everything that had happened in the office, and they both sat mulling their options over steaming mugs of coffee. Sara quietly sat and listened. Sophie had fallen asleep in Fenris's lap.

"How long do you think we'll be exiled down to the basement?" asked Marcel.

Fenris shrugged. "No idea. I feel like I'm catching up with everything myself. I'll know more in a day or two. I hope."

"What about Durgan?"

"I shouldn't have left him as I did," Fenris said. "I was an idiot to not get more information out of him. I just ... didn't see this coming."

"Do you think you should have?" Sara asked.

"Yes."

"How could you?"

"I should have seen it coming," he insisted. "Maybe not this exactly, but *something*. All the warnings, all the signs. He was right, I've been distracted ..."

"Stop it." Marcel slammed his hand down on the table. Both Fenris and Sara looked at him in surprise. "I won't let you do this to yourself, Fen. Not again. I won't let you blame yourself. What you call distraction was living a normal life for once. Having love. A family. You haven't done anything wrong."

Fenris shrugged.

"You going to honestly tell me you regret these last few months? Your marriage? Sophie? Are these things *distractions?*"

"Of course not."

"Then stop it."

Fenris smiled reluctantly. "Okay."

"What's our next move?"

Fenris eased Sophie onto Sara's lap and stood. He paced the room a few times. "I'm not sure. I do know this, I'm tired of hanging back and waiting for them to come after us. It's time to take the offensive."

"What does that mean?" asked Marcel with a worried frown.

"Josephine and her people are going to regret they threatened my family."

IN THE DARK OF THE NIGHT

I t wasn't late, but the sun was setting earlier, and the encroaching darkness was welcome, as were the people walking their dogs or jogging the streets. They were the perfect distraction to allow Fenris to slip through the twilight, the hood of his black sweatshirt drawn up over his head. Casting his Gifts in the surrounding area, he could feel them. Other Gifted lurking about. Shadows in alleyways and hiding behind buildings.

Some of the shadows were his friends, watching over him.

Some were not.

After checking on a pretty little bungalow and muttering a grateful prayer that all looked well, Fenris arrived at a house he knew almost as well as his own. He recoiled at the overgrown yard and untrimmed hedges. The whole place had a neglected air, when in times past it had always been kept clean and neat. He crossed the street, every sense alert to the potential dangers, and skirted around to the back of the house. Peering through a dimly lit window, Fenris scowled at the sight of debris and filth.

He marched to the unlit back door and knocked a familiar code. A muffled yell came from the interior of the house. Fenris hesitated, debating with himself over the best course of action before finally blasting the door off its hinges. He took a few, cautious steps into the house. Turning a corner, he found Durgan sitting on the floor with his back against a wall. He held a half-empty bottle of liquor in his hands and blinked at the sight of Fenris before him.

"Fen, m'boy," he slurred.

"Whiskey?" Fenris asked incredulously. "How drunk are you?"

"Not much."

"You're disgusting."

"Tell me something I don't know."

Fenris growled and threw a paper at Durgan. "Three a.m. Be at that address." Bleary-eyed, Durgan blinked at the paper while Fenris swiped the bottle from his hands. "I want you there sober. You hear me?"

Durgan belched. Fenris took the bottle to the kitchen and dumped its contents down the sink. A couple of beers was one thing, but every Gifted knew too much alcohol had severe consequences on their specialized brain function.

Coming out of the kitchen, he loomed over Durgan. "You going to be there?"

"Yes. If they don't kill me first."

"If they do, it'll save me the trouble. If you don't show up, you had better be dead already."

Durgan flinched. "I deserve that."

"That and more." Without another word, Fenris let himself out through the front door. A car pulled up, and he spotted Hugo in the driver's seat. He slid into the vehicle, and they sped away.

ꙮ

Back at the Aguilar home, Fenris sat alone in the kitchen in a low beam of light, nursing a mug of black coffee. It had been months since he'd drank this much caffeine so late into the night hours, and he wondered how it would affect him later. Fenris needed to keep his mind clear and not get too rattled, so he was glad the light footsteps coming up behind him didn't make him jump. Sara's arms came around him from behind and he caught a hint of strawberries as she gave him a warm kiss on the cheek.

"Sophie okay?" he asked.

"She's asleep. Should be out the rest of the night."

"Good, it's late."

"Where are the others?"

He didn't have to ask who she meant. "Hugo is crashing on the sofa until we leave. Erin is down below fussing at the computers, and Raven is ... well, no telling at the moment."

"Have you heard from Tudor or Cal?"

"No. I'm not worried about Tudor. He's young and probably out partying, clueless to what's going on. He wasn't on call. Cal on the other hand ..."

Fenris stood and together they walked through a few rooms to the snoring heap of Hugo, asleep on a sofa. He gently pushed Sara away and nudged the man, stepping back before a flash of light could strike him.

With a holler, Hugo sat up. "Oof. Sorry, Fen."

"No worries, I expected it. Listen, could you go check out Cal's place? It's unusual for him to be this delayed."

"Sure thing, boss."

"Don't call me that," Fenris growled.

"Fine. But you're the boss now, like it or not."

"Yeah, yeah. Go now and be careful."

Hugo heaved himself to his feet and left. Fenris sank into the sofa, bringing Sara down into his lap. He cradled her in his arms like a child, holding her close with her head on his shoulder.

"I'm scared, Fen."

"Me too," he whispered, squeezing her tight. They sat a long time, and Fenris dozed in spite of the coffee. The soft tone of his phone jolted him awake, and Sara stirred in his arms. He slid her off and stood, answering the phone. After a brief, muttered conversation, he swiped the phone off, his hands shaking.

"Cal's dead."

"What?"

"He and his wife Bethany—dead. Hugo is at their house. Tudor was with them. He's hurt. I need to get Marcel."

"Why was Tudor there?"

"I'm not sure. He and Cal worked together a lot. He may have been there already, or maybe Cal called him when they were in trouble ..." Fenris snapped his mouth shut, aware he was on the verge of babbling. He moaned at the sight of his wife, pale and shaken. He pulled her into an embrace.

"I'm so sorry, sweetheart."

"This isn't your fault."

"I know, but I wish you weren't dragged down into it with me."

"We've talked about this. I wouldn't be anywhere else."

He pressed his lips into her hair. "You make me ridiculously happy."

"No one deserves it more."

"I don't know about that," he said, thinking of his words to Durgan earlier in the evening. "Hugo will be back soon with Tudor. I better go wake Marcel. Why don't you go to bed?"

"No, I would just lie awake, wanting to know what happened."

"I'll be right back. You'll be okay here alone?"

"Of course."

Fenris snuggled her back into the couch, tucking a blanket around her before making his way to the kitchen. Getting a fresh, hot cup of coffee, Fenris decided to message Marcel instead of going into his bedroom.

A few minutes later, Marcel shuffled in, yawning, hair askew.

"Whassup? Sheesh, Fen. Drinking coffee at this hour? What will Sara say?"

"Cal is dead."

Marcel froze before giving Fenris a hard stare. "Couldn't have led up to that a bit more gently?"

"No. I don't have time. Tudor's hurt and Hugo is bringing him."

"Bethany?"

"Dead as well. Tudor found them both ... or he was there. I'm not sure. We'll find out."

Marcel swallowed. Fenris knew what he was thinking. If Cal's wife Bethany was dead, who could say if Frances or his mother were safe? Or Sara—

Fenris shook the thought away. "Do what you can with Tudor. I'm going to need him later."

❧

Hugo's old, beat-up car dropped Fenris off at a dark corner. "I'll watch for your signal, Fen."

Fenris grunted and pulled the hood back over his head.

"You sure you want to do this on your own?"

"I'm sure. Get out of here. Watch out for the others."

Left alone in the darkness, Fenris studied the all-night diner across the street. A slight movement at the building's corner caught his eye. It was Erin, waiting in the shadows and holding one of Josephine's electric guns. He knew Tudor was watching from the back side of the restaurant. A catlike figure moved on the roof—Raven. Hugo would circle the block as long as needed.

Fenris shoved his hands into his pockets to stop the shaking. He couldn't help thinking of Durgan, Cal, and Hugo together—the first of the street fighters. They were there the night Teresa was killed. Cal had been the one to drag him away from her body, holding on to him until his father got there—he stopped that memory in its tracks. He had joined the team himself soon after. Cal had been a good friend over the years and the news of his death had nearly broken Fenris, but he had no time to dwell on his grief.

He strode into the glow of the streetlight, crossing to the diner. A bell chimed as he pushed through the door. As he had hoped, it was almost empty. The bars had let out an hour ago, and those with alcohol-induced hunger had gotten their fix and were already on their way home. Fenris used all his senses to feel out the place. No other Gifted nearby, save his own people and the man he was here to meet. If there were Hunters in the vicinity, well—after Josephine's people, he no longer feared them.

Fenris slid into the booth, his eyes locked onto Durgan's as though daring him to make a wrong move. Durgan licked his lips.

"I want you to understand—"

"No."

Durgan took a breath, his eyes roving about. Some movement in the window caught his attention. "Who came with you?"

"Hugo and Tudor. Raven. Erin."

"I'm surprised you didn't bring—"

"Cal is dead."

"What?"

"And Bethany. They're both dead. Murdered in their home."

Durgan buried his head in his hands. When he looked up again, his face was haggard. "I'm sorry."

"You're sorry."

"Yes."

"That's all you can say? You're *sorry*? You betrayed us! Their death is on *your* hands."

"Fen—"

"I've never killed anyone in cold blood before, but I swear ..."

Durgan smiled weakly. "You've never killed *anyone*, period. Don't play that game with me. If a Hunter has died on your watch, it was an accident. Never on purpose."

"You know nothing—"

"I know this."

For a moment, Fenris's eyes glazed over. There were things they had all done. The fighters. Acts of desperation in the dark of night, done to protect each other. Things even Durgan didn't know. Fenris had never told anyone, and the fighters held silent unto themselves.

"There's a first time for everything," Fenris rasped. He held up his hands, the palms facing Durgan. "We haven't worked in the field together for a long time. You have no idea what these hands can do. All the fun little *tricks* I've picked up over the years."

"That's not who your father raised you to be."

"My father? Don't you *dare* bring him into this. Dad didn't know what I would be facing—what we would all be facing—in this miserable life the Changing gave us. He trusted you to watch over me, to—" Fenris choked on his words, emotions swelling, recalling those days in the hospital after Robert Trygg had that last heart attack. Everyone but Fenris had known he was dying. Robert, using what was left of his energy to ensure his heartbroken son would have support. Charging Alicia Aguilar, Durgan, and Marcel to watch over his boy. Fenris remembered pleading with Marcel to do something, anything, to save his father. Yet he did nothing.

I can only heal so much, Fen.

The old, familiar bitterness against his best friend rose like bile in his throat. Fenris pushed it down, as he always did.

"You are your father's son," whispered Durgan, breaking into his memories. "You always have been. Don't shame him."

"Stop it!" Fenris half rose to his feet, sick feelings churning. Would his father be proud of him? Fenris didn't want to dwell on that. "Dad left me alone to figure all this out. And you—you were his best friend."

"I didn't mean—Fen, it was never supposed go down the way it did."

"Yet it did. She's not done, is she? Josephine."

Durgan slowly shook his head.

"What does she want?"

"All the Fighters. Some others. Erin—"

"You knew all along Erin wasn't with her. Yet you tried to pin it on her."

Ignoring him, Durgan continued. "She wants you and Sophie, and—"

"Why, Durgan? What does she want from us?" asked Fenris, desperation clawing at him.

"Her own army of Gifted. To take over."

"Take over what?"

"Everything. The government. The world. Her ambitions have no boundaries."

"That's ridiculous. There aren't enough of us."

"You don't know that, not with her recruiting all over the globe."

"People don't want—"

"I'm convinced she's a Charisma."

"Even a Charisma can't control a person's thoughts or actions."

"True, but don't underestimate her. She can be *quite* persuasive, Fen. And if you don't go along with it, she'll see you dead. That's probably what happened with Cal. If her minions confronted him, and he refused …"

Fenris fell silent. Cal was as loyal a colleague as one could find. Of course, he refused.

"What's coming?"

"She'll kill me if I tell you too much."

"You're dead already. By her hands or mine. I've only let you live this long to get information and—"

"She has my daughter!"

Fenris froze, staring at Durgan.

"She has Laurel. You—all of you—you're the ransom."

"What?" gasped Fenris. "When did this happen?"

"Two weeks ago."

"She's been holding this over your head?"

"She had been threatening me—it started last winter. She wanted me to turn you over. I thought she was a joke. I didn't take her seriously until after the attack on the Hollingses."

Fenris ground his teeth, willing himself not to kill the man before him. "Were you responsible for their deaths?"

"No! It was her way of sending me a message. To show me what she was capable of doing. Not to mention, her first real attempt to get you and Sophie in her clutches. After that happened... I ... She began to ..."

"And you planted the bug."

"I didn't, but I did give them access."

"Why didn't you come to me?" Fenris groaned. "I've known Laurel since she was a kid. I—we all would have helped. You think we would have let her get away with it?"

"She threatened to kill Laurel if I didn't do it her way."

Fenris slumped. There was nothing left to say.

"I'm sorry, Fen. It wasn't supposed to go down the way it did. She never told me she would do ... what she did to you."

"And Sara?" muttered Fenris.

"Incidental. She was just going to be collateral damage. To them, she was nothing."

Fenris jerked his head up and his eyes flashed. "Excuse me?"

"Sara. She wasn't the goal, but—"

"*Just* collateral damage?" said Fenris, rising to his feet, his hands curling into fists. Durgan fell silent, realizing his mistake. "What's changed?"

"Sara is on her list. With the emergence of her Gift, Josephine has become quite interested in her."

The long simmering temper boiled over and Fenris slammed his fists on the tabletop, rattling the coffee cups. Leaning far over, he invaded Durgan's space. "Pass this on to Josephine. There are many things I will tolerate. Many things I will let go. But if she threatens my wife ... my daughter ... *she will pay.* Touch them and she signs her death warrant. Tell her."

"What about Laurel? Fen, please ..."

Fenris's face softened a fraction, and he gave Durgan a grudging nod. "I'll see what I can do for her. My family comes first, you understand?"

"Thank you," Durgan whispered. "What next?"

"I don't know. Stay put at your house."

"She might not let me live."

"I'll do what I can for Laurel. After I take care of my own family. As for you," snarled Fenris, "that's not my problem."

Fenris crept into one of the larger guestrooms of the house. Sara was awake, and put her finger to her lips when he came in. He checked the makeshift cot off to the side and gave the barest hint of a smile at the sight of Sophie, curled up and asleep with Bun.

He remained at the end of the bed, unable to move. Sara shifted over to him, perched on her knees to put her arms around his waist. He relished the feel of her holding him, but his heart raced. The last twenty-four hours had resurrected horrific ghosts of his past.

What would Sara do if she knew his darkest secrets? Would she pull her sweet warmth away from him forever?

"I don't know if I can do this," his voice rasped. "Can I lead these people? Protect you? I don't think I can stop what's coming. Sara, I—"

She brought his head to hers, their foreheads touching. Still, he made no move to hold her. His chest heaved with suppressed emotions. Sara ran her hands down his back, massaging him gently.

"My sweet Fen, whatever—"

"I've done things, Sara. Terrible things. I've never told you."

She froze.

"Hunters. I didn't mean to, but—sometimes—" he choked, afraid to meet her eyes. Afraid to see her love grow dim. Afraid the light in her eyes when he whispered of his love for her would be gone forever.

"Fen."

He shook his head; his heart lay dying at her feet.

"I know, Fen. *I know.* That day when Marcel came over to heal you. You ... told us."

Tears falling, he didn't dare look up at her.

"You were crying out, talking, you were delusional—Marcel and I agreed to never bring it up, not unless you did first."

"I—I talked about ..."

"Yes."

Fenris remained silent a long moment, struggling to understand.

"But—you're still here with me. Despite knowing ..."

"Where else would I be?"

Bewildered, he finally met her eyes. Clear, beautiful, full of love, brimming with grace.

"Let me hold you," she whispered, tugging him closer.

"I'm so sorry ..."

"Don't." Sara took his face in her hands and kissed him. Slow. Deep.

He broke away, almost strangling on his fears. "No matter what happens to me, to us ... Sara ... Always know I love you."

"Don't do this," she whispered. "Not tonight. Let the next hour be about us."

Sara was kissing him again, her fingers tangled in his hair. She pulled him down with her onto the bed. His arms tightened around her. "Sophie?"

"She was up far too late. She's out."

Fenris wrapped his arms around his wife, wanting the next hour to stretch into eternity.

ↄₑ✳ₑↄ

After Fenris fell asleep, Sara could no longer keep the hot tears from falling. All the grief and terrors of that long day rushed over her, the fears for their future were arrows aimed at her heart. She wept for the sweet, noble man who lay in her arms, who carried the weight of their world on his shoulders. At last she took a ragged breath, wiped away the tears, and held on to him, letting sleep take her in the last hour before dawn.

REGROUP

In the months since their marriage, Sara had learned her husband's sleep pattern quite well. Fenris always started the night snuggling her as close as possible. As his sleep deepened, he eased away, his arm still draped loosely around her. Sometimes he rolled over to his back, often trying to bring her around with him. By dawn he was usually on his stomach with a pillow over his head to block the sound of the birds. However, that morning Sara woke still crushed against his chest. When she tried to move, she was surprised to hear him mutter, "Stay."

Sara slid back enough to see his face. His eyes were shut, with deep shadows underneath. She stroked his temple until his breathing slowed as he dropped back into sleep. She lay there as long as she could, but when Sophie began to stir, Sara inched away. His breathing hitched, and she froze until he rolled over to his stomach. After dressing Sophie, she paused, unsure whether to tell him they were leaving or not. She hated to disturb Fenris after so little sleep the night before but gave him a gentle nudge anyway. He huffed a breath at her touch.

"Mhumph."

"I'm sorry," she whispered.

He lifted his head and gave his eyes a rub. "Washapning?"

"Nothing. Sophie and I are going to breakfast. I didn't want to wake you, but with everything going on, I was worried you might go ballistic if you woke up and we weren't here in your sight."

"You're probably right." A wry smile peeked through before his head crashed back into the pillow. "I need to get up anyway."

"Take your time. I'll make sure the coffee is brewing." Sara bent down to kiss his cheek, and he gave her what she interpreted as an affectionate grunt.

The kitchen was the heart of the entire Aguilar home. Located in the middle of the sprawling house, it had French doors and large windows opening to the courtyard. With so many family members always in and out, the kitchen held both a table near the windows and a massive island with stools. On the other side of the island was a vast rectangular cooking area with an industrial sized fridge, the largest gas-burning stove Sara had ever seen, and two ovens. Sara took a deep breath of contentment. It was hard to not feel hopeful when sitting around the island with the sunshine streaming in, and the aroma of fresh coffee in the air.

Mrs. Aguilar was already at the stove, cooking a copious number of eggs. Tortillas were on the griddle, and Sara's nose also picked out bacon, chorizo, and roasted potatoes. Mrs. Aguilar gave both Sara and Sophie a warm smile. Sara helped Sophie onto her booster seat at the table. "Are you doing all this by yourself? Can I help?"

"No, *mija*. Frances was here, she left to clean up. Everything is almost finished. I just need to keep all this warm until people can eat."

"I'm sorry I wasn't up earlier to help."

Mrs. Aguilar waved a vague hand. "You are a woman with many of your own cares. What happened last night? Everyone must have been up late."

Sara took her time answering, pouring herself a mug of coffee before telling everything that happened during the night. Mrs. Aguilar listened carefully, crossing herself at the news of Cal and his wife.

"This is a madness," she sighed while dishing out some food onto a plate. "We must have faith it will work out in the end." She handed the plate to Sara, who took it to the table for Sophie.

Marcel wandered into the kitchen, his expression brightening at the sight of the food. "This is enough for an army, Mama."

"Isn't that what I have in my home? Our own army. They must be fed well."

"Speaking of which, is there some paper and a pen around here?" asked Sara.

Marcel's mouth was full of egg, but he dug around in a drawer, pulling out some pens and a legal pad. Sara sat, writing down the name of everyone she knew was present at the house. She pushed the paper toward Marcel. "Am I missing anyone? Any fighters who came during the night?"

"Two more came in earlier this morning. Burton and Augie. That's it."

"Is Tobias Grant still with the Guild?" asked Mrs. Aguilar.

"Tobias—you mean Toby? Yes, why? Do you know him?"

"Mama knows everyone with the Guild," Marcel inserted. "She helped train us all."

"What? All of you?"

"Sure, you've worked with her. You know what she can do."

"I didn't know she had worked with everyone. Why did you ask about Toby, Mama?"

"I was curious if he ever did learn to control his Gift. He would be a great asset if he has."

"What is his Gift, anyway?"

Marcel snickered, and Mrs. Aguilar turned back to the stove. Sara knew she wouldn't get any more out of them on the topic. She glanced at the oven clock. "Goodness, it's almost nine. What do you think? Give it until noon and put out search parties for those who haven't shown up yet?"

"That's Fen's call."

"You're second-in-command now, right?"

"I forgot about that." Marcel groaned. "Are you sure you can't—"

"Fen's asleep and I'm not waking him up unless I have to."

"No, I'm not," came a grumble as Fenris lurched into the room. He patted Sophie's head and came to Sara, hugging her from behind. "What's this?" he asked, peering over her shoulder.

"List of who's already here."

Fenris grunted and kissed her cheek. Yawning, he went around the island to Mrs. Aguilar. "Can I help?"

"No, Fenris. Get some coffee."

He nodded obediently and shuffled to the coffeepot. Sara smiled—if it wasn't for the beard, he could be an overgrown teenage boy getting up late on Saturday, with his plaid pajama bottoms and rumpled T-shirt. His hair was all over the place, black waves tangled and tossed, hanging over his eyes. He caught Sara's watching him and paused while pouring the coffee. "What?"

"Nothing. You look adorable this morning."

"More like exhausted and anticipating a terrible day." But a soft smile appeared, the one she knew he saved just for her. It warmed her down to her toes.

"Always the optimist ..." muttered Marcel.

"Give the coffee a chance to kick in, and you'll think that *was* optimistic."

"You should really think about therapy one of these days."

"Now, why would I need that when I have you?"

"Very funny."

"Okay, show me the list." He peered at the legal pad, pushing it back and forth a few times, trying to focus.

"Do you need glasses?" asked Marcel, with a wicked gleam in his eyes.

"What? No! I don't need—you know, I'm *tired.*"

Marcel hooted. "You *do* need glasses! That's hysterical. Fenris Trygg, our own superman, needs—"

"Shut up, Marcel." He winced as Mrs. Aguilar smacked him on the head while passing by with a fresh plate of food. Getting the words focused at last, he sipped on his coffee and murmured the names to himself. "Half the Aguilars—has anyone checked in with the rest of the family? All the cousins?"

"Pops did this morning. Everyone is fine."

"Great. We have most of the fighters. Tudor, Burton, Augie, Hugo, Raven... still missing two. Erin, great. She could be a fighter herself if she worked at it. Vanessa—where the heck are the rest of the office people? They all knew where to go. Where's my phone—blast, left it the bedroom. I need to—Sara? You all right?"

Sara started, unaware she had zoned out. "I'm fine, why?"

"You don't look fine. Marcel, should you—"

"None of us got a lot of sleep."

Fenris set down his mug and came to her with worry in his eyes. He put an arm around her, and Sara relaxed into his embrace. He cuddled her closer when an involuntary shiver went through her. "Of course, you're tired. I've ripped you away from your home and everything has gone crazy. Did you have breakfast?"

"I'm not hungry," she mumbled.

"Sweetheart. Go back to bed and get some rest, please."

"I'm fine, I don't—"

"That's an order from your boss, Red." He pushed her back and forced a smile. "I won't be able focus on anything if I'm worried about you, okay?"

Sara hesitated. The idea of going back to bed was appealing. "What about Sophie?"

Fenris kissed her forehead.

"I can keep her out of mischief. Let's get you to bed."

He walked her to the room and grabbed his phone from the bed-side table. Sara snuggled back under the covers with another shiver, and he tucked her in. His beard scratched pleasantly against her ear as he kissed her cheek and whispered, "I love you, sweetheart."

Within seconds, she was asleep.

⁓✳⁓

Sara woke with a start and sat bolt upright in bed, heart racing. It took her a moment to recognize her surroundings. Her stomach growled and she clambered out of bed. Grabbing her shoes, she trotted back toward the kitchen, wondering at the silence that had descended upon the house. Was everyone down in the basement? She hadn't memorized the passcodes yet. A soft rattle in the kitchen reassured her someone was hanging about. Turning the corner, she saw Frances standing watch over the largest stew pot Sara had ever seen.

"Sara! I'm glad you're awake, you slept right through lunch. How are you feeling?" Frances gave her a sisterly hug.

"Much better, but that explains why I'm so hungry."

"I have a vat of soup going—oooh!" Frances hunched over, her hand on her swollen belly.

"Frances?"

"I'm fine. That was a big kick."

"You shouldn't be on your feet. How much longer?"

"Two months, give or take. This one's got to be a boy. He's huge. Anyway, this soup won't be ready for a few hours yet."

"It smells delicious. I'll dig around for something to tide me over. Where is everyone?"

"Out back on the patio. Big children, all of them."

"What?"

"You'll see. Here ..." Frances pulled out a warmer from the back of the stove and handed Sara a piece of cornbread. She paused, and her eyes raked over Sara, who thought Frances was mastering that same soul-piercing look she must have learned from Mrs. Aguilar. "You sure you're okay, Sara?"

"I'm positive. I needed a bite, that's all. Thank you. I'll go see what Fen is up to. Is Sophie with him?"

"Yes, that child can't be kept away from anything. Be careful out there."

Sara wondered why Frances would issue such a warning as she walked outside through the kitchen doors. A large crowd was gathered, with Mrs. Aguilar in the middle. They were laughing and joking around, not at all behaving as she expected, given the circumstances.

An electric stream shot out twenty feet, barely missing her. Fenris yelled and raced to her, with Sophie tagging after him. "Are you okay?"

"Sorry, Sara!" Erin called out, waggling her fingers.

Fenris took her by the shoulders. "You look better. How are you feeling?"

"I'm great. Don't fuss over me. What are all you doing out here?"

An unexpected grin came over her husband's face. "Well, to be honest, I'm not sure how it got started, but it's turned into a game of showing off each other's Gifts. Mama is helping a few."

"They're displaying their Gifts? I'm surprised."

"Well, I think with everything happening, people needed a way to blow off some steam. They won't be showing them *all* off, I can promise you that. Just some of the more fun ones. Come on ..."

More people had arrived during her extended sleep. Almost everyone from the office was present, including a few people she had never met before. Sara assumed they must be spouses or siblings. She was certain the young men surrounding Erin were her brothers.

Mrs. Aguilar was lecturing Tudor about something regarding his gift, and he listened to her intently. Sara smiled. She didn't know Tudor well, but she liked him. He was the youngest fighter they had, recruited two years ago when he was eighteen. Unlike the rest of them, the Changing had happened in his childhood. Fenris had indicated he was very powerful and had speculated it could be because he received them at a younger age.

"Fen, what does Tudor do?"

"A lot. In fact," Fenris glanced around to ensure no one was near, "I'm starting to wonder if he's like me."

"An Assimilator?"

"Yes, but keep it quiet. That's what he and Mama are hashing out, trying to determine how he's been obtaining new Gifts. Are they manifesting late, or is he picking them up from others?"

"Tobias!" Mrs. Aguilar called out in a commanding tone.

There were some giggles as Toby raised his eyes heavenward. "You know I go by Toby, ma'am."

"You are Tobias in this house. It is a good name. Now, come here."

Mrs. Aguilar gestured toward the pool, and Toby groaned. Red-faced, he took a solid stance and appeared to put great deal of thought into what he was about to do. Throwing out his hand, a vast ball of fire shot out and rolled into the pool. Everyone gasped and applauded. Fenris rubbed his hands together.

"I *need* that one. Has he been practicing, Marcel? He shot that one pretty straight."

"He told Mama he hasn't had much opportunity. It's not like he can practice in his apartment."

Fenris snorted. Sara watched as Toby shot out another fireball. This time it bounced around and came back like a boomerang until Raven swiped it into the pool.

"And there we go." Fenris sighed. "This is what always happens. He can shoot them out but can't control them."

"Just like a man," Raven murmured nearby, and all three of them jumped. Sara gasped. Raven had been across the patio seconds before.

Fenris glared at her. "Blast it, Raven! Will you stop doing that?"

"You're only jealous because you can't do it," Raven taunted.

"It's also unnerving."

Sara wandered about, watching various people showing off their Gifts. What surprised her the most were the office people. She had always assumed they had mundane meaningless Gifts, but in fact, they were incredible. Another fireball raced past her, and Sara laughed at the sound of Fenris yelling at Raven to get rid of it.

"It's a regular island of misfit toys, isn't it?" Marcel said as he approached her.

"I'm so confused."

Marcel took her arm and led her and Sophie away from the fray. "I need to get you two over here before Fen has a conniption. He's watching fireballs and electric streams and ice daggers coming at you from all directions."

"Ice daggers? I missed those."

"One of Augie's more fun Gifts."

They sat on some pool chairs away from the others and watched them for a while. Sara was amazed at some of the Gifts she was seeing for the first time.

"Why have all these powerful Gifts been kept under wraps?"

"Powerful Gifts, yes. Control? Not at all." Marcel chortled. "We can't take them into the field, but neither were we going to waste a warm body in the office without the ability to protect."

"Oh, I see. That's why the office was safe even if Hunters dared attack without the fighters around?"

"Right. Every single office worker has solid defensive Gifts that could be used in a pinch."

"As long as they didn't burn the office down in the process."

Sara and Marcel fell silent as Fenris called out to the group. "Okay, folks. Let's gather in and have a talk about what's going on. I think most of you are aware of the basics of why we're here, but I know there might be missing gaps of information for some. Especially for the office people who aren't privy to the information the fighters must know."

Fenris proceeded to outline all that had happened in the last few months, starting with the day the database system was infiltrated. The hardest parts were when Fenris told them all about Durgan's betrayal and the death of Cal and his wife, causing anger and sorrow to sweep through the group.

A silence fell among them until Hugo spoke up. "What's next, Fen?"

"Well, this is where it gets tricky," Fenris said. "I'm not sure. We have this location, and it's as secure as we can make it. Your homes may not be safe to go back to—at least, not for a while. The Aguilars have welcomed us to stay here, and there is room. When you all signed on to work at the Guild, you knew this was always a possibility. That said, none of us saw this coming. It's okay if it takes you some time to acclimate to the situation and make the right decision for you and your families. Where we go from here, I—I have no idea. I'm working on it.

"Fighters, none of you have fought against Gifted before, and I tell you, it is a whole different ballgame. You'll need to learn to rethink your entire process. I'll go over this with you later. At this point, I've dealt with them the most. With Cal gone, I want Hugo in charge of the fighters, under me. Erin? I want you with the fighters."

"Fen—you can't—" Erin protested.

"I can, and I will. Don't worry, it'll be a last resort thing, but you are more than capable of doing ... whatever it is you do. Toby, I see you still can't control those fireballs, can you?"

Sara whipped her head around to Marcel. "Wait," she whispered. "Fen has always made jokes about not shooting fireballs in the street. Is that—"

"Yeah," Marcel grinned. "Toby started off as a fighter until there was an incident downtown, and ... Well, Fen had no choice. He had to take him off the team."

Stifling a giggle, Sara turned back to Fenris, who was giving them both an exasperated look. He continued, "Toby, keep working with Mama. Or anyone else who might be able to help. Erin, maybe you can help him learn to manage those things. It would be incredible if we could make use of it."

Erin gave an exaggerated groan, but Sara noticed her eyes were sparkling.

"All right, people. Settle into your quarters as best as you can. Everyone, even the fighters, are going to be on phone duty for the next few days as we communicate with all our people. As soon as I ... have figured out what to tell them ..." This last was said with a huff. No one was listening anymore. Fenris followed the collective gaze to the courtyard gate.

Their attention was riveted on a figure staggering into the yard, trailing blood.

LOSING IT

F enris swore and ran to Durgan, breaking the man's fall as he collapsed. "Marcel!"

Marcel pushed through the crowd, but Raven grabbed his arm, holding him back.

"Let him go help!" Sara cried.

"Why? He as good as murdered Cal."

Murmurs began among the others. Marcel jerked free of Raven's grasp. "I'm no judge and jury. I'm a Healer—that's what I do."

"He's probably led them right to us!" another voice shouted.

The rumblings grew louder. Fenris recognized the beginnings of a mob mentality and panic bubbled up in his chest. While he didn't blame them for feeling that way, neither could he allow them to tear Durgan to pieces. Fenris knew he had seconds to decide one way or the other before the choice was wrested from him.

A burst of gold light shot forth, and everyone but Marcel fell back. He stood there in shock, contained within Sara's Shield with her grasping his hand. She maneuvered her Shield toward the two men on the ground. Reaching them, she let it collapse.

"Help him." She turned to the others, her voice ringing out. "If we start this, we are no better than they are."

Fenris stood, flexing his hands, ready to rip apart anyone who threatened his wife. To his amazement, Erin came forward.

"As much as I hate to admit it, she's right." Erin spat in Durgan's direction. "Besides, he may have information we need. We don't know what's been happening on the outside for the last twenty-four hours. We have to keep our heads."

"He can't—"

"Enough," Fenris commanded. "I won't have him killed in cold blood by any of you. If it needs to be done, I'll do it myself."

"You don't mean that," said Sara.

He shook his head. "I don't know anymore."

"Doesn't his coming here jeopardize us?" Toby asked.

Fenris rubbed the back of his neck. The late hours of the night before were hitting hard. "I doubt it. With everyone arriving, my guess is they already knew we were here. It isn't the location that protects us. It's all of us together, with the additional defenses the house provides. Let's get to work. We'll get more information when he's back on his feet."

"He can't come downstairs," insisted Toby.

"No, I'm with you there. We'll find a place in the main house to hold him."

Satisfied, the others backed away in little knots of twos and threes. Sara whispered in Erin's ear. She nodded and took Sophie's hand, leading her back to the house.

Fenris took a deep breath of relief. That had been too close. He crouched down near Marcel. "How is he?"

"Multiple stab wounds. Lots of blood loss. I've started the healing process, but it's going to take a few sessions. He's stable, at least."

Fenris flinched when Durgan reached for him. "Fen ... thank you."

"Thank Sara," he snapped. "She's the one who protected you. Heaven knows why, after you gave her up to Josephine. Hugo!"

His colleague approached. Even though he appeared calm and steady as always, Fenris couldn't help but wonder what must be going through the man's head, this betrayal after years of working together. He pulled Hugo off to the side. "I can rely on you, right?"

"Always, Fen. You know that."

"Thank you. Ask Mama where we can put him that's secure. Stay with him until he and I can talk. Erin's right. He may have information we need."

Hugo hauled Durgan up to his feet, supporting the older man with ease. Fenris watched them go before collapsing onto a patio chair. "When is this ever going to stop?" he moaned. "I was finally getting a grip on things, but I have a bad feeling this is just the beginning. I don't know if I can do this."

Sara sat beside him and took his hands in hers. "You can, I promise. You were born for this."

"For what? Born to lead a rag-tag group of freaks into battle against a world that doesn't want us, while our own kind betray us?"

"No," she said with a kiss to his cheek. "Born to be a warrior. A hero. *My* hero."

"I would have preferred to be the kind with a horse and a sword."

"Well, none of us are perfect."

He laughed at this and drew her into his lap, kissing the top of her head. "How are you feeling? Tell me the truth."

"I feel fine after catching up on sleep."

Fenris tucked her head under his chin. "Thank you for last night."

Sara let the barest whisper of a laugh escape her. Fenris chuckled himself and rushed to correct her assumption. "Not *that*. Although that, too. No, I mean after what I said—for forgiving me."

She considered his comment before speaking. "I don't think it's up to me to offer forgiveness. You know very well who to ask for that. But Fen, you've compared our situation many times to being at war. If that is true, you're a soldier, and soldiers sometimes need to do ... things. To defend themselves or defend others."

"I guess I never saw myself that way. In my head, I'm a college drop-out who wishes he was still playing baseball."

Sara smiled and cupped his cheek with one hand. "You are so much more than that. Do you know why I used my Shield back there?"

"To protect Durgan."

"No. To protect *you*."

"Me? I don't understand."

"I could see you treading water, not sure what to do. Protect him or let them take over. Despite everything he's done, you still love him. If you'd allowed him to be killed that way, you would have never forgiven yourself, and the last thing you need is more guilt. I couldn't let that happen."

He swallowed hard and pulled her tightly against his chest. "I love you," he whispered.

"I love you, too. And I meant what I said about things done in self-defense." Sara hesitated. "However, I won't let you damage yourself—your heart—by doing anything deliberately. That isn't you."

Fenris was quiet, dwelling on her words. His voice shook when he finally spoke again. "I can't make any promises, Sara."

"I will fight you on this, if I must. For your own sake."

"Let's hope it doesn't come to that." He eased her out of his lap. "We have work to do."

☙✳❧

The rest of the afternoon passed in a blur for Fenris. He lectured the fighters on battling other Gifted. Everyone else spent hours on the phone, updating their people on the events across the region. Most were frightened but resigned. The years since the Changing had always been fraught with tension. They were all understandably curious, asking questions about Josephine and her intentions. Some were *too* curious, too enthused about the idea of rebelling against the system that had long treated them as something to be reviled. The team did their best to emphasize the dangers and potential long-term consequences if Josephine's quest was left unchecked. Worst were the silences—the phones that rang again and again, the voice mailboxes unanswered.

Fenris could sense a subtle panic building, further complicated by his own anxieties forming a permanent tight ball in his chest. He organized patrols for the area and began to send fighters out alone to keep an eye on things. All the while, he kept a close eye on Sara. Something wasn't right, despite her insistence everything was fine. She was pale and wan. Fenris was all too aware of her tendency to bury down her own needs for the sake of supporting others—supporting him.

Passing Mrs. Aguilar in a rush, he skidded to a stop and called her name. She was harassed and flustered on her way to prepare the late dinner, but her gaze softened at the obvious worry on his face.

"What is it, my little wolf cub?" she asked, placing a hand on his cheek.

The simple gesture shook him, with his emotions simmering far too close to the surface, and he tugged her hand down. "Sara. Does she seem all right to you?"

She searched his eyes, then gave him a small smile. "She is fine."

"What is it? Do you know something?"

"She has told me nothing. Make sure she rests. She is working too hard."

Dissatisfied with her answer, Fenris nodded curtly and began to leave, but Mrs. Aguilar stopped him. "Fenris. You cannot do this alone. You need to delegate."

Frustrated, he burst out, "How? Who can I trust anymore?"

"Pshaw, that's nonsense talking. You lack trust because you have been hurt by Durgan. Use that head of yours. It's a good one. Think it through, and you will know who you can trust. There are many to choose from."

Fenris groaned and spun away, heading back to the basement. He met Marcel at the closet door.

"Fen! I was looking for you. Durgan can talk now."

Startled by the sudden interruption of his own brooding thoughts, Fenris exploded. "What do you want me to do about it?"

"Whoa. Dude."

Fenris slid down against the wall to the floor. He buried his head in his hands, trying to hold himself together. "I—I'm sorry."

Marcel joined him on the floor. "Hey, it's been a long day, and you barely slept last—"

"How do you do it?" Fenris snapped, irrational anger boiling up toward his best friend. "No matter what happens, you're always so blasted cheerful! Does nothing ever get to you?"

"What are you saying?"

Hauling himself to his feet, Fenris jammed the passcode in. The door slid open, but Marcel grabbed his arm and pushed into his space.

"No! You don't get to do this. Not to me. If you've got something to say, then say it."

"Forget it," growled Fenris, entering the passageway. "You wouldn't understand."

"Shut up, Fen. No one understands you better than I do. Better than you understand yourself."

"Is that right?"

"Yeah, because you've never taken the time to really sit with yourself and process all the crap that's been churning around for years."

"Whatever, Yoda."

"And you get all over Sara for not talking things out? Look at you!" Marcel waved a disgusted hand at Fenris. "The master of self-deception. For years I've watched you. No more baseball? Fine, brush it off. College? Drop out like it wasn't ever your dream to teach. Teresa—"

"Don't." Fenris's eyes flashed, and he gritted his teeth, breathing hard. They had entered the main basement and stood at the top of the stairs, voices growing louder and louder as they argued. A small crowd had gathered at the foot of the stairs, watching them.

"Do you have any idea how selfish that was? Not being a part of our grief? We lost Teresa too, and we almost lost you. You hid from the rest of us, grieving alone. After that, your dad—"

"We are *not* talking about Dad," snarled Fenris, rearing back. The stench of antiseptic, the beeps of the machines—no matter what he did to keep those memories at bay, they were always there, waiting for a chance to break free.

"Yes, we are. We are getting everything out today, because you can't—"

"You let him die!"

"What?" Marcel gasped. "You—after all this time, you still think that?"

Fenris heaved air in and out. It had been years since his last true panic attack, and he couldn't afford to give in to one now. He gripped the rail of the stairway, willing himself not to fall while the room spun. "It's true! He was right there—for days in the hospital—and you didn't do a thing!"

"Fen—"

Fenris swung before Marcel could say another word, his fist crashing into him. Marcel fell backward against the railing of the stair landing. Recovering, he rushed back and threw Fenris down, the metal of the staircase clanging. Standing over Fenris, his usual gentle eyes were ablaze.

"He was my whole world!" Fenris cried out, horrified to hear a sob escape him. He tried to stand up. "You let him—you let him—"

"Stop it!" Frances yelled, moving up the stairs with surprising speed, given her condition. She launched herself at Fenris, shoving him back down. "You know nothing, Fenris. *Nothing*! All those days your dad was in the hospital, Marcel worked over him in secret. He didn't dare tell you, for fear you would be disappointed. He would come home brokenhearted because he could do nothing for Robert. Every night, feeling like he failed his best friend. Every night we prayed, hoping your dad wouldn't go so soon after ... it was just his time! No one can stop death."

Fenris froze, staring at her. Memories long buried beneath years of grief and denial raised themselves up from the dead. He tried to pack them away again, but Marcel had pushed him too far and the memories began rushing in.

He had raced out of the hospital after his father had died, out of control and dangerous, blasting things left and right. He wanted to die right there, to be with his dad, with Teresa ... even his mother. His anxiety and terror after her death had hidden her memories behind a wall so thick, he could barely reach into the blackness of his voided childhood to remember her.

Fenris had fallen, weeping, utterly alone, crying out to whomever would listen. Wishing he could use his Gifts—these terrible, horrible Gifts—to end his own life and join his father. Then, someone was holding him. Marcel—whom he had cursed and poured his venom upon, Marcel had not let him run out alone. He was there, holding on to his best friend, weeping with him, not letting him fall into the blackness.

"You followed me," Fenris rasped, pushing himself up to his feet. "I don't know why I didn't remember. You stayed with me. You've always...stayed with me." The part of his heart he kept frozen and locked away burst free in the warmth of this new memory. How often had Marcel rescued him from the brink? Countless times. Keeping him going long enough to start to heal, to be worth something. Without Marcel, he would never have been ready for Sara.

Without Marcel, he would have nothing.

Marcel seemed confused over this sudden change, but he softened at the sight of his friend's broken expression. They stood awkwardly for a moment, until Fenris cleared his throat. "Why didn't you tell me? About Dad?"

"Like Frances said, I didn't want you to be disappointed. You were already dealing with a lot." Marcel massaged his jaw.

Fenris blinked back the tears that stung his eyes and swallowed. "You okay?"

"Might as well be in second grade again."

"Yeah, well ..." Fenris turned to Frances. "Thanks for not letting me kill him."

Frances rolled her eyes in exasperation. "I'll kill both of you if you can't behave yourselves. As if we don't have enough happening already, without me having to babysit you two?"

Fenris put on a shaky smile and gave Marcel a tight hug.

"Whoa," said Marcel with a surprised chuckle.

"Thanks, buddy," Fenris muttered. "Sorry."

"It's okay. But you really pack a punch, Fen."

"You'll get over it."

BE THOU MY VISION

F enris could take Mrs. Aguilar's clucking over the whole affair.
He could grit his teeth and listen to the snickers of everyone
as he got lectures from both Frances *and* Mrs. Aguilar. However,
he almost broke under Sara's silence. He knew she had heard the
story, for her green eyes went all soft and sad as she looked at him,
but she never said a word.

The evening meal was far later than typical, and everyone clam-
ored for a spot in the kitchen to inhale large quantities of soup. Sara
remained quiet and withdrawn. Fenris squeezed into a place next
to her at the island, glad to see she was eating. There was enough
chatter going on around them that they could talk between themselves and not be overheard.

"Anything you want to say to your emotionally stunted husband?"

"No."

"C'mon, Red." He jostled her with a forced joviality. "Talk to
me."

"You first," she challenged.

Fenris swallowed down the temper that wanted to react to her
tone. He had no right to be angry. Instead, he pushed his bowl
away, appetite gone.

Sara took his hand in hers and squeezed. "I'm not angry, Fen. I'm worried about you. And I'm terribly sad you've been holding on to so many things without talking to me about them."

"I don't mean to," he said. "You know, Mom died before I was old enough to see how my parents worked through things together. I don't always—know how to do this. Communicate."

"Shocking," she said with a smile, and he stifled a laugh. "You never talk about your mother. Just your dad."

"I was young when she died."

"You weren't *that* young."

"True, but it was ... Did I ever tell you I was in the car when it crashed?"

Sara shook her head, her eyes wide.

"I wasn't hurt but ... It messed me up. I don't remember much before the accident or my childhood. It's all a big nothing. The doctors said I blocked it, trauma or something. I don't know. But it was after the crash when the anxiety and panic attacks started."

"You should have told me. I know something about panic attacks and suppressed memories, as you might recall."

"It's not the same thing. That one time was a very reasonable reaction to a particular set of circumstances. I had them all the time for years."

"Marcel told me once you could never play pitcher."

His eyebrow quirked at the sudden topic change.

"He said the pressure was too much. Is that how you are feeling right now? The pressure of leading everyone sending you over the edge."

"Maybe. Do you think I have a choice?"

"No, but I wonder if it might help to acknowledge where this is coming from."

"A good night's sleep wouldn't hurt either." He yawned. "I'm working off maybe three hours from last night. Today has been the longest day ever."

"It's not over yet," boomed Hugo, coming upon them. "Fen, you've got to talk to Durgan."

"Can't we put this off until tomorrow?" asked Sara, with a worried look at Fenris.

"Sorry, Sara. We need answers, and the everyone is getting restless."

"He's right," said Fenris. "Can't put this off any longer."

⁓❋⁓

Durgan was sitting on the edge of the bed when Fenris, Hugo, and Sara entered the room. His eyes darted between all three before landing on Fenris.

"Marcel says you'll live," said Fenris tonelessly.

"I know they were ready to do me in. Thank you for stopping them."

"Well, I haven't decided how long I'll hold them off. Depends on how much use you are to us."

Sara shivered. There was something dangerous in her husband's voice, but she didn't dare interrupt. She had hung back upon entering the room, knowing Fenris wouldn't thank her for interfering. Not that she felt inclined to participate. This was a fragment of their world in which she had no experience. The best thing she could do was offer support with her silent presence. Hugo stood near her while Fenris paced the room.

"Didn't take them long to find you, did it?"

"Told you they would be out to kill me. For talking."

"And like the fool you are, you came here, leading them straight to us."

"You're the fool if you thought they didn't already know where you were," Durgan snapped. "I didn't lead them here. They practically dumped me outside the door."

Fenris stopped pacing. "Say that again. No, wait. Start from the beginning."

"They came at me before I even got home from the diner. Those electric guns—once they hit me with those, I couldn't do a thing to stop them."

"Tell me about it," Fenris growled.

"They dragged me off to Josephine, and she interrogated me. I swear, I didn't tell them anything about this place, she already knew. She had her lackeys blindfold me and put me in a car. We drove awhile, and they pulled up, removed the blindfold and knifed me. I was a quarter mile away."

Fenris swore under his breath.

"She's toying with us," Hugo muttered.

"Yeah," said Fenris, both hands rubbing his eyes. "What's her plan? You can't tell me she didn't give you a message to pass on before you met your untimely end."

"She's giving you one more chance to join her."

"If we don't?"

"War. None of you will be able to stir a step out into the world without being attacked. You won't be able to help any of our people. You will be blocked, no matter which way you turn."

Fenris stared hard at Durgan, and Sara wondered what was being said but not spoken between the two of them. He whirled around.

"Who's patrolling, Hugo?"

"Raven was the last one sent out."

"Call her back. Right now."

Toby stuck his head in the room, his face pale. "You guys need to come with me."

A strange energy was traveling through the house. Fenris could almost smell the fear. He collided with a dozen other people as he sped down the hallway. Rounding a corner, he came upon grey-faced Marcel holding a sobbing Frances in his arms. His friend pointed to the bedroom door.

Fenris placed a hand on Sara's shoulder and squeezed it. "Stay here."

Jerking his head at Hugo in a silent request to have his back, he stepped into the room. Seconds later, Hugo cried out at the sight before them and pushed past Fenris. He fell to his knees, hands over his face.

Raven lay on the bed, dead.

Smeared in blood on the wall above her was the word *Ragnarök.*

Fenris swore and golden light surged from his hands, vibrating the room. The light faded, and he took a step back, shaking. It had been years since he had lost control of his powers. But this ... He crouched to whisper a few words into Hugo's ear before spinning away from the macabre scene to check on Frances. She was calmer, even if tears still streamed down her face. "You okay?"

"Yes. It was just shocking."

"Whose room is this?"

Frances gestured at the still figure. "Hers. Raven's."

"Are you telling me someone not only killed Raven, but got her back into this house and to her own bed without anyone seeing it?" A long silence followed as the full implications began to settle in. Durgan entered the room and groaned at the sight.

"This is it. It's beginning."

⁓※⁓

Sara couldn't keep up as Fenris dragged her down the hallway. He almost threw her into the bedroom before yanking a suitcase from the closet.

"What do you think you're doing?"

"You're leaving. You and Sophie."

"Where are we going?"

"Texas."

"Texas! You've got to be kidding me. Why?"

"Because of all the country, Texas has the most liberties for the Gifted. We should've hauled out of this miserable state years ago. Down there they have protections, and the Hunters are considered criminals."

"You know, they might support Josephine's mission."

"Her mission, maybe. But I doubt they would care for her tactics. They've never appreciated being bossed around much."

"A regular showdown at the Alamo."

"It's not funny. You're leaving tonight."

"Don't be ridiculous. We aren't going anywhere."

"Sara, I swear, if you are going to act stupid—"

"Be careful, Fenris," she hissed, her temper sparking. "You know what happens when you bully me."

He pulled up short, rubbing his nose. "You wouldn't."

"Try me."

"Sara ..." he pleaded. "Did you *see* what happened to Raven? Killing her is bad enough, but I have no idea how that witch got her body back here, unseen, to her own room. This isn't normal. Even for us. You aren't safe!"

She took a cautious step forward and hugged him, resting her head on his chest. His heart thumped hard against her ear. "I'm not leaving you. We face this together."

His arms came up around her, and she heard him swallow. "And Sophie? Isn't it on us to protect her?"

"Not like this. If we start running, when will we ever stop? You think Josephine will give up? This is personal for her now. She'll hunt us all down."

He squeezed her tighter and a small moan escaped his lips. "Promise me, when it's time, you will go."

Sara remained silent, locked in his embrace.

❧✳☙

The attacks began the next day.

Teams of fighters were dispatched to check on the people from their database who had not responded to repeated phone calls.

Everywhere they went, they met Hunters backed by Josephine's growing army of Gifted. In the beginning, these hybrid groups were disorganized and chaotic, drawing the eye of the law to themselves while the fighters remained hidden, doing what they always did best, watching over their people from the shadows. But as phone calls remained unanswered, the enemy became more organized with increasing aggression.

The new headquarters was a shambles. Finding places for everyone to sleep caused mayhem nightly. Trips to the store to gather enough groceries to feed the group took energy to plan. Fenris struggled to maintain a solid grip on a world that was rapidly spinning out of control.

To make matters worse, he wasn't sleeping. He had his own anxieties to manage, and now there was Sophie. Those precious few months of family life following their wedding were a distant memory. Disturbed by the change, the little girl's visions bombarded her without mercy, and she woke every night screaming. Her hysteria became so great she would lash out at Sara who tried to comfort her.

"Please, darling, let me hold you," Sara pleaded one night, attempting to restrain the child. Wild-eyed, Sophie thrashed against her. Fenris stepped in, taking Sophie into his own arms.

"Sophie," he whispered, stroking her hair. "Sweetheart, we're here. Breathe with me, Soph."

He put her hand on his chest, inhaling and exhaling slowly, their little exercise for working through the panic together. She moved as though to strike him, but instead she gripped his head with both hands. Sophie stared into his eyes until Fenris cried out and tried to jerk away. She held him fast, and their eyes met once more.

Long moments passed. Sara's heart raced, watching the two of them, frozen and unaware of anything around them while they continued to maintain intense eye contact. Fenris shuddered and moaned as Sophie's eyes drooped heavier and heavier. She was almost asleep when he whispered, "They're all gone now, Soph." He wrapped his arms around the child as she sank against his chest. Fenris shivered violently and reclined back against the headboard. Sara took hold of his hand. It was ice cold.

"Fen!"

He rasped, "I'm okay. Water."

Sara jumped up and grabbed a glass of water, handing it over to her husband. He drained it before handing it back.

"More?" she asked.

"Not yet."

"Can you tell me what happened?"

"Hold on. Trying to think how to explain it." Fenris dragged in a long breath. "Do you remember what happened to Sophie's mom, Mary?"

Sara's own breath caught. "She killed herself. You said the visions drove her mad."

"I was wrong. Well, partly. There was something else, something I didn't understand until now." Fenris paused to drop a kiss onto the sleeping Sophie's head. "Is she okay? I can't see her face."

"She's fast asleep. She looks ... peaceful. Do you want me to put her on her cot?"

"No, she's fine. I—I want to hold her a bit longer."

Sara waited, taking his hand in hers once more. It was still cold, although some warmth was creeping back. "What about Mary?"

"I don't think it was having the visions that drove her mad. I think they were locked up inside. Ted and I always talked about how Sophie was too young to communicate her visions. Mary had a difficult time as well, even as an adult. After a vision, she would spend days in her room, unable to talk. I think—I think the visions drove her mad because she couldn't understand them—couldn't explain them. They were trapped in her head. I think that's what happens to Sophie."

"What do you mean?"

"She—released her visions to me. Her visions became mine."

"Are you saying Sophie is a Telepath?"

"No, but I think me being one gives me ... access. Or something. When she took my head in her hands and locked her eyes on mine, she ... poured the visions out. Everything she Sees. Remember when I said that after spending time with her, I used to have flashes of things? I've become more sensitive to it since the two of you moved into the house. It's been easy enough to push back. But this was overpowering. I couldn't stop them. Sara—what I saw—" His eyes became frantic, and he reached for her.

"Don't, Fen. It will be okay. Whatever you saw, the future isn't written in stone."

"Isn't it?" he groaned, squeezing her tight.

"No," she said firmly.

The three of them remained together until slow, deep breaths told her Fenris had fallen asleep. With each breath he took, the child's head rose and fell on his chest. His face was pinched, as though anxious even while sleeping. Sara stroked back the hair that had fallen over his eyes. At her touch, his furrowed brow relaxed. A smile ghosted across his face before disappearing.

"Oh, Fen," whispered Sara. "My sweet Fen, how I do love you." She burrowed against him, and after a long time praying, all three of them slept.

SECRETS

For years, Fenris had kept a tight hold on his street fighters. He gave them two rules: Don't take it to the streets and don't die. The onslaught of the next few days wrecked the first rule. After Raven's death, Fenris held his breath, waiting for the second to fall again.

The Hunters had become more aggressive than anyone could recall. Initially they stuck to the usual night attacks, but soon things escalated into the daylight hours. Aided and encouraged by Josephine's crew hiding in the background, they had little to fear from local law enforcement, which already tended to look the other way when it came to assaults on the Gifted. It wasn't long before there were open fights in the heart of the city. Fenris shuddered as the evening news showed his own people fighting back in full daylight. He himself had been in the thick of these battles, for he never let any of his fighters out unless he was willing to go himself.

He was almost never seen at the Aguilar home over the next two weeks. When he left with fighters, Sara didn't know when she would see him again until he reappeared exhausted, often hurt. Dragging himself into their room, he would hug Sophie and hold

Sara for a long moment, whispering that he loved her before collapsing on the bed.

The others were in similar situations, throwing themselves into their work like never before. Erin proved herself to be an excellent fighter, and Fenris chided himself for not appreciating her skills before. He remained hesitant to allow those with unrefined skills to participate, even though they were eager to help. Try as he might, he couldn't shake the image of massive fireballs rolling down the street.

Fenris was unrelenting about the safety of Marcel and Sara. He refused to let either of them leave the house. Anyone who was injured was brought to Marcel, or if absolutely necessary, he was sent out with a full protection detail. There was no question he was kept busy, between his work as a Healer and his increased load as the media liaison. Despite this, his frustration was acute. He understood why Fenris insisted on keeping him grounded—his best friend was terrified of losing those closest to him—but that didn't stop him from demanding more freedom to help. Fenris refused to listen. While it puzzled him that Josephine was blind to the value of having a Healer on her side, he wouldn't allow her the opportunity to consider it.

Sara was under the same restrictions. She fought it as well, for her Gift was powerful as both an offensive and defensive weapon. However, her protests were weak at best, and the fact that she didn't fight Fenris more on this point added to his worries for her. But he had no time to dwell upon it. Deep down, he increasingly believed they were fighting a losing battle, and once more he tried to send Sara and Sophie away. His wife infuriated him by walking off mid-argument. Yet a part of him was relieved—as much as he wanted her safe, he was thankful she remained by his side.

Then the phone call came, and everything crashed down around them.

◦❈◦

It had been many months since Fenris last entered the state capitol building, and he fidgeted in the elevator. Durgan made him jump with a telepathic message. *It will be fine.*

The man was a traitor *and* an idiot.

Fenris wasn't sure which he despised more. Nothing about this was *fine*.

Angry with himself for letting Durgan into his head, Fenris shot him a glare. Durgan ignored him. Fenris clenched his jaw tightly but managed to not grind his teeth. He resented that Durgan was even there, much less forcing his thoughts at him. Hugo, Sara, Marcel, and Erin had overridden his wishes and determined that for this meeting alone, Durgan would appear as the head of the Shadow Guild once more.

He knew it was for his sake they had made that decision. Durgan had nothing more to lose, and they all knew they couldn't afford to have anything happen to Fenris. It made sense, even if it rankled him.

A movement to his right snapped his focus back to the present as Hugo shifted his feet. At least Hugo's loyalty could never be questioned. Since Raven's death, he had been intensely focused on bringing down Josephine. Although there had never been a known romantic link between them, Fenris wondered if Hugo had carried deeper feelings for Raven than he had ever let on.

The elevator dinged, and the three men exited. Fenris swallowed down his unease. Nothing about this meeting with a government official was normal, in the dead of night and an unmarked room in the capital building. They reached the door, and he hesitated, taking a deep breath.

"I won't let them bring you down," Durgan said. "If they are going to arrest us, I'll create enough of a diversion to get you out. Take Sara and get out of the city."

"And leave the others to rot? That's your M.O., not mine."

Durgan sighed before knocking on the door and opening it himself. Fenris followed with Hugo at his heels, close enough to bump into Fenris when the younger man skidded to a halt.

Senator Jacobs. Of course. It all made sense that he would be the one to call this meeting. He had most likely spent weeks sharpening his knives for the kill. Jacobs was flanked by two men who stood several feet behind him. *Security detail*, Fenris thought. Or FBI.

Durgan approached the desk while Fenris hovered over the threshold of the door, unsure of his next move. Hugo eased around him to enter the room.

"Do close the door, will you, Mr. Trygg?" Jacobs requested. "I promise, you will leave here unharmed."

"You think I believe that? You've done everything to stand against us. I have people other than myself to consider if I don't get back."

Jacobs glanced back at the men behind him. With a slight flick of his hand, the door behind Fenris closed on its own. Fenris jumped in shock, putting his back to the wall. Even Durgan gave a start of surprise. A wry smile appeared on the senator's face.

"Didn't see that coming, did you?"

Durgan and Fenris exchanged looks and Hugo shrugged. "You didn't know he was Gifted? I knew as soon as I walked through the door."

"How did *you* know?" demanded Jacobs, non-plussed.

"I can read the non-Gifted. The other two popped out at me right away. You didn't. I don't understand why Fen couldn't read you though."

"Because I have spent a great deal of time and effort learning to hide it. I was unaware my efforts didn't work for someone with your particular talent. Bravo."

"All this time ..." muttered Fenris. Shaking his head, his fury mounted. "All this time, you did everything you could to—"

"To what, Mr. Trygg? Think carefully. What have I done?"

Fenris opened his mouth and shut it again.

"Come on, Fenris. You are one of the most intelligent young men I've ever encountered. What exactly have I done?"

Jacobs had belittled and interrogated Fenris at every committee meeting, pushing the limits of his temper and tolerance. Which made Fenris burn to improve and come back better. To fight better ... *fight smarter* ... each time.

While Jacobs had argued with Fenris on the committee floor over and over again to prevent self-defense measures for the Gifted, he himself had been absent the day that bill had been voted on years ago.

He had introduced multiple bills to undermine the citizenship of the Gifted, only to pull them before elections.

Senator Jacobs had been on their side all along.

Fenris had never seen it. Just like he never saw Durgan's betrayal coming. How blind could he be? The senator smirked, seeing everything connect.

"Why now?" Fenris whispered.

"Because we have a serious problem on our hands, and the time has come where we must join forces."

"Gifted or no, how can I trust you?"

"I suppose you don't have to, however the alternative would be far worse. Do come sit, Fenris. We have much to discuss."

Like an animal caught in a trap, Fenris ventured to the remaining empty chair, every sense on high alert. Senator Jacobs sat back in his chair, satisfied.

"Shall we begin?"

⁓⁕⁓

"No!"

Sara's cry pierced his heart.

"I won't let you do this! Why can't Durgan—"

"Durgan's going, too."

"Why isn't that enough?"

"If he's shows up at Josephine's camp alone, they'll kill him. He has to have me to have value, to get in. I'm the bargaining chip."

Sara looked helplessly around the room, desperate for someone to back her up. Marcel sat, white-faced and stunned, gripping his wife's hand. Mrs. Aguilar watched Fenris with a thoughtful gaze. The rest were quiet, soaking in the news.

To Fenris, there was no choice. The plan was sound and the best option they had been given since the whole mess had begun. To infiltrate the enemy and bring Josephine down from the inside. To buy the rest some time to regroup and come up with a good defensive plan, should he and Durgan fail. However, the cost had been made clear—the odds were low they would ever make it out alive. If they even got in.

Durgan and Hugo had volunteered at once, but Hugo's Gift, while useful for tracking down non-Gifted Hunters, was useless to Josephine. His other Gifts weren't anything that she didn't have already. She would want someone extraordinarily powerful, like Fenris. Or Marcel—and for Fenris, that wasn't an option.

He took some measure of hope that Sophie appeared unperturbed by the news. He clung to the idea that he would know if a vision came to her. Fenris was thankful Sophie wasn't upset, because his heart was already breaking as Sara sobbed in his arms, begging him to stay.

"Sara ..." he whispered, running his fingers though her hair.

"It's not fair."

"Never has been. You know this plan makes sense."

"I know," she said, burrowing her head into his chest. "But why does it always have to be you?"

⁓∗⁓

After a subdued dinner, Sara and Fenris retired to their room. Time lay heavy on their hands. The two FBI agents who had been in Senator Jacobs's office would be coming to fetch Fenris and

Durgan at dawn. Sophie went to sleep after a bedtime story, and Fenris began to pack a single duffel bag.

"No room for the coffee maker, I guess?" he joked weakly.

She began to weep then, and he held her until she cried herself to sleep in his arms. His heart cracked to pieces as he gazed upon her face, not knowing if he would ever see her again. When she started that light snore he always loved to tease her about, he chuckled even as his eyes glazed over with tears. Fenris traced the outline of her face with his fingers, wanting her features to be imprinted forever in his memory.

"You've made me incredibly happy. Do you know that?" he whispered as she slept. "I wish I had asked you out long ago. The first day you came into the office, you were so pretty, so feisty. And *funny*. I hadn't laughed in a such long time, but half an hour talking to you had me laughing more than I had in years, even if I didn't show it. Remember when I pulled you away from the taxi running up the sidewalk? I didn't want to let you go, even then. I should have been braver and asked you out that day. Should have married you by Christmas. I really wanted to spend a Christmas with you. I was supposed to take you to the Nutcracker this year. Also Sophie ... You're both the gifts I never saw coming ... I'll forever be grateful."

He huffed a shaky breath.

"No matter what happens, I'll always love you."

Her breathing caught, interrupting her snore, and she whispered his name in her sleep, breaking his heart further. He held her close and lay awake until sunrise, not wanting to miss a single, precious moment.

∽❋∾

"Where is Marcel?" Fenris asked as they stood in the driveway, waiting to leave. Frances was rather pale and said nothing. When Marcel came out of the house with a backpack, Fenris almost snarled.

"No."

Marcel grinned and gave both his parents a hug.

"I said no, Marcel."

"You're not the boss of me."

"As a matter of fact—"

"You might be the boss, but you and I both know this is well beyond the job. You can't order me around this time."

Exasperated, Fenris turned to Mrs. Aguilar who shrugged.

"He is a man free to make his own choices."

"First time for everything," Fenris snapped. His face blanched as he turned to Frances. "Please ... don't let him. Not him. Not with you like this."

Frances stood straight. "And make him stay behind like a child?"

"Frances ..." he pleaded, catching both her hands into his own. "I might not be able to protect him."

"I know. This time, his place is with you."

Marcel smiled and put his arm around his wife's shoulder. "Always told you she's the best."

"Besides," Mrs. Aguilar inserted, "He can do more than healing."

"No!" Fenris said, frantic. "I won't let him."

"Too late, Fen. I already hashed it out with Frances last night, and I'm not going to go through that torture to back out now."

Frances rolled her eyes and smacked at her husband before taking him into her arms. Fenris scrubbed a hand over his face in frustration. He was losing control of this excursion already, and his temper was simmering. His emotions were all over the place, and he couldn't grasp one to hold onto. He looked helplessly at Sara.

"I love you," he rasped, jerking her into his embrace. A muffled sob told him she was weeping, and he clung to her even tighter.

"Time to get moving," called Dellaney, one of the FBI men.

"Sara, sweetheart ..."

She kissed him. It was a long kiss, salty with tears, but Fenris savored every second. A tug at his hand broke him away, and he knelt down before Sophie.

"Don't go," she pleaded.

"I have to, for all of us."

"Do you want to?"

"I will never, ever *want* to leave. Sometimes, we have to do things we don't want to do, to help others. You need to stay here and take care of Mommy." He hugged her and whispered in her ear. "I love you, Sophie. Don't try to find me. Not where I'm going. I don't know if—you shouldn't look for me. Do you understand?"

"Yes," she whispered.

He kissed her forehead. Fenris gave Mrs. Aguilar and Frances a hug, shook hands with Pops, and pulled Sara close for one last kiss. There were no more tears, but her eyes were distraught. He walked straight to the car where Marcel was already sitting and got in.

⁓✳⁓

Sara was strangling, trying not to cry out his name, to beg him to come back to her, to never leave. A brush of movement caught her attention as Frances came near.

"You never told him, did you?"

Sara shook her head.

"Why? He would have stayed if he had known. Nothing would have made him leave."

"She knows that," said Mrs. Aguilar, hooking her arm around Frances's waist. "She also knows he has a warrior's heart, and she must let him go. Same as you and me with Marcel."

Frances snorted. "Marcel is no warrior."

"He fights his own way," Mrs. Aguilar murmured.

"Mommy ..." Sophie cried out. "I can't see him. I can't see Daddy."

Sara bent down to put her hands on Sophie's shoulders. "Your Dada is gone, remember?"

"Not Dada!" The child stamped her foot. "Dad-*dy*. I can always see him, but now I can't."

"Daddy—" Sara's mouth dropped open. "You mean Fen?"

Tears spilled from Sophie's eyes. "He's gone from my dreams."

"What is she saying, Sara?" Frances demanded.

"She—she can't see Fen in the future."

"What does that mean?"

Sara couldn't choke out an answer. She looked up to catch one last glimpse of the car before it turned the corner. Crying out, she took a step forward before the earth started to whirl before her eyes. Frances caught her before she fell, sobbing.

ROAD TRIP

F enris fell back on the cheap motel bed with a groan, one hand rubbing his eyes. They had spent the whole day in the car, driving in endless loops and backroads only to arrive at a small town not far from Mt. Shasta. From there Fenris, Durgan, and Marcel would travel alone, seeking out Josephine and her cohorts.

He loved this part of California. Fenris had brought Sara and Sophie here for a surprise weekend getaway not long after their wedding. But there would be no lazy hiking trails or cozy cabin this time. No hot tub after Sophie went to bed...

Marcel's voice carried over from the adjoining room where he was chatting it up with Dellaney. Despite his mood, Fenris stifled a chuckle. Leave it to Marcel to remain his usual, obnoxiously cheerful, extroverted self even as their world fell apart. While he still had misgivings about Marcel joining them, Fenris was thankful to have his best friend at his side for this last adventure. He prayed that at least Marcel would make it home.

Durgan entered the room and sat on the opposite bed. "The other guy is heading out today, but Dellaney is with us until morning. I'll crash with him next door. I assume Marcel is bunking in here with you?"

"What do you think?"

"Fen—"

Fenris jumped out of bed, aiming for the hotel coffeemaker. It was the smallest he had ever seen. Scowling, he jerked out the miniscule packet of coffee and went to the bathroom to get water.

"I should go to the office and ask for more. That coffee pot doesn't even make enough for you to have in one sitting," Durgan quipped.

Fenris grunted.

"We have to be able to talk. At least about business, or this whole project is going to be dead in the water before it starts. We need to work together if you boys want to get home."

"You think that's even possible?" Fenris asked in a low voice.

"I do. I agree the odds aren't good, but I think ... It's possible."

The heavy silence was broken when coffee began to burble and drip into the pot. Fenris turned around, his arms folded over his chest, leaning against the dresser. "You've ruined my life, you know that?"

"Don't be stupid."

"Excuse me?"

"I didn't ruin your life. I didn't start this. Josephine did."

"You—"

"What I did was unforgivable, I don't disagree. However, I didn't cause any of this that's happening. If I had died that day they dumped me on the curb, would anything be different?"

"This goes back much further, and you know it."

"Perhaps, but I can promise you, Josephine would have found a way to get to you, with or without me. No man with the powers you have could escape her notice forever."

Fenris stood silent.

"Now my daughter is their hostage, and we are meat for the slaughter. Because of her. This woman."

"So, what now?" Fenris asked.

"We do what we can. Get Laurel back. Bring this witch down. Get you boys back to your families."

"And you?"

Durgan looked him directly in the eyes. "I don't think there's anything for me beyond this. One way or the other, I'll be dead before this is over. I'm okay with that if you can get Laurel to safety."

"What am I supposed to do about you in the meantime?" Fenris rubbed the back of his neck. One of the muscles had a crick, and it ached.

"What about me?"

"You! Us. I'm still trying to figure out how to process this new dynamic."

"There is no new dynamic, Fenris, except the one in your own head."

"Blast it, Durgan. Stop getting Zen on me. You betrayed us. Sara almost—"

"In my defense, I thought you and Sara were over at the time."

"Even if we were, it doesn't excuse you for putting her in danger."

"No. I suppose not. What can I say? I was desperate to protect my daughter. I'm sorry."

Fenris opened his mouth to snap back, but Marcel sauntered in through the connecting door. "You guys are getting kinda loud in here, you know? Dellaney and I are going out for a bite. You coming?"

Durgan picked up the jacket he had thrown across the bed. "Fen?"

"You go. I need some time to myself."

"You sure? You haven't eaten all day," Marcel fretted.

"Yeah," Fenris mumbled. "Go on."

⁕

"Fen ... wake up."

Fenris groaned and rolled over in bed, putting his back to Marcel.

"C'mon, get your butt up. I brought you a club sandwich. I know it's your favorite, and this is absolutely the best club I've ever had."

He propped himself up on his elbows, blinking at Marcel. "You brought me a club?"

"Extra bacon." Marcel waved the container in front of Fenris, who grabbed it and took a peek. His eyes brightened at the sight. Marcel chuckled. "Also, I brought back a full thermos of *good* coffee for you. None of this hotel crap."

"Thanks, buddy. I appreciate it."

"No problem. Say, listen. In the morning, I'm going with Dellaney to pick up a rental car for us to use while we're out searching for Josephine. Is that okay, or are you going to be stressing over not having a say?"

"Nah, it's just a car."

"Hmm ..."

"What's that supposed to mean?"

"Um, nothing. Eat your sandwich."

Marcel got up with a grin on his face. He had a plan, and for once Fenris wouldn't be there to mess it up.

⚹

"What is this, Marcel?"

"A car."

Fenris glared at his friend. "A Toyota is a car. *This* is a hot rod."

"A hot rod? Okay, boomer. It's a beautiful car. And *fast*."

"It's a gas guzzler."

"Who cares?"

"The planet might."

"Ugh, Fen. Have you ever considered having fun? You used to understand the word."

"Pardon me if I think our lives are in enough danger already, but you want to drive this death trap down the interstate?"

"Yes! We only live once, Fen. Let's live it!"

"What did Dellaney say about this frivolity?"

"I think he's a bit jealous, to be honest."

"It's flashy."

"Even better." Marcel gave the cherry-red convertible a loving polish. "After all, we want to catch her attention, right? It isn't like our goal is to be discreet."

"I bet it's uncomfortable."

"It has a seat warmer."

Fenris's eyes flitted to Marcel. "It does?"

"Yup."

"Hmrph."

"Great sound system. You can turn up those fancy speakers."

"I get full control of the music?"

"Absolutely."

"Fine," Fenris huffed. "I can't argue with you about this all day. Let's get her loaded. Dellaney?"

The FBI man stepped up, his eyes glinting in amusement at the exchange between the two friends. "Remember, from this point on you're on your own. Stick to the protocols we told you about communicating with anyone."

Fenris sighed, patting the burner phone in his pocket. "I'll remember."

Dellaney handed him the car keys and clapped him on the back. "Right. I think that's about it. Good luck, men. I hope you get in and out as quickly as possible."

"Well," said Marcel, rubbing his hands together, a wicked grin on his face. "Let's get this show on the road. I'm driving!"

He bounced away to the driver's side. Durgan and Fenris looked at each other.

"After you," Durgan offered, with an incline of his head.

⚬✻⚬

"Marcel ..." Fenris growled.

"What?"

"We are *not* stopping again."

"Yes, we are. We're out of snacks. A road trip requires snacks."

"Are you kidding me? This isn't a *road trip*. I swear—"

Marcel ignored his friend entirely, hopping out of the car. Durgan smothered a smile. "He'll never change, Fen. Don't know why you even want to try."

Fenris huffed, fighting his temper. His senses went on high alert as Marcel ran back, full of excitement.

"Guys! There's a ... a ..."

Jumping out of the car, Fenris raced around and grabbed Marcel by the shoulders. "You okay?"

"Of course I'm okay. You've got to come see this!"

Relieved but exasperated, Fenris glared at Durgan, who squeezed out of the tight backseat. They followed Marcel into the gas station. It was like any of a thousand in the country, with a basic market for coffee and snacks. Marcel kept going however, and rounding a corner, Fenris and Durgan both slid to a stop.

"No way," Fenris muttered.

"It's beautiful," said Marcel.

It was a bowling alley. Not large, just four lanes, but an honest-to-goodness bowling alley in the middle of a gas station in a flea-sized town on the western edge of Nevada. Marcel cackled and rubbed his hands.

"You're not thinking what I think you're thinking," said Fenris.

"Absolutely I am. We're going to have a game."

"Marcel!" Fenris lashed out, his impatience hitting maximum capacity.

Marcel whirled around with a stubborn expression.

"Listen to me, Fen. You're not the only one who's stressed and left everyone he loves to go on this wild goose chase."

"You had a choice—"

"So did you!"

"No, I didn't, I had to—"

"You had a choice! You *chose* this. It didn't have to be you. You could have sent someone else."

"No one else would have—"

"Yeah, yeah, yeah ... I've heard this one too many times, and I'm sick of it. You *chose*, Fen. You chose to be here doing this. That's okay. It's who you are, taking on the danger. I get it. But don't you dare act like you had no choice. Now. Stop feeling sorry for yourself and grab a ball."

Marcel spun around and went to the counter. Fenris trudged behind grumbling while Marcel shouted out shoe sizes.

"I'm not wearing bowling shoes. Who knows how many feet they've been on."

"Yes, you are. Shut up."

A little chuckle escaped Fenris.

Marcel glanced back. "Was that a laugh?"

"No."

"C'mon. You used to love bowling, Fen."

"That was a long time ago."

"And you will love it again today. I promise."

"We don't have time ..."

"What do you mean?" Marcel grinned. "We have all the time in the world. We have no idea where we're going or where Josephine is. We are literally wandering the country."

"Marcel—"

"Fen. I need this. *We* need this. Some fun, some joy."

"Fine. One game. Be prepared for me to whip your butt."

"You can't use your Gifts."

"I don't need Gifts." Fenris smirked.

꒰৺꒱

Multiple games and hours later, Fenris and Marcel were kicking back with nachos and sodas, laughing hard as they exchanged old stories. Durgan smiled on occasion but didn't say much.

"Oh, and Fen—" Marcel giggled madly, interrupting himself. "That game, when you did the thing with the baseball bat ..."

Even Durgan laughed at the memory. "I remember that game. I was there. It was your last one, wasn't it?"

"Yeah," Fenris said with a rueful smile. "I was out anyway. I figured I might as well have fun."

"That poor ump kept trying to pick up the bat, and it would scoot away a few inches just before he could get it—and then—and then—" Marcel dissolved in laughter and couldn't go on.

"I let him have it, and it conked him in the head."

Marcel howled and reached for a nacho. "The best part was—"

But Durgan and Fenris had both straightened and were looking over Marcel's shoulder. He turned and saw what had captured their attention. Two men had entered the bowling alley section of the pit stop and were setting up in the lane furthest away.

"Don't quite seem the type to be bowling, eh?" Marcel mused.

Fenris snorted. "Like we do?"

"Well, I do anyway ..."

"They're Gifted," Durgan said in a low voice to Fenris.

"Caught that, too?"

"Hmm ... Can you read them?"

"Give me a moment." Fenris bent over and untied his shoes, casting out to the two men nearby. "Funny."

"What?"

"One can talk to plants."

Marcel chuckled. "Really?"

"Think so. That's a new one. Well, maybe not talk to plants, but his Gift is centered on them. The other is ... odd. He's hard to read, all shadows and light."

"What do we do?"

"I'm thinking."

"Let them know who we are," said Durgan.

"You sure?"

"What do we have to lose? If they are with Josephine, they may lead us to her. If not, does it matter?"

"Okay. Hold on."

"Don't be too aggressive."

"I know, I know. Sheesh, Durgan ..."

It was something all Gifted could do, but it had to be taught. Fenris hoped they would understand his intentions. A gentle ping. Not like a Seeker, although the difference was subtle. A Seeker invaded one's mental space without regard to privacy, whereas this was more like knocking at the door. At his silent greeting, one took a step back in surprise. The taller of the two tipped his dark head in greeting. Marcel waved cheerfully.

"Will you stop it?" Fenris hissed. It was a normal exchange in their world, but his nerves were on edge. He picked up his shoes and stood.

"I think they're okay," said Marcel.

"Me too. Still, it's time we moved on."

"Right."

Before they could move, the two strangers approached. They were younger than Fenris had first assumed, no more than twenty, maybe. The taller one took the lead.

"From out of town?"

"How can you tell?"

The man chuckled. Fenris heard Marcel take a breath as if to speak and nudged him to stay quiet.

"Is there any ... community around here?" Fenris asked.

The shorter one shook his head. "Not much. A few."

Fenris read him loud and clear: *And we like to keep it that way.*

"Fair enough. We're road tripping from Sacramento."

"Sacramento?" Both men were suddenly alert. "Look, we don't want any trouble ..."

"I guess you've heard things?"

"That's one way to put it."

The shorter of the two began to show some nervous agitation, tugging on his friend's arm. "C'mon, Wyn ..."

"Can you talk to plants?" Marcel blurted out.

"Marcel!"

"Well, it's different. I'm curious."

Fenris offered an apologetic look. Wyn chuckled and glanced at his companion, who shrugged with a reluctant smile. "That's not how I would put it but I suppose I do. I'm Brose, and this is Wyn."

Fenris rolled his eyes as Marcel began a conversation with Brose the plant man. In turn, he and Durgan had a quiet conversation with Wyn. As Fenris had hoped, the man had information about Josephine.

"Last I heard, she was in the area, making her way down south. Well, hold on. Let me show you."

The three of them worked over a map until Fenris and Durgan had a good idea of where they needed to go next. Before they parted, Wyn shook hands, and Fenris was surprised to feel the sensation of light spill into his palm.

"I don't know why you want to find that woman but be careful. You're good people, and you don't want to get caught up in her crowd."

"No, we don't," Fenris agreed. "Maybe someday we'll reconnect, and I can tell you about it."

"How do you know we're good people?" Durgan asked curiously.

"My Gift. I sense those with the Light, and those without." Wyn studied Marcel and Fenris. His eyes lingered longer over Durgan until he finally nodded. "You all have it."

Fenris took one last, long look at the two men before heading to the car. A thought struck him, and he turned back around in their direction. "Hey, if you—"

The two men were gone. A strange feeling skittered down his spine, but it wasn't disturbing. Instead, for the first time since they had set out on this trip, Fenris felt a sense of peace.

⌒⥽❋⥿⌒

At the car, Fenris hesitated and muttered, "Keys."

"What?"

"Give me the keys, Marcel."

"Are you driving?"

"One usually does with keys."

"But you said—"

"You know I don't *need* the keys. I'm trying to be polite. Are you going to hand them over or what?"

Speechless, Marcel passed the keys to Fenris and slid into the passenger's seat. Durgan grinned from the back. Fenris settled in and adjusted the seat and mirrors, stroking his hands along the smooth leather of the wheel before inserting the key.

"Let's see what this baby can do."

"Who are you?" gasped Marcel. "And what have you done with my best friend?"

"Well, we only live once, right?" Fenris said with a smile as he revved the engine.

⁘

That evening, they sat on the hood of the car, devouring take-out fried chicken. They were parked at an overlook, watching the sun set over a vast landscape.

"There," said Durgan, pointing to lights twinkling on the horizon. "That town to the southeast. That was the most recent sighting, according to Wyn."

"I guess that's where we'll go," said Marcel.

"I wish you would go back," sighed Fenris. "You can still get out of this before it's too late."

A chicken bone flew past his head.

"Shut up, Fen."

Fenris chuckled, thankful he wasn't alone.

UNTETHERED

S ara awoke, startled to find herself in bed. A gentle hand lay on her shoulder.

"Shh, take it easy," said Frances.

"What happened?"

"You fainted, sweetie. Or something close to it."

"Oh no, I didn't," Sara moaned, covering her face with her hands in mortification.

A masculine cough broke through her embarrassment, and Frances turned her head to speak over her shoulder. "She's going to be fine, Hugo. You can go."

To Sara's amazement, Hugo gave her a brief nod and left the room.

"What was that?"

"I think he sees himself as your protector with Fen gone."

Sara's heart wilted. Her husband gone, perhaps never to return. She pushed herself into a sitting position and tried to hide her emotions. "Well, this is embarrassing. Fainting in front of everyone. People will think—"

"People will think nothing less of you." Frances gave her a knowing smile. "Some of us will understand better than you might suppose."

Sara's eyes widened. "How did you know anyway? About ..."

"Please! For one thing, you've lived with us off and on for months. You've always had a lot of energy and a good appetite, both of which have been lacking lately. Plus, a woman gets a good instinct for this kind of thing."

Sara could feel heat staining her cheeks. She twisted her hands up in the sheets.

"Why didn't you tell Fen?" asked Frances.

"I—I don't know. At first, I waited because I wanted to be sure. I knew he would be so happy. I didn't want to disappoint him if I was wrong. Right when I was sure, we found out that horrible woman was still alive, and things have spiraled out of control ever since."

"You aren't showing, but it takes a while with the first one. After that you show almost right away. I mean, look at me! I'm a whale at seven months. How far along are you?"

"Ten weeks, I think. Maybe a little more."

"Well, you two certainly didn't waste any time," Frances laughed. She stopped when she saw the tears in Sara's eyes. "They'll be back."

"It's my fault if they don't. He would never have left if he knew. I—I didn't want to hold him back just because I was afraid. I did that once and it almost ruined something precious between us. Now Marcel's gone too, because of me. Frances, I'm sorry!"

"Stop. It will be okay, sweetie."

"And I'm crying. *All the time.* This is ridiculous," sniffled Sara.

"It's the hormones and stress. It's normal. You need to—"

"What is this?" Mrs. Aguilar demanded, as she came into the room.

"Nothing, Mama. Sara was telling me ..."

"The baby?"

"You knew, too?" Sara groaned. Mrs. Aguilar gave her a kind smile. "Oh my word, does everyone know?"

"No, *mija*. It takes the right eyes to see such things. How are you feeling?"

"Embarrassed. Heartbroken. Exhausted. The usual."

"You are beginning to sound like Fenris."

At the mention of his name, Sara's heart cracked, and she leaped out of the bed. At the other women's exclamations, she waved them aside. "I can't spend my day in bed. There are many things to do. With Fen gone, someone needs to take charge."

"There are others for that," insisted Frances.

"No, she is right. She must take the lead with Fenris gone," said Mrs. Aguilar. "But that does not mean you must lead alone. You know my love for Fenris is deep, but he always felt the need to carry the burden. It does not need to be this way. Let others help you. You must take care of yourself and the little one. Fenris would want that."

"Yes," Sara whispered, swallowing down the painful lump in her throat. "He would."

⤔❋⤐

Sara had never considered herself a leader in their group. That had always been Fenris and Durgan. For so long she had not been one of them, the Gifted. While they were aware of her newly-found Gift, no one from the office had ever seen it in action until the day she had protected Durgan. Now with Fenris gone and hearts raw over death and betrayal, Sara knew it was time to step up.

Sara had no trouble locating Hugo, who had remained near the door to her room. "Hugo, could you ask the others to meet in the courtyard?"

"On it."

"Hugo?"

"Yes, ma'am?"

"I never told you how sorry I was about Raven. I know you two were good friends."

Hugo hesitated before nodding his thanks. Something about the expression in his eyes made Sara's heart ache even more.

"You weren't ... more than friends, were you?"

His throat worked. "I had hopes. That someday we might have been. Fen knew. Can't keep that dang kid out of my head. I never really considered it until you two got married, and he would yammer on and on about how happy he was—"

"He did?"

"Heck, yeah. Couldn't get him to shut up about you. All these years working with him, and I never knew he could talk that much. I like you, Sara, I always have, but sometimes I got sick to death of hearing about the two of you. No offense. Anyway, it got me thinking more about the idea ..."

"I'm so sorry, Hugo."

Hugo raised his eyes to the ceiling, clearly struggling to control his emotions. After a long, shaking breath, he cleared his throat. "I'll get the others. And Sara? Take care of yourself and the ... You know, Fen talked all the time about wanting a big family. He's always loved kids. I don't want anything to happen to that dream. Don't worry. I won't tell anyone."

"Thank you, Hugo," said Sara. She watched Hugo leave in stunned silence. How much had he heard while waiting outside the door? And his revelation about Raven. So much waste. How his story could have been hers. Sara caressed her stomach, her heart aching.

"I promise to take care of you," she whispered. "I hope you're like him. You may be all I have left."

⊰✳︎⊱

Sara counted the heads of those surrounding her. A few of the office people should have remained downstairs for the phones. Those that held lesser Gifts. Replaceable. She flinched at the word, even though it was true.

Anyone could answer phones.

It was the fighters she needed, and they were all here. Yet ... Sara eyed Toby talking with Erin and smiled. Yes, anyone could answer phones, but not everyone could throw fireballs or manipulate electricity. Sara ran over her mental list of those in the office who had special powers that could never be refined enough to use on the streets. Toby. The other attorney, Eden, whose cool demeanor belied her inner heat that burned so hot she could melt gold in seconds. Sara studied the pool as she walked around it, thinking. The office assistant Megan was rumored to have control over water. Sometimes.

Misfits, the lot of them. Except now, every Gift counted. They had been hired for a reason—as the last line of defense, should the fighters be taken out. She needed a list of everyone and their Gifts, no matter how small, how inconsequential, how little control they might have over their powers.

Sara's eyebrow raised as she watched Mrs. Aguilar bring out a tray of sandwiches with Frances close behind her. Why had she never been told what Frances could do? Or Pops? Or any of the Aguilar family? What had Mrs. Aguilar meant when she mentioned Marcel having other Gifts?

Fenris had always impressed upon her it was the height of rudeness to inquire about Gifts. They were private things, he said. She was willing to risk being impolite at this point. Besides, he was sometimes prone to exaggeration. It couldn't be such a terrible thing to ask under the circumstances.

The group was gathered around in a half-circle, and she approached the break in the center. All eyes were trained on her, and her courage almost failed her. A whisper of a familiar deep voice floated up in her imagination. *You can do this, Sara.* She took a breath.

"Thank you all for gathering together. I think it's important we all be on the same page and work together as a team for what is coming."

"What is coming, Sara?"

"War. Durgan told us Josephine would not stop until she had us all under her control or dead. I know there are many reasons to not trust him, but everything we know supports this claim. Part of the reason why Fen left was he hoped it would track her attention away from us. It would be foolish to kick back and assume we're safe. We have to continue believing there is an attack coming and plan accordingly."

There were nods and murmurs.

"As I see it, we have two immediate tasks. First, to somehow make contact with our people on the outside and continue to ensure their safety as best as possible. Second, to prepare this compound for a strong defense. I'm not sure how to do that."

"It's not up to you to know," Erin spoke up, and Sara's heart sank. She and Erin got along most of the time, even if her temperament was unpredictable. But Erin wasn't finished. "What I mean is, it's not up to you to figure this out alone. We are a team, a family. Fen always wanted to take the lead. He was good at it, more than I liked to admit. On the other hand, he can be overly controlling."

Sara grinned. "Maybe a little."

"My point is he didn't always have to do everything on his own."

"This is true," Tudor said. "He was always holding me back too much."

"You are young," Sara said.

"Ugh, not you too? You all think I'm the same age I was when I joined at eighteen. I can do a lot more now that I'm older."

Hugo's voice boomed. "We can all do more. You don't need to feel you carry this alone."

"This is great. Thank you. We'll figure this out. I know many of you are grieving—or angry—and I want to give you time to work through that. So for today, I need one thing from all of you. I want to pass out a paper, and I need everyone to write out their Gifts. I don't care if you think they are important or not, we need a record of them all ..."

Her voice faded at the look of horror on their faces. She didn't quite understand the problem. They had put on a display in this very courtyard two weeks before. Their own database was full of

Gifted from the region and all their powers. Or was it? Were they *all* listed? Maybe it was the act of writing them down.

"I—tell you what. Instead of writing them, we can start with demonstrating our most powerful ..."

The consternation grew even greater, and the friendly faces grew dark with suspicion. Sara didn't blame them, but it frustrated her. No wonder Fenris was always exasperated, managing this lot. Even some of the Aguilars on the fringe of the crowd seemed worried.

Turns out, Fenris hadn't been exaggerating this one.

Her eyes met Mrs. Aguilar across the courtyard, who gave Sara an encouraging smile and a nod. With a breath of air, Sara cast out her enormous golden bubble. What had in the past caused pain and no small amount of fear in her was larger, more powerful than ever, yet contained and controlled with ease. She grew the bubble, its bottom flooding out from her feet and along the ground to the edge of the group and overhead in a vast sphere. Bringing it in tighter, she hurled golden light bombs at a potted plant nearby, shattering it. Another at an old citrus tree she knew Mrs. Aguilar had been trying to convince her husband to rip out. She built up the tension of the sphere's core, and air around her began to whirl, becoming a small tornado of controlled destruction. Before she lost her grip on it, she brought the bubble back in with the familiar whoosh, and everything went quiet.

Sara turned to see everyone staring at her in awe and confusion. She had never used her Gift so well. She didn't even feel the usual exhaustion that came from practicing. Sara smiled at them all and called out, "As I was saying. If we could all demonstrate our Gifts, that would be fantastic. Then, we can get organized and plan for what's coming."

⊂•✳•⊃

Sara teetered to the kitchen on her own, barely able to stay on her feet. She grabbed the fridge handle, but another hand pushed her away.

"You are dead on your feet. Sit down and I'll get you something," Frances scolded.

"You're more pregnant than I am."

"Yes, and I didn't just spend hours organizing a war plan and demonstrating one of the most powerful Gifts I've ever seen over and over again."

Sara sighed and fell into a chair. It was true. She had been repeatedly asked to give an encore performance of her Gift, even as the others demonstrated their own. It had been worth it. She had a full record of almost everyone's Gifts either by seeing them for herself or a quiet verbal acknowledgment, as well as a good idea of their control. More importantly, she, Erin, and Hugo had worked together on the first stage of a defense plan.

Multiple small teams had been made, each with a full range of duties. Some were assigned to go afield to check on the Gifted in the region and perhaps even do some recruitment. Others were on watch and had the duty of preparing the house for battle. Each team of three had two experienced fighters and one who needed mentorship. On top of this, those who lacked control of their Gifts were required to work with Mrs. Aguilar on a daily basis. Every three days, their assignments switched out, allowing each team to gain experience for every job available. This way, in the heat of battle, no one would ever be caught dealing with something new.

She watched Frances move with assurance around the kitchen. Funny. Not one of the Aguilars had added their name to the list of Gifts, nor had they demonstrated anything. Sara knew what Mrs. Aguilar could do—or did she? Sara corrected herself: She knew of *one* Gift. Maybe there were more. What of the others? Why were they so secretive about it?

"Frances, does pregnancy stunt our Gifts?"

Her friend looked up with surprise at the sudden question. "Why ever would you ask me that?"

"Sorry, random thought."

"Pregnancy brain, how wonderful it is." Frances chuckled. "To answer you, no. Not at all. In fact ..."

"Yes?"

"I think pregnancy can enhance our skills. My theory is a baby already has their own powers and it adds to ours. On the other hand, we are also super hormonal, which can mess with our brains and emotions. It's a double-edged sword."

"Isn't it always," said Sara.

Frances filled two bowls full of soup and sat down next to her. Sara blew on hers to cool it, thinking with a smile about how Toby had insisted he be put on Erin's team. There were sparks there, she was sure of it. Now, how to fan the flames ...

"Eat!" Frances commanded, breaking Sara out of her reverie. "I won't have Fen coming home to a wraith."

Sara nodded listlessly.

"He'll be back, Sara. Both of them. Unless Fen kills Marcel along the way. Can't say I would blame him ..."

"Here I keep thinking someday Marcel is going to be the one to get fed up, once and for all. He has the patience of a saint."

"He really does," Frances mused. "He's put up with so much over the years, between Fen and being married to me."

"He adores you. He talked about you all the time in the office."

"I got lucky. It could have been Fen. I love that boy, but being married to him would have made me crazy. You handle him much better."

"What do you mean?"

"Oh! I never told you? I had a huge crush on him. This was before Marcel asked me out of course."

"I never heard this. Does Fen know?"

"No, and don't you dare tell him. When Teresa ..." Here her voice faltered. "The moment Teresa caught sight of Fen, she was done for. She didn't know how I felt. Fen—my stars, he was clueless. He brought Marcel along on his first date with Teresa."

"What? Oh my word, Fen." Sara laughed helplessly.

"Granted, we were all just kids. I guess he was terrified at the idea of taking a girl out alone, so he brought Marcel with him. Teresa had the smarts to make it a double date, talking me into going, too. Marcel was so sweet and funny, especially considering he wasn't expecting a date that night. I never thought I would hear from him again, but he called me the next morning to ask me out himself."

"That's so fun!"

"The crazy thing is, we knew almost immediately we were right for each other. But Teresa and Fen only went out off and on for a while. I think it was seeing Marcel so happy that convinced Fen to really make an effort. And once he decided, he—" Frances choked up and shook her head. "I'm sorry. Thinking about those days, and when Teresa ... Marcel has always been my rock. And now ..."

Sara took her friend's hand, her own throat closing up.

"Now, we are untethered," she whispered.

THE ARENA

S cattered images.

    The roar of the ocean waves.

Scent of salt in the air.

Driftwood on the fire.

It was their honeymoon and that last hike to the beach, when Sara had jumped up on his back and he dashed into the cold water. She had squealed at his playful threat to dunk her. Falling into the sand together, laughing. Her sweet kisses, pulling him to her ... They had forgotten a blanket but didn't care ...

He had never been so happy in his life. She filled his heart with laughter and joy.

The image blurred, and he desperately tried to hold onto that moment. Sara, sweetheart, please stay ... The scene shifted into a long hallway with many doors. He wondered if he was back in the hospital. He hated those dreams. But this was different, with colors swirling ... It was a Gift in action, not a dream.

A familiar little nudge. Sophie. What ...? She was showing him ...

"Fen. Wake up."

The colors faded, and Fenris groaned as Marcel shook him by the arm.

"You awake yet?"

"Yeah."

The crackle of plastic and the dank smell of bad hotel coffee assaulted his senses. Fenris squeezed his eyes shut and clutched a pillow to his chest, wanting to be back in the warmth of his bed with his wife. Holding Sara in his arms as he kissed her. The touch of her. In the mornings, he would bring two mugs to the bed and they would sit, Sara snuggled against him as they enjoyed their first coffee together. Although, if it was before Sophie was awake, those cups of coffee would often grow cold beside the bed ...

"Here you go."

Fenris sat up and took the Styrofoam cup and stared into it—the coffee looked disgusting.

"Happy birthday, buddy," Marcel said. Even his smiles were forced now.

Fenris grunted. Twenty-six. This was not how he had hoped to spend the day.

"You okay?"

Silence.

"Fen?"

"I miss them. Sara. I—" Fenris rolled his eyes at the emotions that pricked and stung.

"I know," Marcel whispered. "Me, too. Keep thinking about Teresa. They grow so fast even in a few weeks."

For four weeks they had been on the road, trying to locate Josephine. Fenris thought about what Durgan had said: They would find her when *she* chose, not the other way around. He had been worried her trail was leading them further away from Sacramento, setting their loved ones up for a trap. Then her trail spun around. They were in essence making a wide, circular sweep several hundred miles around the city.

Today, they were near to where they started, a hundred miles north of the city. Whispered conversations with Gifted in the area spoke of an encampment hidden deep in the forest. Meetings, too perfectly timed to be accidental, led them to believe her minions were watching them—herding them even—and they allowed it to happen. The previous night they had risked a quick communication with Dellaney and pleaded for information on their families. All was well, they were told. No attacks had taken place at the Aguilar home. In fact, all violence in Sacramento had ceased.

They debated long into the night after Dellaney told them the news, unsure of what it meant. On the one hand, there was a sense of relief that their families were safe. They had led Josephine away, but Fenris feared they were playing a deadly game of chess. Josephine was aware something was afoot, and she was watching everything play out. If she knew Fenris not home, she also knew his powerful Gifts no longer defended the group. It was all he could do not rush back home and sweep Sara into his arms.

Blasted woman! He should have forced her to Texas. Tied her up and packed her on a plane, bus, whatever he had to do to get her out. Even that last day together, too many hours had been spent with them arguing over her refusal to go somewhere safer.

"You'll be gone! I have to stay and lead."

"You aren't a queen leading a kingdom, Sara," he snapped. "Don't be stupid."

That had been a mistake.

Later, they had ended up in bed together ... Fenris shut his eyes against the memory. It was both a treasure and a curse to remember those hours. His arms ached to hold her again.

He started when Marcel clapped a hand to his back.

"Drink your coffee, Fen."

"Marcel?"

"Yeah?"

"How do you do it? The constant positive outlook. I'm not being snarky. I really want to know."

Marcel sighed and sank down on the bed opposite Fenris. "I don't know. There's darkness in me, too. It's in all of us."

Fenris swallowed hard.

"The world wants to say we all have some goodness in us, no matter what. I don't think that's true, Fen. I think it's the opposite. We all have the darkness that wants to take over. It's up to us to overcome it. To aim for the higher things. I guess being positive is my way of combating the darkness."

"I'm glad you're here with me."

"Me too, Frodo."

"You *are* a bit like Sam." Fenris chuckled. "Okay. Let's go find Sauron."

They grabbed their bags and stood outside of Durgan's door, banging on it. The door opened and Durgan came out, his face white. Behind him stood another man, holding a familiar weapon.

"Well, that didn't take long," Marcel quipped.

Fenris swore.

⸻✳︎⸻

They had always known they could be captured by Josephine's henchmen at any time. Their story had been set even before they left Sacramento, and they went over it most nights before bed, rehearsing every detail. Now, blindfolded and shoved into a vehicle, Fenris reviewed the plan over and over again for the next few hours.

Except once they were before Josephine, the memories of the torture she had inflicted overwhelmed him and his courage almost failed. He forced his thoughts on the one memory that broke him more than any other—the tip of that sword pointed at Sara's heart. That was enough to dispel his fears, and Fenris threw himself into the plan with enthusiasm.

He watched as Josephine circled him. It was his first chance to get a good look at the petite woman. Excruciating pain had not provided an ideal opportunity to examine her. While her accent was rooted in eastern Europe, her features reflected a complex background of both European and Asian descent. She seemed ageless under a mask of exquisite makeup. She could have been thirty or fifty. Her black hair was cut in a short bob, never reaching her shoulders. Red—she always wore red, with crimson lipstick that matched. And that sword that always hung from her back. Fenris wasn't afraid of the sword. Physical weapons were harmless to him. Her Gift, though ... that gold whip. The one time he had met the tip of that cracking whip, it had disabled him completely, and Fenris wasn't sure how to defend himself against it. Never mind with those guns in the hands of her soldiers.

"Fenrir, you have come back to me."

"I suppose," he replied. He hated the way she twisted his name.

"I would think this was some kind of trick, but you've never been this good at holding back your emotions."

"Or I'm better than you thought."

The room puzzled Fenris. The walls and carpets were a dull grey, reminding him of a commercial office building, but comfortably furnished like a living room. He threw himself into a nearby arm-chair and sprawled across it sideways, his demeanor one of utter boredom. "If you have a Telepath around, send them in. I'm an open book."

Josephine gazed upon him, curious. Fenris held back his surprise when he felt her poke into his brain. She was no true Telepath. Anything she attempted was learned from others, not a Gift. She couldn't dig in deep. Nevertheless, he was relieved when she turned and sank into the chair opposite.

"I'm wondering," Fenris mused. "How did you pull that trick off? Getting the body of my fighter into the house without anyone seeing. Someone with a gift of Invisibility?"

"I can't tell you all my secrets, my love."

"Teleporting something the size of a human body would be unfeasible."

"Tick tock, tick tock … Is this how we are going to spend our time together?"

"I don't think you had an infiltrator."

"No, Fenrir. Traitors are not my way. Unless it's my dear Durgan here."

It was all Fenris could do to not kill her. He needed to know how she had gained access to the house, but a death blow required him to be much closer, and he knew her instincts for self-preservation were strong. Their cover would be exposed, and they would be dead before he got close enough. While mulling over the options, her next question caught his attention.

"I hear you married that sweet child. Sara, yes?"

"Yes ..."

"But?"

"Marriage is a bit of a drag after all. Dull business."

"And yet, you still wear a wedding band?"

Fenris snorted and yanked the ring off with an easy tug, tossing it to her. "Take it, I don't care. I'm done with that." Josephine fingered the ring for a moment before flicking it away with a laugh. She stood and sauntered over to Marcel and Durgan.

"Thank you, Durgan, for this gift. And Marcel! I never dreamed of adding a Healer to my collection."

Durgan inclined his head in a slight bow. "I hope you are pleased?"

"Most pleased, yes. I may even release your daughter for this. After all things are considered."

His eyes flickered to Fenris for a fraction of a second, but otherwise Durgan's expression remained impassive.

"I do have ... one problem." Josephine smiled back at Fenris once more, but her eyes held a steely coldness. "I'm not sure if I require you anymore. Which would be sad if that were the case, for you to lose your value."

"Ah, well." Fenris rose from the chair. "We'll be on our way then."

"That's not what I meant. I merely want proof you are as valuable as I always believed." Desire almost oozed from Josephine, and her eyes glinted. "A demonstration of some sort, shall we say?"

"Whatever." Fenris shrugged.

Durgan's voice popped into his mind. *Be careful, Fen.*

Fenris ignored him. It was too late to turn back now.

Josephine waved to one of her guards. "Markos. Gather everyone to the arena."

Fenris exchanged a startled look with Marcel. "Arena?"

⌀✳⌀

The arena was nothing more than a circular glade in the forest,
surrounded by trees. No grass grew there. It was all dirt and—

"Are those—bones?" Marcel whispered.

"Yeah."

"Fenris. Listen to me," Durgan commanded. "This will be a
fight to the death, you understand? You must not hold back. Even
if you could defeat them without killing, she will think you are
weak and make you pay. You hear me?"

Fenris stood frozen, his pulse pounding against his eardrums.

"Fen!"

"I hear you."

"I won't be able to help you. I can try, but she'll find a way to
block me."

"I know."

Josephine approached them, with a coy smile on her face. "The
rules here are simple. You may use anything you wish. Gifts,
weapons as you see fit, your own intellect—I don't care. The goal
is to survive until I end this."

"How long?" Marcel asked.

"As long as I wish," she replied silkily.

Fenris grabbed Marcel by the arm, pulling him off to the side a
few paces. "I'm sorry I dragged you into this."

"Fen ..." Marcel's voice was thick.

"If I go down, get out of here. By whatever means necessary. Even if means using—do whatever you have to do to get out alive."

"I could use my Gift to help you!"

"No! I need you to get back to them—to her. Make sure they're safe. Sara and Sophie, you hear me?" Fenris gave Marcel a quick hug, whispering, "Take care of yourself, buddy. If I don't make it."

He then turned to Josephine with an easy smile. "Let's do this."

⁓⋅✳⋅⁓

Fenris stepped out alone into the circle. If nothing else, his powers were strong. There had been little to release them over the last few weeks, and they were bubbling beneath the surface. He flexed his hands. He had once wondered if being married would take the edge off his Gifts, but they had grown stronger since. Now, weeks away from Sara ... He was a dragon with a simmering fire, ready to launch his flames.

Two men and a woman entered the far side of the field. Fenris opened his mind up completely, not caring if one was a Telepath. He needed to read and feel the minds of the others with ease. Neurons firing a warning, he whirled around to shatter a lone assailant creeping from behind. There was a pause as the stalker's body skid a furrow into the dirt before coming to a stop at Josephine's feet.

Both Fenris and Josephine stared at the body until, dreamlike, Fenris lifted his eyes to meet her gaze. She smiled and blew him a kiss.

With that, everything let loose. The three figures sped at him. He stood there, his body tense, waiting.

Timing was everything.

A whisper of movement to his left. He threw his arm out, sending an ice dagger into the chest of another man sneaking up on him. Fenris spun around, swiping both hands to the right, across the line of sight of the three runners. They both fell, tumbled rag dolls collapsing on each other.

"Child's play," he whispered before being crushed into the dirt by an unseen person. A foot rammed down upon his spine. Bones crunched. He gasped in pain. A large hand yanked him upright. Strangling as an arm wrapped around his neck, Fenris reached behind and placed his hands on his opponent's head. He poured out lava heat, melting the attacker's skull from within. The strongman jerked away with a cry and fell writhing to the ground. Fenris grimaced. His own fingertips had blistered with the heat. Taking in gulps of air and looking around, he froze.

Half a dozen people were rushing at him. He threw out two large fireballs, scattering the group. A woman raised her hand, thrusting one fireball back at him. Fenris swore in surprise before the flaming orb struck. He screamed, rolling with the fireball once, twice, before it dissipated. Fenris lay there gasping, the burns searing his body.

With a shocking lurch, an invisible power dragged him along the ground to the feet of another woman who gawked down at him, unblinking. A dagger came at his chest, but he rolled before it struck. The woman was unbelievably fast. Even with Telepathy, he could only just anticipate her next thrust. Her movements were a blur. Again and again he dodged the flying weapon. He cried out as the dagger found its target at last, sinking deep and ripping across his waist. She cackled, holding up the bloody knife before the cheering crowd.

A wave of nausea flooded through Fenris. Grabbing a handful of dirt, he threw it in her eyes. She reared back. He leaped at her, twisting the dagger out of her hands with enough time to throw it into the stomach of a charging assailant. Then a touch to the woman's temple. She sank against him, making him stagger before letting her fall.

So much pain. Fenris grasped at his wound and his hand came away slick with blood. He fell to his knees, his vision clouded. Marcel's warning yell echoed in his ears. Through the haze, he saw four more figures barreling toward him.

Everything slowed as he lurched to his feet. A blow, a kick. A spin to evade. A slicing maneuver to kill. Another rush. Fenris poured out his Gifts. Some were new, acquired without awareness. They rose up instinctively in his desperation. An arm of iron slammed him into the dirt again. Instead of struggling, he lay there, done. The ground beneath him wet with his blood, his consciousness fading.

He was spent. Exhausted. Sara's face flashed before his eyes, and he bucked against his latest attacker. Positioning himself into a crouch, Fenris placed his hands on the ground and sent ripples spreading ... spreading ...spreading in waves upon the ground, in circles with his body as the center. Repeating and strengthening until trees began to topple. Screams echoed from the people gathered around the arena.

The earth beneath him cracked and began to break apart. Fenris stood on trembling limbs and with a heave, blasted Sara's weapon at them all, her golden sphere coiling fire and heat. He dropped bombs of molten lava into the crowd, while the protective sphere wrapped itself around him. The bubble grew, and fire shot out in streams. The ground continued to split before him, creating a chasm. A mighty wind whirled all around him with fire and fury.

Then he let it go.

The bubble sucked back into him and Fenris stood, sick and shaking. The arena was empty. He staggered around. Marcel and Durgan stood beside Josephine, their eyes wide with shock and awe. She, too, appeared stunned but calculating even in her surprise.

He limped toward her, coughing up blood. Marcel took a step in his direction, and Fenris held up a warning hand. He looked straight at Josephine, wheezing with every breath.

"Satisfied?"

Her eyes gleamed.

"Quite."

She raised a gun and shot into his chest.

A HOUSE PROTECTED

G rim-faced, Toby stood before the small group around him at the table. The hour was late; tensions were high. His eyes scanned the faces, lingering on Sara.

"I didn't know I would be the one doing this. To make this announcement ... It may come as a shock to some of you."

They all held their breath. Waiting. Sara tried to subdue the scream of frustration that wanted to break free. Why was he taking so long?

"Spit it out," Erin demanded.

"Right. Here we go." Toby took a deep breath. "Colonel Mustard, in the library, with the wrench."

Every eye went to Pops as he pulled the cards out of the envelope. There was a long pause before he tossed them to the table. All correct. Yells and shrieks of laughter erupted over the table, with Sara throwing her own cards down fuming. "I had it right and was going to be next!"

"I had no idea you were this competitive, sweetie," chuckled Frances.

Toby laughed harder than any of them and casually looped his arm around Erin's shoulders as he sat back down. "Were you close?"

Erin, who was about as competitive as Sara, shot him a glare. "No. I was convinced it was Professor Plum with the knife. At least I guessed the library."

"Not too bad." Toby winked.

Frances stood up and swayed, grabbing hold of the table's edge. Everyone gaped at her. She rolled her eyes at them all. "Good stars, people. I got up too fast. I'm eight months this week, it's not like this baby is going to pop out anytime soon."

"Soon enough," Hugo muttered.

"You should let us clean this mess." Sara jumped up. "We shouldn't have stayed up so late, but it was such fun. This was exactly what I needed."

Frances shrugged. "There's not that much to do. Toby, grab the popcorn bowls, dump out the leftovers, and put them in the sink. Hugo, wipe down the table, will you?"

Sara let out a loud yawn and several people laughed.

"And you! Get yourself to bed!" Frances commanded. Exhausted, Sara couldn't muster up the energy to argue. She toddled off like a child, ready for another night of not sleeping.

It was always something. Sophie was better, although she still woke often enough. With Fenris gone, she had no outlet for her night terrors. Mrs. Aguilar had begun working with the child, teaching her how to make her visions manageable, and encouraging her to talk about them instead of holding everything inside. It seemed to help, and Sara was relieved to see she was sleeping.

Sara lay down in bed, happy to get off her feet although she knew sleep didn't come right away. She thought of Frances and rubbed her own belly. "Fourteen weeks," she whispered. Sara couldn't believe she had already finished her first trimester. Even though she was weeks away from showing, there now was a tight knot indicating the tiny presence growing warm and safe within. There was no question her body was changing. Things weren't fitting quite like they used to. Eating all that popcorn tonight probably hadn't helped.

She smiled. The evening had been ... fun. She felt guilty, not knowing what Fenris and Marcel were facing, but a break in the tension had been something desperately needed by them all.

Things weren't bad on the surface. A few days after the men had left, the attacks around the city had come to a screeching halt. They had been able to re-establish a tenuous communication with most of the Gifted. To their surprise, almost all the violence had been directed to the street fighters when they ventured away from the house, and no one else.

The sudden quiet and silence held its own terror, taunting them. Sara feared it was the calm before the storm, and when the storm would arrive, no one knew.

Sara shivered and buried her head into her husband's pillow, breathing in his lingering scent.

༄⚜༄

"I dreamed of Daddy last night," Sophie spoke up, her face messy with oatmeal.

Sara and Mrs. Aguilar glanced at each other. Sophie was calm, even happy with her statement. She had slept well, and her eyes were bright.

"What did you dream, little one?" Mrs. Aguilar asked, leaning over the opposite side of the counter to peer into Sophie's face.

"It's his birthday."

"That is correct, *mija*."

Sara walked around to sit beside Sophie, trying not to think of all her former plans to celebrate her husband's birthday, the first time they would have celebrated it as a couple.

"We were in each other's dreams."

"You mean ... he was in your dream?" Sara asked.

"And I was in his." Sophie picked out a raisin from the oatmeal and set it in a small pile she was collecting. It was a habit she had demonstrated since Sara had known her, saving all the best parts of a meal for one delicious bite at the end. "We talked to each other."

"What—what did he say, darling?"

"He misses us."

"But he's safe?"

"Uh-huh. And Uncle Marcel." Sophie picked out another raisin. "They're close to finding her."

Sara's heart raced. There was no need to ask who Sophie was referring to. She fought the urge to shake the child and force her to say more. Fenris had insisted no one make Sophie look for him or to try to See what was coming, but his order didn't stop Sara from listening to whatever Sophie volunteered to tell her.

"Anything else?"

"He said ..." the child's face squinched as she thought. She stiffened and her face went slack.

"Sophie? What is it?"

"Get her off the stool, Sara. She's having a vision and might fall." Mrs. Aguilar's voice was urgent.

When Sara touched her, Sophie screamed, "Daddy!"

It was one thing when she woke in the night, but Sara had never seen this before. Sophie, wide awake, eyes glazed over in a waking nightmare. She eased the child from the stool to the floor, and Mrs. Aguilar knelt beside her. Sara gently shook Sophie to pull her out of whatever held her captive, but the older woman stopped her.

"Wait." She knelt before the little girl and whispered to her, going from Spanish to English, urging her to practice all she had learned to control her visions. Sophie's face cleared, her mind returned from wherever her Gift had taken her.

"What did you See, *mija*?" Mrs. Aguilar asked, her voice tight with fear.

Sophie heaved gulps of air, struggling to get the words out. "Daddy. He's hurt. Bleeding."

"Where is he, darling?" Sara whispered. "Can you tell us?"

"Lots of trees. Uncle Marcel ..."

"What about Marcel?" asked Mrs. Aguilar, her face set and pale.

"He's trying to help Daddy, but it's not working. He's crying."

"No ..."

Sara could handle the bad dreams—not this. The image of her husband lying on the ground, bleeding. Dying. The life ebbing from him. She swallowed it down and took Sophie up in her arms.

"Mommy. They're coming. To the house."

"Let's get you dressed, darling." Sara turned to Mrs. Aguilar and for the first time saw fear in her eyes. "Mama? Will you assemble the fighters?"

༄ ⁕ ༄

"Do you think Sophie can be relied upon?" asked Erin.

Sara fought the urge to snap at her friend, but she had been expecting this. After informing everyone of Sophie's vision, she was aware it would open up a new round of endless debate on what to do next. Everyone adored Sophie. She was a sweet child and forever popping up to someone with a smile and a hug. However, there was no question many of their group viewed her as ... odd.

"Her mother was a Seer—"

"Who went nuts and killed herself," inserted Augie.

Sara flinched.

"You told us yourself you never know what she's saying."

"That's not—"

She stopped when Hugo rose to his feet and paced back and forth a few times. The big man had not been the same since Raven's death, and she wasn't sure what she expected him to say. At last, he turned to face them.

"You all know me. I'm not a strategy man. When Fen and I worked together we had a saying, *brain and brawn.* Everyone knew he was the brain, I was the brawn. I would have followed Fen anywhere, faced anything. I know most of you felt the same way about him."

There were nods and looks between them. Sara swallowed past the tight lump in her throat. Why was he talking about Fenris in the past tense? They didn't know if he was dead. They knew nothing! With a great effort she tried to focus on Hugo's words.

"You're right. We don't know enough to be able to interpret what Sophie is Seeing. I'm not saying Fen is ... Our duty is to do the best we can with the information she has given us. As I see it, the problem is we don't know if she is talking past, present, or future. Right, Sara?"

"Correct."

"Well, heck. We know it's not past, unless it just happened. Fen has never had injuries like she described. And she clearly saw Josephine's men here, at this house, which has also never happened. That narrows things down. I think it's safe to say what she saw was in the future, and something is coming.

"Sara, you've always said Sophie's visions of the future were not set in stone. The future can be changed. Maybe if the Josephine vision is the future, so is the one with Fen. Maybe if we ... I don't know, do something ... we can prevent both visions from ever happening."

Sara fought back the tears. She wasn't sure what she believed about the timing of Sophie's vision, but she appreciated Hugo's attempt to find any potential hope.

"What does that mean for us today, Hugo?" asked Tudor.

"Well, I'm not sure. Again, that's not my—"

"Do we attack first?"

"No." Sara was sure Fenris wouldn't approve of this idea at all. "We have no idea what their numbers are, and I suspect they've been watching us all along. Even if Sophie could give us clear predictions, which she can't, they would see us coming long before we got to them."

"If it's a defensive game we're playing, how is that any different from what we've planned already?" asked Toby.

"Before, the attack was a vague possibility we were hoping to avoid. Now, we need to approach it as something inevitable, and adjust accordingly." Sara's mind raced to consider what Fenris would do. "We need to contact everyone in our database. Tell them we will be unavailable for the foreseeable future. It's high time some of them learn to take care of each other. I think they'll be safe enough as long as we are the main interest to Josephine, but ... if we should fall ... they should be prepared. Anyone without a fighting Gift, or a Gift useful for our current needs, take over the phones. The rest of us will gather together and come up with something."

"We have confidence in you, Sara. You, too, Hugo," called out Tudor.

Sara glanced at Hugo. They had talked before informing the group and both agreed they felt woefully inadequate for challenges ahead. Waving Erin over, Sara said in a low voice, "I'm going to need you. Will you help?"

Erin started to walk with her but was stopped by Toby's hand. He opened his mouth once and shut it. He reached around her waist, jerked her closer and planted a kiss on her lips. Breaking away he whispered, "I wanted to make sure I did that before anything exciting happens. You never know if you'll get another chance or not." With a wink, he was gone.

Erin spluttered her shock. She glared at Sara and Hugo. "I don't want to hear a word. Not. One. Word. You hear me?"

Sara grinned until her attention was drawn away to Mrs. Aguilar walking from the courtyard and out onto the open lawn.

"It is time." Mrs. Aguilar beckoned her husband, who joined her.

With their backs to each other, they both raised their hands and complicated swirls of light sprouted forth. To Sara, it seemed as if she was looking through soap bubbles at a distorted reality. The light bubbles grew and began to merge. Husband and wife spun around the courtyard, and the large bubbles continued to join together until the courtyard was surrounded. With a push, the bubble flew upward and out, around the entire house and grounds.

Sara turned around, gazing up at the sky. It was there, clear blue with hints of rainbow hues dappling the sides of the giant soap bubble that held them.

"What is this?" she asked in wonder.

"You are not the only one who creates Shields, *mija*." Mrs. Aguilar said with a smile. "This will not hold against everything, so we must have faith. Now, Frances."

Frances appeared less confident than usual. "Mama ..."

"What is it?"

"If I do this, and Marcel comes back ... he won't ..."

"He will understand and will wait."

"Yes, but—"

"He would want you to be safe more than anything. Fenris would say the same for Sara."

"What is she going to do?" asked Sara.

"Watch and see."

Frances stood alone, her back straight and head bowed. One hand was pressed to the outline of her womb, and the other was raised. She was speaking in a low voice with her arm raised.

Sara shivered. "Is she—what is she saying?"

"Talking through it," said Mrs. Aguilar. "Some find verbalizing their Gifts makes them easier. Surely you've seen Marcel at work? He can't keep quiet, even when Healing."

It was true. Marcel murmured, prayed, and hummed when deep in the healing process. If Sara hadn't been so amazed at what was happening before her, she would have been amused that both Frances and Marcel approached their Gifts in the same way.

Frances also spun around several times. Sara saw no light, no distortion, nothing to tell that anything was happening, until a gasp came from someone in the group. Her own heart skipped a beat. There was ... nothing beyond the courtyard walls. Light shined through, but there was no sky. No vegetation showing from the opposite side of the wall. It was strangely suffocating to not see what should have been there.

"What's happening?" she demanded, her voice shaking. Mrs. Aguilar placed a steadying hand on her arm.

"Don't be frightened. Cloaking Gift. Very powerful and rare."

But there were glitches. Pockets of the outside world. Sara wondered if they were because of the difficulty of the Gift or reluctance on the part of Francis to shut out her husband. If Marcel and Fenris came back—*please come back*—they wouldn't see the house, and there was no way for those inside to know the Shield must be brought down.

Walking to Frances, Sara saw there were tears on her face.

"I'm sorry. I couldn't—I couldn't do it completely. I can't leave them out there. I have to believe they'll need to see the house to come back." Frances wiped her tears away and the two women embraced.

⁂

That night, Sophie slept while Sara lay wide awake in the darkness, nerves jangling. Heart breaking. Aching to be with him. To hold him.

What was happening right now? Was he even alive?

"My sweet Fen," she whispered.

Sara ...

Her heart stuttered. She sat up in bed and looked at Sophie. The girl was fast asleep. Why had Sara heard his voice, wafting to her in a hushed breath of wind?

Was he saying goodbye?

She clutched his pillow tightly against her own body, imagining he was with her. Hot tears fell from her eyes as sobs overtook her.

"Fenris ..."

THE NOOSE TIGHTENS

M *y sweet Fen ...*

"Sara ..." he mumbled.

Her arms were around him and he groaned. She should not be here, not with ... Her hand stroked his cheek, fingers brushing through his hair.

Fenris ...

Another voice pushed through. "Fen! Please, buddy, help me out here."

Marcel. He sounded frantic.

Fenris's eyes flew open, and he bolted into a sitting position, gasping for air, soaking in sweat. Marcel sank back on his knees with a sound caught somewhere between a groan and sob.

"I thought I was going to lose you. *Again.* Stop doing this to me!"

"Sorry ..." Fenris said, closing his eyes. Everything confused him, and he wanted Sara back. Dream or no, she had felt so close ...

"Lie back down. You're a mess and there's more to do here."

"Okay."

He was on some sort of cot. Marcel eased him back down and began to murmur healing words over him. Sleep overtook Fenris, but he didn't dream of Sara again.

⚹

When he woke again, he felt like he was in relatively good shape. Marcel snored on another cot nearby. Fenris stood, wobbling until he found his balance at last. Then the aches hit him, all the residual effects of the previous day's battering of body and soul.

He took in his surroundings. An empty room, windowless and spare. There were several empty cots and a table holding a pitcher of water and glasses. He tottered over and poured himself a glass, draining it dry. He returned to his cot and sat with a hard thunk and a grimace of pain.

Looking himself over, he wondered how long Marcel had worked over him. The burns were gone. Fenris was surprised to see no scarring—Marcel's healing sometimes left remnants, and he had the scars of past injuries to show it. He craned his neck down and ... yes, there it was. An angry, red scar remained to show where the dagger had almost gutted him. Fenris wondered how Sara would react to that one. It didn't matter. He would take whatever she had to say, if it meant being with her again.

There were no signs of the gunshot that had brought him down. The sudden memory of a blue crackle came back to Fenris. Not a regular gun then. He shuddered. His powers were present and steady inside, so it must have been a single surge and not the barrage he had endured before. It wouldn't have taken much to bring him down after the arena.

Marcel's snore broke, and he stirred. With a weary groan, he sat up and brightened at the sight of Fenris awake. "Fen! You doing okay?"

"I'm alive, which is more than I was expecting by this point. How are you?"

"Bushed. Working over you wiped me out."

"Sorry, but thanks." He eyed Marcel, noting the worry and exhaustion in his friend's expression. "Was it bad?"

"Blood everywhere. I—I don't want to talk about it. You were amazing, Fen. I had no idea you could do all that."

"That's what you get from years of taking on other people's Gifts. Where's Durgan?"

"I'm not sure. They dragged us both in here, and I haven't seen him since the arena."

"Can you tell me anything about where we are?"

"We're in an office building."

"What?"

"Yeah, some place in middle of the woods. We can't be that far from civilization, though. There's an empty parking lot with a road leading out and everything. The road must go somewhere."

Fenris took a deep breath and glanced around the room.

"Thinking?" asked Marcel.

"Barely."

"What now?"

"I have no idea. Let me know if you come up with something."

"What a mess. Are your Gifts still working?"

"They are, surprisingly. How long did she shoot that stuff at me?"

"Just one solid blast. What was up with that? You think she didn't fall for the ring trick after all?"

"I don't know." Fenris dug into his shirt and pulled out a long chain with his real wedding ring hanging from it. He grinned at the sight. "You know, this was Sara's idea to switch them out."

"You never told me that. Clever."

"Yes," said Fenris, fingering the ring. "She's incredible."

Marcel groaned. "You're getting that goofy face again."

"Shut up."

"That's better. Didn't she put some sort of inscription in it? She mentioned something to Frances, but never said what it was."

"Yes."

"And?"

Fenris shook his head. "It's between us."

They sat in silence, both thinking.

"Can you blow your way out of here?"

"I could but ..." Fenris battled through the brain fog that lingered. "We have no idea what's beyond that door. If I do that and get shot worse than before, I waste an opportunity. No. I need to wait until I get a better grasp of our situation."

"What about Sophie?"

"What about her?"

"Can you ... talk to her?"

"She's a Seer, not a Telepath."

"I know, but you two have that weird special connection. Can't she send you a vision or something?"

"I don't know ..." Fenris thought about the way she spilled her night terrors into his head. "Maybe? Except I did tell her not to be looking for me."

Marcel snorted. "Sure, and a five-year-old is always going to do exactly what she's told."

A chuckle broke free from Fenris and he lay back on the cot. "Be quiet and I'll see. I've never tried this before."

"Like that's ever stopped you," muttered Marcel.

Fenris closed his eyes and cast his mind out. Reaching. No, she was too far away, that wouldn't work. What else? Mind and heart. That had always been his battle. This overactive brain of his, every conceivable neuron firing, soaking in every Gift, finding a way out of every obstacle. But his heart—his heart had been left cold and stagnant for years. Until Sara … and Sophie. For Sophie had stolen it, too, in her own way.

He thought of his dream before he had woken up. Her familiar nudge. There was a way to reach her; he just had to figure out how. He bent his heart to her, pouring all the love he held for the child out, envisioning a flood of it enveloping her.

"Sophie," he whispered. "Can you hear me at all?"

There! A spark of connection. Or was it? Fenris pushed harder, his heart thumping before he blacked out.

Sara weeping in bed, saying his name.

That sweet little nudge …

A hallway. So many doors. Which one, Soph? What are you showing me?

He stopped in front of one door and tried to open it …

A loud bang sounded. Fenris struggled to hang onto the vision. *Sophie! Don't go. Tell Sara—*

The door opened and broke him out of his self-induced trance. In a daze, he came back to the present in time to see Durgan pushed into the room. He fell in a heap upon the floor. Fenris and Marcel raced to the man, turning him over. Marcel's hands traced over him.

"He's roughed up. Not bad."

Fenris sat back in relief.

"Were you able to connect with Sophie?"

"Maybe, but it ended when they came in. I'm not sure. I'll try again later."

"Let's get Durgan up on a cot."

They heaved, and Fenris broke out in an instant sweat hauling up the older, heavier man's dead weight. He cursed his weakened state. "How much blood did I lose anyway?"

Marcel didn't meet his eyes. "A lot."

Fenris recalled Marcel's reaction when he had regained consciousness the first time. "That bad, huh?"

"Pretty bad. I'd put you on two weeks bedrest if we were home."

"Fantastic. He's out cold. You sure—"

"He'll wake up soon."

On cue, Durgan groaned, and his eyes blinked open before closing again. "You two."

Marcel helped him sit, while Fenris fetched a glass of water. The older man took it with a mutter of thanks. As he became more alert, Durgan's eyes widened seeing Fenris.

"Fen! Last time I saw you was in the arena. I thought you were—"

"Disappointed?"

"Don't be stupid."

"What happened to you? Can you tell us anything about this place?"

"All I know is—"

The door banged open again. Two men entered first, both with electric guns. Close behind them came Josephine.

Fenris couldn't stop the shiver that ran down his spine at the sight of the weapons. At this point, he feared them far more than the woman, although her Gift was terrifying enough. At least he had a fighting chance against her, but those guns—capable of stripping away all his powers in a few moments. He couldn't afford to give her a reason to use them.

Four more men followed her, unarmed. Two strode over to Marcel and Durgan, slamming each of them against the wall. The other two made a grab for Fenris and jerked his arms behind him. Josephine studied him a long time before a smile ghosted across her face.

"Such games we play, Fenrir. Such petty little games."

He kept his face a mask. She *did* enjoy her games, and he wasn't entirely sure which one they were playing now. She paced in front of him.

"Let's gather the facts, shall we? I know in late June you married Sara Gardien, and the ring you so callously tossed at me was not, in fact, your wedding ring. My sources have told me you were quite distraught to leave her. It saddens me that you lied, Fenrir." Josephine stopped pacing to sidle up to Fenris and got within a scant few inches of his face. "I was hoping we could be more, working together. I have much to offer, as you might have guessed."

One flash of power and Fenris could be free of the men that held him, of the woman before him, and they would be out of the room. But to face what?

She smiled as though she knew what he was thinking. Panicked, he searched his mind. Josephine shook her head with an indulgent smile. "No, I can't get in there. I wish I could. It would be a such delightful place to play. I just know how you think. I would not recommend trying to leave. It would be death to your friends, if not yourself."

Fenris felt a sting and a jerking sensation from his neck. Josephine took a step away from him, the chain with the wedding ring dangling in her hand.

"How romantic," she cooed. Her voice dripped with venom as she held the ring up to the light. "Why, my dear, did you know there was an inscription here? Shall I read it aloud?"

"Don't," he growled.

Her mouth moved silently as she worked out the word. "Winterpast? What does this mean?"

Fenris squeezed his eyes shut, not wanting to associate the wicked creature in front of him with his beloved wife. Josephine spoke in a sing-song voice that made his flesh crawl.

"Fenrir, you must tell me, or I shall become quite upset."

"No," Fenris swallowed hard, his breath coming fast. "You will not take this from me. Not this."

"What if ..." Josephine approached him once more, her breath hot on his face. "If you could tell me she meant nothing ..."

Fenris jerked back in alarm, but a strong hand held him fast. Josephine closed the space between them and rested her lips on his. She would *not* do this, would not steal his treasured memory of Sara's kisses. Something feral in him broke loose, and he snapped at her.

Josephine leaped back, staring at him in shock. Her hand rose to take a slow swipe at her lip and came away with blood. She laughed and handed the ring over to the guard to her left.

"This is Gerard. He's one of my pets, aren't you?"

The guard never moved. He kept his eyes on Fenris, his finger ever ready on the trigger. He was a muscular behemoth of a man, with cold, grey eyes.

"Gerard loves to play cat and mouse, don't you?" Josephine stroked her hand over the man's bicep. "There's a group of mice in Sacramento, my dear. Why don't you round up all your cats and go chase them."

Marcel moaned at these words. Fenris held back a scream of frustration, knowing he could break free if he wanted. His powers surged, though weakened from the previous day. Maybe ... maybe if he could ...

Stop, Fen.

Durgan's words pulsed through his head.

The armed men raised the guns to their shoulders, ready to fire.

Not yet. Not the right time.

Defeated, Fenris sagged. Durgan was right. He was too weak. To fight now would mean to lose his powers or worse. Separation from the others. Torture. Maybe death. All for a momentary loss of control. His gaze flitted to Durgan, who gave him the barest of nods.

Josephine watched the exchange and broke into laughter. "I see we have quite tamed the beast. Negative reinforcement is, after all, quite effective with animals." She turned to Gerard. "Do what you wish with the others. Save the redhead for me. You can *play* with her if you like but keep her alive."

"No!" exclaimed Fenris, desperate. "Please, I'll do anything."

She gestured to the guards restraining Fenris, and they increased their grip on him. She leaned in to whisper in his ear as one hand trailed along his cheek. "Too late."

With another laugh, she sent the remainder of the guards out of the room. Gerard called over his shoulder, "I look forward to meeting your wife. She must be something."

Josephine lingered a moment longer. "Three days. You have three days to decide. On the third day, you will join me, Fenrir, or I will let Gerard loose on those back home. And all three of you will be dead."

With those words, she left the room. Released from her presence and the restraint of the guards, Fenris fell to his knees, groaning.

Sophie. You have to tell them ... Sara ...

"What do we do, Fen?" Marcel asked, his voice strained.

Shaking, Fenris got back to his feet. "Tell me everything you know, Durgan. Marcel said we are in an office building?"

"Yes. I know we aren't far from Lake Almanor, but that's all I can figure out."

A mere few hours away from those he loved. Who needed protection.

"What about Laurel? Do you know anything?" Fenris demanded.

"This is their current headquarters. I know she's here somewhere."

"Right. We stick to the plan. Get Laurel out, hand that woman to the Feds. Get home."

"Brilliant, Fen," Marcel rasped. "How?"

"Your hearing as good as ever, Durgan?"

"Yes."

"Good. For now, we wait. Durgan will use his ears. Try to pick up what guards are outside, how many. Find the patterns. If we break out and they blast us, we're dead. Or soon will be. If we can figure out a window of opportunity, maybe we have a shot at getting out. If we can find Laurel, even better."

"After that?"

"Armageddon."

THE SIEGE

T wo days had passed since Sophie's warning, and Sara hoped they were ready.

Vanessa and Molly were preparing the basement as the last refuge of escape if fighting on the surface became too much. Ventilated and stocked with food, plus one crucial escape hatch that opened far from the house, it was the best place for a final stand. Sara prayed escape would not be necessary.

The three men were on everyone's mind. Sara insisted someone be always near the phones in case one of them tried to make contact through the landline. It had been over a month since their departure, and the strain of not knowing anything weighed heavily on Sara and Frances. Even Mrs. Aguilar, who had remained confident of their return, began to wilt. Sara sometimes caught the woman in a frozen stance, her eyes far away and silent lips moving before crossing herself and moving on with her work.

"Is Mama a Seer?" Sara asked Frances, late that afternoon.

They had both been on their feet for hours until mild contractions had forced Frances to sit. Sara flew into a panic, but Frances had waved her off with a rueful chuckle. "Braxton Hicks. Early pains. I've had them before. It's fine."

Now she looked up, startled, as Sara arranged a pillow behind her back. "A Seer? Not at all. Why would you ask such a thing?"

"I don't know. Sometimes, she says things that makes me wonder."

"I know what you mean. I think ..." Frances's eyes went distant.

"What?"

"I think the Gifted have a heightened intuition about things. Don't you feel it? With Fenris? Like you are this close to speaking, to connecting, even from a distance, but can't quite manage it?"

Sara sat down on the nearby sofa. "I thought it was just my imagination," she whispered.

"No, I sense it with Marcel as well. I have no doubt Mama can feel it with them both. She's highly attuned to those she loves, and after Pops, there is no one she loves more than those two boys."

Sara smiled at this and tugged an afghan off the arm of the sofa to drape around Frances. The weather had been unusually cold that entire autumn season, and the late afternoons were chilly. She said a quick prayer for the men, hoping they were warm and safe, wherever they might be.

A question crossed her mind, but she hesitated, unsure of how to ask. "I was wondering ... I don't know if I'm even allowed to ask this. Fenris always said I shouldn't."

"What are you talking about?"

"It's about Marcel. The day they left, Mama said something about him having another Gift. What did she mean?"

Frances was silent a long time, playing with the tassels of the afghan. She sighed and kept her eyes down. "Marcel has another Gift. One he has been forbidden to use."

"Forbidden? I've never heard of such a thing. Who decided this?"

"Well, Fen. It's a very powerful Gift, and it can drain the healing powers. Fen and Marcel agreed he needed to focus on being a Healer."

Sara pondered this information. She could see there was something—perhaps several things—Frances wasn't telling her.

"What's so terrible about this Gift? What does it do?"

Frances met her gaze at last. Sara thought her eyes looked haunted.

"Death. His other Gift is Death."

⸙

Sara's stomach had long since settled, and she had begun to eat more, but she still was unable to rest. Either Sophie or her own racing mind kept her awake long into the night. Mrs. Aguilar fussed over the shadows under Sara's eyes the next morning.

"Fenris will think we didn't take care of you. We'll have to use your Shield to block his anger at me for letting you get into such a state."

"As long as he comes back."

"Don't say that, *mija*. Trust me when I say he's well. At least, he was this morning."

"What?" Sara started at the words. "How do you—"

"Sophie."

"Sophie?"

"Look at her."

Sara grasped what Mrs. Aguilar was trying to tell her. If something had happened to Fenris, Sophie would have shown some sort of distress. It had been three days since her vision, and despite her tears at the time, she had insisted that Daddy was okay. She spent her time playing with the much younger Teresa and pattering about the house insisting she could 'help' with all the things to be done. Sara could believe Fenris was safe for now, but she also remembered the sudden onset of the last vision. It had come without warning, without any sign. The visions were not tied to anything. There were no guarantees.

This morning, Sophie was sitting at the table, focused on watercolors, the tip of her tongue sticking out in concentration. It had been Mrs. Aguilar's suggestion for Sophie to paint seashells instead of paper. Sara had been captivated by the idea. The white shells were glistening in bright purples, greens, reds. When she was done painting, they could be rinsed off and returned to their former pristine state, ready to be painted again another day.

Sara's own fingers itching for her paints and brushes. She had never painted before her parents died, but it had become a form of therapy for her long before she discovered she had any talent for it. She made a rush for her room and began feverishly sorting through the paintings she had brought for safekeeping until she found the portrait of her husband. Sara sank to the floor with the painting propped up against the bed. She smiled as she remembered when Fenris almost discovered the painting, that night they first kissed. It had been hidden away, and she would have been mortified had he discovered it then. Sara brushed her fingertips along the ridges of the thick oil paint she had used to give his hair texture. She closed her eyes, remembering the feel of his hair in her fingers ...

The sound of someone yelling her name broke her from the reverie. When she stood, she was surprised by the twinge below her stomach. Despite the urgency of the voice that had called for her, she paused as a sweet warmth flooded through her. Her practical mind knew it wasn't movement, not yet, but it spoke of a ... presence. Tears filled her eyes. "Please keep him safe," she prayed, not even knowing if she was praying for the baby or the father. Maybe both at once.

More voices joined the yelling, and Sara raced down the hallway back toward the kitchen. A small crowd had gathered around Tudor. He was bent over, gasping for air.

"Is he hurt?" asked Sara.

"No, let him catch his breath," said Erin.

"The Shield's back up?"

"Yes, of course."

"What did you see, Tudor?"

Fighters had scheduled watch duty outside of the compound. At pre-determined times, Mrs. Aguilar and Frances would lower the Shields surrounding the house to let one fighter in, while another dashed out. It was always a moment of tension, not knowing what might be right outside the wall when they made themselves vulnerable.

"Tudor!"

"Sorry," he gasped. "I was circling the house about two miles out and ..." He caught another breath. "I sprinted the whole way back. They're coming. It won't be long."

"How do you know?" demanded Erin. "It isn't like an army marching on a castle."

Tudor shot her a rueful smile. "No. Sometimes I can See things."

Sara and Erin exchanged looks. If Tudor was an Assimilator, being around Sophie might have given him her Gift. He was powerful, and the number of his Gifts seemed to be increasing.

Tudor caught their expressions. "No, it's not what you think. Not like Sophie. It's more like certain things will trigger flashes."

Just like Fenris.

"Ok, fine. What *triggered* you?" Erin snarked.

Anger flushed the boy's face and Sara intervened, leading him a few feet away.

"What did you see, Tudor?"

He closed his eyes and one hand raised as though pointing at something unseen. "Flock of ravens scattering. Trucks on the highway ..."

"What kind of trucks?"

"I'm not sure—"

"What's in the trucks?"

"I don't know ..." Tudor opened his eyes, wide and frightened. "I know they're coming, Sara. Please, believe me."

"I do. I promise."

Mrs. Aguilar stepped into the room and caught Sara's eye. "*Mija*, we need you outside."

Sara groaned. "What now?"

⁂

Out in the courtyard, Sara and Mrs. Aguilar found Frances weeping in frustration and fear, a hand to her womb. At the sound of their footsteps, she whirled around. "I can't do it, Sara! The Cloaking—I can't—"

Sara could see the Aguilar Shield, all the faint iridescent colors in the bubble surrounding them. Unfortunately, she could see far more. The Cloaking was gone. They were exposed to all eyes.

Icy cold prickles ran down the back of Sara's spine despite the morning sun shining down. While it had at times been suffocating to see nothing overhead, Sara had found rest in the knowledge they could not be seen. There had always been pockets where it didn't work, but they had been sparse and inconsistent, not something that could be tracked by outsiders. Now it was gone. If what Tudor said was true, losing their invisibility was the last thing they needed.

"It's been getting more difficult every time." Frances gulped in a breath, tears tracking down her face. "I think it's causing the contractions, and—they're getting worse, Sara! I'm always afraid to keep trying, and it won't—"

Mrs. Aguilar wrapped her arms around her daughter-in-law, shushing her.

"How is your Shield, Mama?"

"Never fear, *mija*. It is strong."

Sara wondered if it would be strong enough for what was coming.

⁓❊⁓

The next hour was tense. Sara felt like they should be preparing but had no idea how or what they were preparing for. If there had ever been an outright battle between two large groups of Gifted, she was unaware of it. She paced in the courtyard with Erin, Toby, and Tudor nearby, watching her.

Without the Cloaking, they could see everything surrounding the house once more. When a flock of ravens shot up into the sky, Sara's heart skipped. She and Tudor glanced at each other.

"Go get the fighters," Sara said. "Bring them to the patio."

Toby took Erin by the hand. "Erin, I—"

"You will NOT die on me, Tobias," said Erin fiercely. "Or I will have your head."

"Yes ma'am." He grinned outright, then pulled her close for a kiss. Breaking away, he whispered something in her ear, causing Erin's face to blush.

"Can we *try* to focus?" Sara said, torn between her stress and amusement. "No wonder you people drove Fen crazy."

"Sorry, Sara. I had to make sure Erin knew how I felt before all this goes down."

By this time the fighters had gathered around them, they could all hear diesel engines approaching. One of Erin's brothers had climbed a tree and was trying to peer out over the walls.

"What do you see, Carl?"

"Two trucks. Big but not huge, like moving vans—oh hey, there's people coming out of them."

"Can you get us a count?"

Sara paced as they waited. Carl called down, "Twenty-five, give or take."

A murmur spread through everyone on the patio. Their numbers were equal, but all of those on the other side would have extraordinary powers. As for their own people, well, not so much.

"Do you think they are all Gifted?" asked Augie. "Or do they have some Hunters mixed in?"

"No," said Sara. "They won't waste their time with Hunters at this stage."

The tension was too great. Sara jittered and placed a hand over her abdomen as it twinged again. A strange crackling sound filled the silence. It built and grew over the next few seconds.

"What is that?" Frances gasped.

Sara and Erin looked at each other. They both knew what it was.

"Electricity. A lot."

The first barrage hit the Shield around the house, and a tremor sank into Sara's bones. Mrs. Aguilar cried out and ran forward, her hand raised to maintain the force keeping the Shield in place. Another giant stream of blue light crackled, and without her husband to help, the older woman fell to the ground, shuddering.

"Mama!" Frances cried, racing to her.

"Where's Pops?" demanded Sara.

"He's down below in the basement, shoring up the emergency hatch!"

Sara spun around. The fighters were all gathered, but a few were edging away in fear.

"Hold!" she commanded. "We have everything we need to fight them on equal footing, as long as we avoid the electric guns."

"How many guns they have, Carl?" Toby asked, looking askance at the trembling Shield.

"Three, I think. They're really big!"

Another round of blue streams struck the Shield, and Mrs. Aguilar shook violently upon the ground with Frances doing her best to hold her steady. "Sara, she can't go on like this!"

"I know! Everyone hold your ground and be prepared. The Shield is coming down. They'll break through the wall first. Get into the positions we talked about. Take cover. We don't know what kind of Gifts they will be using. Watch for anyone who can take over the mind—they'll turn us all into zombies before we can fight back."

Sara paused. Tudor. They had to protect Tudor at all costs, since he was the one person they had who could fight against those with mental Gifts. "Toby, you and Erin—guard Tudor, you understand?"

"What will you be doing?"

"Using my Shield, but offensively."

Another barrage of electricity, and Mrs. Aguilar screamed at the pain.

"Let it go, Mama!" cried Frances.

"No ..." muttered the older woman.

"Mama! We've got this. It's our turn," Sara said.

"Sara!" Erin called, gazing up at the Shield.

All three guns must have been pointing upward, focusing the streams against a single point in the Shield. Cracks showed, the bubble wavered, and Mrs. Aguilar's body was assaulted by violent convulsions. With a final burst, blue flames erupted along the entire dome, splintering the Shield around them until it dissipated entirely.

Silence fell, broken by the sound of Frances weeping over the still body of Alicia Aguilar.

Seconds ticked by.

An explosion tore through the air, and the wall to the courtyard shattered.

The fighters readied themselves, coughing in air choked with fire and ash. The hulking figure of Gerard appeared in the smoke, followed by two dozen of Josephine's Gifted army.

The enemy was upon them.

A DANGEROUS MAN

*D*own one flight of stairs, exit. That long hallway again. All the doors. Fenris spun around, surrounded by doors.

Which one?

She led him to a door. How would he find it again? It looked like all the others. She tugged at his hand, pulling him down to the floor. A sparkle of glitter flashed, embedded in the carpet.

Really, Soph? Glitter?

He could almost hear her giggle. He put his hand to the doorknob—

Jerking out of the vision, Fenris gasped for air. Marcel was sitting beside him.

"Well?"

"We're getting better at it. More details. It's almost like she's here with me."

For three days, they had remained in their office prison. Food and water were brought to them, and they were escorted to a bathroom at regular intervals. Every time they left the room, they kept their eyes peeled for any hint of their location or the layout of the office, but little revealed itself to them. The building was nothing more than a basic office floorplan, except the windows were blacked out.

There was nothing to see.

Fenris's mind knew fewer boundaries. Through sheer will and determination, he and Sophie had joined up several times, enough to give him some information about the outside world. Those sheltering in the Aguilar home were tense, preparing themselves for something ...He could never quite see what.

Sara missed him as much as he missed her. For some reason, that made him feel better. Except she was frightened, and there was something wrong with her. Something Sophie couldn't communicate. He ached to be with her again, to catch her in his arms and kiss away her fears.

The hallway. Always that blasted hallway with the doors! Fenris wasn't sure how Sophie could pass on information on a place she had never been. He assumed she was taking a vision of the future and replaying it back into his own mind.

"What did she show you this time?" asked Marcel.

Fenris opened his mouth to speak, but Durgan waved at them to be quiet from his position by the door. Haggard and worn, he had been there constantly, always listening, taking mental notes of the time from his watch. Fenris recalled how often he had teased Durgan for continuing to wear a watch, but without phones that watch had become a lifeline. With it they kept track of the time and sounds. The sounds of individual feet—Durgan had learned which footsteps belonged to which guard—the sound of breathing, quiet shuffling. He could even hear the sound of heartbeats if they stood close to the door. One of them had an arrhythmia.

What Durgan waited for was the sound of silence.

The first day, the guards never left. Once they decided Fenris wasn't going to force his way through the door, they relaxed and became less vigilant. The times of their absences stretched longer and longer. To Durgan's disappointment, there was no pattern. However, there were tells—the muttered comments about too much to drink told him the fading footsteps were headed to a bathroom and would soon be back. Stomach growls were important. That meant a decent stretch of time was coming, unwatched and unguarded. These were the kinds of openings they waited for.

It was now early in the morning of the third day, and time was running out. Worst case scenario would be a desperate fight for freedom, and Fenris wanted to avoid that at all costs. Marcel and Fenris watched Durgan, tense and still, waiting to see what he might signal. Durgan remained at the door for many minutes, then waved to the other two. "Now."

With the long hours of waiting and planning, Fenris had given much thought to the best way to break out of the room. A single blow would be faster, but a quiet escape would buy them more time in the long run. He knelt down before the door handle, staring into the key slot. It was like moving a flower or floating a pen; he pushed his mind into the lock and searched for the right mechanism. There was a soft click, and Marcel jiggled the handle. Fenris pushed him aside and yanked the door open.

"Go."

Marcel and Durgan scuffled out of the room, and Fenris paused to relock it behind him. Anything to slow down the discovery that they were missing. He shoved past the others to take the lead. "Me first. I can protect you two better."

Marcel shot him a look of exasperation which Fenris ignored. He peered around in both directions and pointed to the left. All three jogged toward the exit sign and entered the stairwell. Fenris held up a finger. One flight down.

Before they opened the door at the landing below, Durgan put his hand on Fenris's arm. "You sure about this? You've built this whole plan on the erratic visions of a five-year-old Seer."

"Got any better ideas?"

Durgan shook his head, resigned. Fenris turned back to the door and sucked in his breath. As he opened it, there it was—that long, narrow hallway. The same hallway he had seen all those times in his mind. "So far, so good," he whispered.

It was silent in the dimly lit hallway, and the many doors contributed to an eerie atmosphere.

"Creepy," said Marcel. Fenris agreed but said nothing in response. He kept walking to the general vicinity of the door in his dream, keeping his eyes on the floor for that funny patch of glitter. The lights had been brighter in his vision, and in frustration he dropped and crawled. The echo of a noise from far away sounded in their ears, and all three froze.

"Durgan?"

"Not our floor. Not coming down the stairs."

"Okay."

"Fen?" asked Marcel, pointing to a spot. "Is this it?"

Fenris crawled a few more feet to where Marcel had sunk into a crouch. Something sparkled in his line of vision, and he almost laughed. He wished he knew why there was a smudge of glitter in this spot of all places, but he had no time to dwell on it. "Yes! Good job."

He got back to his feet and tugged on the handle. Locked.

A sob could be heard from within. Durgan's eyes went wide.

"What do you think?" asked Fenris. He was more rattled by the whole experience than he cared to admit. The silence surrounding them was too much. Felt too much like a trap. He knelt before the lock and closed his eyes. After an impatient effort, he grunted. "Can't do this one." Before either Durgan or Marcel could respond, he blasted it open.

"Sheesh, Fen," whispered Marcel. Durgan pushed past them both, and by the time Fenris and Marcel stepped into the room, the older man was holding his daughter, who was crying in his arms.

"Oh, Dad. They hurt you! I didn't mean to drag you into this, I—"

"I'm fine, dear. Just so thankful to have found you."

Laurel wiped at her eyes and smiled at the others. "I can't believe you all came."

"Hey, Laurel," Marcel grinned. "How've you been? Long time, no—"

"No time to chat!" Fenris snapped. "We need to get out of here."

"How?"

"I—" Fenris stopped, confused. Sophie's visions had always led him to Laurel. Never what came afterward. He turned to the girl. "Can you tell us anything helpful?"

"No. I have no idea where we are."

"Great. Well, back to the stairs, I guess."

As soon as they reached the stairs, a thunder of footsteps coming down had Fenris spinning around in panic. "Back!"

They raced down the hallway, trying in vain to open various locked doors. Turning the corner, and they found themselves facing another long corridor. Fenris was hopelessly lost. He could map his way back the way they came, but the path ahead was unknown.

At what he assumed was the opposite end of the building, they pushed through a door into another stairwell. The sounds of voices from below urged them upward. *How many floors were there?* Fenris wondered. They came out onto another hallway, and Fenris swore.

Marcel was ahead and found an open door with an interior lock. They piled in and locked the door behind them, trying to slow their heavy breathing. Fenris went to a window and jerked down blackout shades, blinking at the morning sun rising over the treetops. Marcel had been right. They were surrounded by forest, but a road leading away from the empty parking lot looked promising.

Durgan had remained by the door, catching his breath and listening. "We're good for the moment."

"Right. Durgan, you get Marcel and Laurel out of here."

"Whoa." Marcel held up his hands in protest. "What about you?"

"I'm going to stay here. Distract them. Give you a chance to get out."

"You've got to be kidding. No way are we leaving you here."

"It's a good plan, and Durgan knows it."

"He is right, as much as I hate to admit it," Durgan said. "Fen's the one they want. They'll prioritize catching him over us."

"No! I won't do this."

"I can get away from them, Marcel. Stop acting—"

"Like you've gotten away the last three days?"

Fenris raked his hand through his hair in frustration. He should have known Marcel would put up a fight over this. "We don't have time to argue—"

"Then we don't argue. It's all four of us or nothing."

"Don't be stupid! You think I couldn't have gotten out before today? I could have blasted my way through this entire building, but not with you guys tagging along."

"What?"

"You heard me. You're always holding me back, always hanging about. For once, let me do what I need to do, Marcel!"

"I'm not that helpless, you know. I can—"

"No!"

"You can't tell me what to do."

"I tell you this. I will *not* allow you to use that Gift."

"I can help you. You're not the only one who can—"

"What, kill? Is that what you want, to have blood on your hands?" Marcel snapped his mouth shut. Fenris saw his hesitation and hammered it home. "You have no idea what it's like. To use a Gift to kill. Sitting in the office most days, sailing in to be the Healer. You know *nothing* about getting your hands dirty. What that does to a person!"

"So, even now, you have to be the hero."

"What did you say?" Fenris snarled, hot anger bubbling up.

Marcel's jaw was set, and he was undeterred. "You have taken on this martyr complex for years. I thought with Sara—"

"Don't bring her—"

"But no, you're always the same. Fenris, the hero. The one who gives it all. Sometimes, I think you would rather go down in flames of glory than deal with this life we've been given, even after you've been given a real chance at happiness."

"Shut up!"

"No, I won't shut up! For once in your life, you will listen. I'm coming with you and—"

Fenris brought his hands around Marcel's face, power streaming. Marcel's eyes widened in surprise before turning sorrowful as the full sense of betrayal struck. "Fen?" he whimpered, and Fenris let out a sob. In another second Marcel slumped against him, unconscious.

"I'm sorry," whispered Fenris, tears falling down his face. "I'm so sorry. After Sara, you're the one person I can't lose—if this is the only way to keep you safe—" Fenris laid him down and knelt beside him. "You're the best friend a man could ever hope to have. Love you, buddy. I need you to do one more thing for me—take care of my girls, please."

Fenris stood and wiped the tears away before turning to Durgan. "He won't be out long. Just a few minutes. You need to be ready to deal with him. Get him out with Laurel."

"Got it. Fenris? I'm sorry about everything."

"I know. I think ..." Fenris thought of Sara and Sophie. The Aguilars. The realization of what he would sacrifice for those he loved hit him forcefully. "I think I understand. Why you did what you did. Now, make up for it by getting Marcel out of here. I can do what I need to do if I know he's okay."

"The hallway is clear, as is the nearest stairwell. Good luck, Fen."

"Too late for that."

With one last look at Marcel, Fenris slipped out the door. He made his way to the stairs and climbed all the way to the top. It took some exploration to find the right door on the top floor. He jogged up a narrow, hidden staircase to the roof.

He found himself alone on the rooftop. The stillness was almost shocking. He had almost expected her to be waiting for him. A breath of relief passed through him; she really wasn't omnipotent. He had been beginning to wonder ...

Glancing over the edge, he saw the building was smaller than he expected—five stories. He considered dashing back downstairs. Maybe it would be easier than he thought to get them all away. The roof door opened, and he flinched.

Fenris turned to face his fate.

First came the guards. He counted eight. Josephine followed. Her demeanor was casual—she almost ambled. Her confidence in the situation was obvious. "Fenrir. I wondered when you would disentangle yourself from them. The two of us, alone at last."

"Hardly alone." Fenris's eyes searched his surroundings, calculating. Now that he was facing her, his attitude shifted. He had to buy the others time to get away, but he intended to at least *try* to survive this.

"True," she laughed. Her face grew serious. "Don't you ever wonder why I've done all this?"

"It's not that complicated. You're a narcissist."

Josephine tsked, irritating him. "I'm not *merely* a narcissist."

"Psychopath?"

"I believe the correct term is antisocial personality disorder."

"I appreciate your precise use of words."

"I thought you would. But again, do you never question *why*?"

Fenris paced, antagonizing the guards. She held her hand up, indicating to let him move about. "I've heard things."

"I'm sure you have."

"You want something beyond taking over." She shrugged, and Fenris paused in his pacing. "You like science. You like to study. You want to know why—why we are the way we are. What happened that day."

"Don't you ever wonder?"

He pulled up short. Memories flashed through his head. The day he was told he couldn't play baseball anymore. Teresa's murder. His father's health getting worse. Everything after the Changing. *Because* of the Changing.

"Don't you question it at all, Fenrir?"

"Yes," he breathed. Durgan was right, she was a Charisma, and she was turning her Gift loose on him fully now. Her words were a delicious poison, luring him to consider her way as ... reasonable.

"We've lost a great deal, you and I."

Fenris swallowed hard. "You can't—nothing you do can bring them back."

"Look at you. In your heart, you are still a nineteen-year-old boy who just lost his father. Who can't even remember his mother."

Fenris gulped, swaying.

"Oh Fenrir, I could make all this so much better."

"Stop it!" He lashed out, clearing her toxic stench out of his head. "What did *you* lose?"

"Everything," she whispered. Her mood shifted, eyes growing calculating. "I study the Gifted, yes. To understand. To find a reason for why this happened. With my army, I will have my vengeance."

"On who?"

"You think the Changing was an accident?"

"I... don't know."

"You can't be that naive. This was *created*, forced upon us."

"That doesn't mean there isn't a reason ..."

"A *reason*? You can't be serious."

"Something at work beyond our understanding."

"Here I thought you were intelligent. You can't tell me you've never wondered."

"Of course I have," he snapped. He was struggling to argue, wanting to give into the one thing he had in common with this woman—bitterness. Another memory flashed through his mind. Sara's smile. The sound of her sweet laughter. The way she kissed him ...

At the change of his expression, Josephine's eyes gleamed with curiosity. "What is it?"

"I've been so stupid ..." he muttered. "All this time, all these years, the anger I've held. Dwelling on everything the Changing took from me. But I've never considered what it has *given* me. Without the Changing, I would have never known Sara."

Josephine snorted in derision. "Does that even matter?"

"Oh, yes," he whispered. "It matters. Because I know now—*I know*—there is always a reason. Always a greater plan at work. Whether I understand it or not. For everything I've lost, I have also been given something precious." At her scoff, he lasered his focus back on her. "Was this natural? Science run amok? Aliens? It's done, and we are here. We can't turn back the clock."

"Indeed. We cannot." Josephine snapped her fingers. One guard brought her a tablet. "Are you at all curious about what's happening back home? The Aguilar defenses were impressive, but did they think they were impenetrable?"

Frigid fear washed over him. "What have you done?"

"Come see. Gerard is quite efficient."

Fenris took a cautious step forward, reluctant to come closer, but the images flashing on the screen called out to him. Another step. One more, and he could see the feed clearly. Smoke and fire. Prone bodies on the ground.

Frozen, he watched, unaware as Josephine took a few steps closer, giving the images a startling clarity. Several figures—one might be Hugo—were running in one direction, and a determined redhead stepped in front, her golden Shield powerful. He had never seen her use it with so much control and yet ...

"Sara ..." he whispered. "Run."

"She has nowhere to go."

A sudden explosion shook the camera and he saw Sara flying back. He cried out and made a grab for the tablet, but Josephine jerked it away. Handing it to the guard, she laughed. "Sara is gone. They will all soon be gone. Last I heard from Gerard, most of them were dead already. At this point, he's cleaning up the trash."

Over and over, the scene he had witnessed on the screen played in his mind. Hot, burning rage crept upon him.

"If what you say is true ..."

Josephine's eyes glittered, waiting.

"You have made a serious miscalculation."

"What is that?"

"If my family is truly gone, I have nothing to lose. Which makes me a very dangerous man."

Whatever she had expected to hear, it wasn't that.

Protect. Always defend and protect. But his priorities had changed with what he saw on the screen. The rage in his heart called out for blood. What would it be like to go on the offensive for once? To attack without mercy. Without regard. Only two of the guards had guns. *Idiots.*

The clatter of more footsteps on the stairs told him time was running out. Not a problem. If Sara was really ... he would go out taking as many as he could.

"For all your cunning, you really are stupid." He laughed outright at the surprise on her face. "You set dozens against me in the arena, and I survived them all. You think this handful can stop me?"

"You—" She licked her lips, glancing about.

"Get ready to die."

Fenris circled, hands upraised, jerking the two guns out of the hands of their owners. They skidded across the rooftop toward the stairwell door as several people burst through. He somersaulted, avoiding a Paralysis wave from one of the guards. With a smirk, he threw a fireball back at him. The burning sphere landed directly into the man's chest, and he fell back over the edge of the roof with a scream.

"Chose the wrong side, buddy," Fenris said with no regret. But as he spun about, his heart stopped at what he saw. There weren't more guards coming onto the roof. It was Marcel. And Durgan, who was pushing Laurel back into the stairwell.

The unexpected sound of a gunshot rattled him. A bullet slammed through his thigh, and he fell to his knees with a groan. It would be a great joke if a regular human gun turned out to be the thing that finally took him down. Bullets could kill him if he didn't have a Shield up. Would have been good to remember that.

Before he had another thought, he was thrown to the ground as the world exploded around him.

A STORY TO REMEMBER

G erard was flanked by the three Gifted with guns. The rest stood near the broken section of wall, hovering like specters in the smoke.

"Sara Trygg?"

Sara lifted her chin, her jaw set. She would not let this monster intimidate her. Still, her voice quavered as she responded, "Yes, and you are?"

"Gerard Hamilton."

"Well, now that we are acquainted, would you care for a cup of tea?" she snapped.

"I have something for you."

"What is it?"

"Come closer, and you'll see."

"Do you think I'm that stupid?"

"Fine. I'll just keep this ..." He dangled a long chain with a ring looped through it.

Sara gasped and took a step forward. Erin grabbed her arm. "Sara—"

"I have to see," she said, desperate.

"At least take a few of us with you. Come on, Hugo."

They each stood on either side of Sara. She edged closer and held her hand out. Gerard dropped the ring and chain into her waiting palm. Sara backed away but made no move to inspect it. Instead, she kept her eyes on Gerard.

"Well?" he asked.

"Well, what? A gold ring tells me nothing."

"Maybe you should give it a better look. There's an inscription inside. Winter-something."

Sara stumbled, cold chills running down her spine. With fingers that trembled, she held the ring up to the light. There it was. *Winterpast.*

Fenris would have never given this up on his own. Which meant ... well, what *did* it mean? Sara narrowed her eyes at Gerard.

"Where is he?"

Gerard shrugged. "Dead, as far as I know."

Sara was grateful for Hugo holding onto her arm. His grip tightened at Gerard's words and kept her from collapsing. "As far as you know?"

Gerard grinned at her discomfort and raised his voice louder so all could hear.

"Josephine gave him a choice. He and his friends. They had three days to join us or be executed. Given it's the third day and Josephine's flair for drama—" Gerard snickered. "I expect she killed them at dawn." He let his words sink in before glancing up at the sun. "Dawn is long past."

Not true, Sara told herself, frantic. It couldn't be true. Sophie would have known. She would have communicated something, anything, if Fenris was dead. He had found a way out. For a second,

Sara hoped he *had* joined Josephine to stay alive, but on that fact alone, she was confident. He would never have compromised.

Her hand closed over the ring. A flash of memory—the brilliant light of happiness in his eyes at their wedding, when she had slipped the ring on his finger. ... She shook herself free of the intangibles and faced the man in front of her. "What do you want?"

"What do you think?"

"Join you or be attacked?"

He snorted. "This won't be an attack. It will be a slaughter. And an easy one."

"We might not be as powerless as you think."

"Kent!" called Gerard.

Sara didn't see the man named Kent, only the streaming flames that erupted, scorching along the ground right up to her feet.

"Oh."

Gerard laughed and turned. Over his shoulder he called, "Half an hour. Be ready."

She stood her ground until they had disappeared beyond the walls. Then she fell to her knees, pressing the ring to her chest. "Please be alive, please ..."

"What do we do?" asked a voice from the crowd.

She had to hold it together a little longer. It would all be over soon, one way or the other. Sara pushed herself up to her feet, swaying against Hugo. The smoke and dust had settled, exposing the fear on everyone's faces. She teetered, regained her balance, and went straight to Frances. Pops had appeared in the last few moments and was holding Mrs. Aguilar.

"Is she—?"

Frances gave her a grim smile. "Very weak. She kept the Shield up far longer than she should have."

"But she's alive. Thank heavens. We need to get her below. You, too."

"I can help!"

"No. I will not risk you and your baby, and for what? Are you going to make them invisible? That would be a funny way to fight a battle." Sara turned to Hugo. "Get Pops and Mama to the basement, please." What next? Her middle twinged again. Sara wished she knew if these were natural sensations or if something was wrong.

"You okay, Sara?" Toby asked her.

"Yes ... yes, I'm fine." She had told no one about the baby; only Hugo, Frances, and Mrs. Aguilar knew. "We need to get ready."

"For what?"

She set her jaw. "To fight."

Toby took Erin's hand. Sara saw doubt on almost everyone else's faces. Everyone except Tudor, who looked fierce and ready to go down fighting. Sara lifted her chin in defiance. "What else would you do? Join them and live? Well, I'm not stopping you."

There was a long pause.

"Go ahead! Run away. Do you think they'll greet you with hugs and kisses? I don't even want anyone here who is that stupid. Even if they did let you live, is that what you want for the rest of your life? Attacking Gifted all over the country, forcing compliance or death? How are they any better than what we've dealt with already? At least before, our enemy was always clear—Hunters. A small sect of hateful people, but in general, we aren't do-ing badly against them. If we stay together, we have a chance.

With Josephine's army, you'll become something hated and feared. You'll be part of something that will eventually be the downfall of all the Gifted."

Sara paced over to a large chunk of the collapsed wall and stood upon it. "But if you stay, you will be a part of something bigger. A story they will write and remember. When the Gifted stood their ground against evil—when they stood against their own people to do what was right. To protect themselves and the non-Gifted alike from dangerous powers that serve no good and promises harm to everyone."

Her fingers tightened around the ring in her hand. Her voice lowered and people had to strain to hear her. "And if we die, we die. I know where I'm going after this life. I know who's waiting for me, and who will be following, someday. I'll go with no regrets, knowing I did what was right on this side of the veil." Voice breaking at last, Sara shook away the tears that were gathering on her eyelashes. She took a deep breath. "Go if you want. But I would *really* like it if you chose to stay."

Not a single person left and the enemy on the opposite side of the wall was left wondering what the cheers meant.

⟜✳⟜

Sara walked back up the basement steps, her heart aching. She had given Sophie one last hug, telling her over and over how much she loved her. Sara wanted to take her and run. If Fenris was here, that's what he would demand—get to safety. Except he wasn't here, and Sara knew she couldn't leave the rest to their fate. All her life, she had hidden away. Hidden when her family was murdered. Hidden away from Fenris for fear of losing him. Hidden in the office when others were out fighting.

She would not hide again.

Sara left Sophie in the care of Frances. Mrs. Aguilar was recovering, and the woman spoke lovingly to her as they embraced. *Remember who you are. A Guardian for those you love ...*

Leaving the passageway through the closet, she ensured all was locked and well-hidden before she walked through the house, speaking to the few who were set to guard and fight from the interior. She glanced at the oven clock, noting it was almost time. Picking up her pace, she grabbed an apple while passing through the kitchen, steeling herself against happier memories in that room, afraid they would weaken her resolve. Then she changed her mind and paused, allowing the memories to soak into her bones. Sara found that, after all, when you know what you are fighting for, those memories give you strength.

Time was running out.

She bit into the apple, the sweetness exploding into her mouth. Heart rate increasing, she stepped into the courtyard and made her way to the patio. Eyes followed her. She remembered when Fenris wished he could be the hero with a horse and sword. A sword would be pretty awesome about now.

Fenris.

"Please be alive ..." she whispered, clutching at the ring that hung about her own neck thanks to a quick repair job. What would he do to prepare for what was to come?

Encourage them.

That's what he would do. Even on his worst days, those caustic moods with biting sarcasm, Fenris knew when to inspire. Imitating his good example, she walked among them all. Sometimes to whisper a word in someone's ear or a bit of advice, assuring herself they knew their roles and what was to be done. She motioned for Augie to follow her, joining Tudor, Erin, Toby, and Hugo to face the break in the wall.

Gerard was already approaching with a crowd behind him. He took one look at their defiant stance and laughed. "Is this seriously how it's going down?"

"Toby," Sara said, without taking her eyes off the man before her. "Give Gerard our answer."

Toby nodded, and Augie tensed, waiting. Half a dozen enormous fireballs shot out, five directed with remarkable precision toward Gerard. He disappeared with an angry yell behind the wall, but the fireballs went into the crowd. Sara struggled not to weep at the sounds of screams. The last fireball went askew as though caught in a pinball machine, bouncing around. Augie was ready with a well-aimed ice dagger, the fireball exploded into a cloud of steam.

"Wow," said Erin. "Those fireballs were huge."

"Just for you, baby," said Toby with a nervous wink.

The screams fell away to silence. Hugo stepped up behind Sara, placing a large hand on her shoulder.

Waiting.

Sara and Erin tensed at the sound of a familiar crackle. "Down!" screamed Sara as her Shield exploded out to meet the electric streams. They ricocheted off the Shield in a multitude of directions, while Tudor crouched outside the Shield's protection, throwing his hands in the air and jerking the three weapons out of the hands of the enemy. They flew, one slamming into a tree and shattering. Another landed in the pool, butt end first, and water exploded upwards in a fountain of blue and silver light until the entire gun sank to the bottom.

The last gun fell to the ground. Sara sucked her Shield back in. Erin ran and reached the weapon as the crowd of enemy Gifted flooded the breach. She tossed the gun to Hugo, who aimed at the invaders. Erin shot electric bolts from her hands.

Sara took a step back, assessing. Erin and Hugo were to her right. Toby was shooting fireballs from her left, with Augie watching for strays and throwing ice daggers into the hearts of those who came too close. The enemy was falling left and right. Sara couldn't believe it could be this easy. Had they so completely overestimated what was coming at them?

Gerard stepped forward with a mocking smile that sent a shudder to Sara's own heart. Instinctively, she sent her Shield out once more as an explosion rocked the ground beneath her. Sara fell, her Shield collapsing. Erin screamed.

"Erin!" Toby cried out. Sara gripped his arm.

"Focus. I'll see to her."

Erin was on the ground, clutching her head, screaming over and over again with agonizing mental pain. Someone was torturing her from the inside out. Sara yelled out for Tudor, "Find who's doing this!"

Sara shot her Shield out to cover him as he sank within himself, his mind bouncing off the enemy, seeking ...

"Let me out!" he yelled.

Sara pulled the Shield away from Tudor so he could attack. Erin stopped screaming and lay still, gasping for air. Sara helped her up while trying to bring the Shield back over Tudor.

"Toby! Take her and go—take Tudor, too."

"We can't leave you, not when—"

"That's an order!"

Hugo ran up beside her and shoved Toby in the chest. "Go! I'll stay with her."

The ground shook again. Toby gave Sara one wild-eyed look and helped Erin away.

Each tick of the clock lingered as Sara took in everything around her. Fighters were everywhere, battling each other. Hugo was screaming in her ear to get away. What was she forgetting?

Something important.

Her Shield. Defensive *and* offensive. Sara sent golden bombs of light surging into the enemy.

Gerard met her gaze across the courtyard. For the first time, he had a wild fear in his eyes. She saw him dig deep and braced herself for the blast. The explosion sent her flying across the courtyard. Someone screamed her name. But her last thought was another memory of Fenris, holding her close on their wedding night.

"Tell me a secret," she whispered.

"A secret?"

"Yes. Something just between us, something no one else will ever know."

"Fenris," she whispered.

Silence enveloped her.

FULL CIRCLE

S ounds distorted. Vision blurred. Fire raged.

Chaos surrounded him, and Fenris remained on his hands and knees, trying to discern what was happening around him. Durgan shot an icy cannon ball into a guard. Another guard reached for one of the electric guns. Marcel kicked it away, catching his attention. The guard threw out his hand, sending something at Marcel.

With a groan, Fenris forced a Shield out to block whatever was coming. He tried to clamber to his feet but fell back to his knees. The bullet had ravaged though his thigh, and he nearly screamed at the fiery pain that tore through him. Marcel raced to him, hooking one arm through his and dragging him back a few feet, near the edge.

"What happened?" mumbled Fenris. "Explosion."

"I'm not sure. Something got launched at us from a distance."

"Great. Where is she?"

Marcel didn't need to ask who *she* was—he pointed toward the other side of the roof, where Josephine was yelling at two of her guards. More gunshots rang out.

With a growl, Fenris pushed past the pain and got to his feet. Staggering, he shook off Marcel's arm. "I'm going after her, before she—"

He never saw the gun raised, just Durgan racing toward him, yelling. The bullet ripped through Durgan as he leaped in front of Fenris before falling over the edge of the building.

Laurel screamed. Marcel froze, staring over the edge of the building in shock. Fenris let out a feral yell of rage, whirling around to face the rest. Another explosion rocked the building, shaking them all. When the dust cleared, he saw half the guards had been taken out, one way or another. Two were racing toward him. Fenris had taken one step when the psychic blast hit his brain, shattering all thought. An inhumane shriek filled his head, blocking sound, sight.

Fenris collapsed, screaming. All sense of time and space distorted. On and on ... would it never end?

"Fen!" Marcel cried out from far away.

Pain. Nothing but pain. Surrounding him. Engulfing him.

Then the screaming stopped. The pain faded away. Lying there, his vision returned to see a black mist creeping across the rooftop.

"Get out of it, Fen!" Marcel yelled.

Fenris sat up, horrified. It had been years since he had seen this. "Marcel?"

Marcel stood firm, toxic vapors emanating from his hands and speeding toward the guards. The darkness of the cloud, and the poison it contained shocked Fenris. All the healing, all the noxious buildup of blood and injuries, death avoided, pain gathered, all rolled into this miasma pouring out of Marcel.

The guards came to a sudden stop, staring at the mist as it traveled to them, up their feet, wrapping itself around their bodies. In the end, it shot into their mouths and nostrils, filling their lungs, death entering the bloodstream.

"No ..." groaned Fenris. It was a horrible way to die.

One guard fell, clutching his throat, gasping for air, eyes bulging. The other guard kept his head long enough to try to escape, but the mist whirlpooled around his body, throwing him down until he moved no more.

Marcel withdrew the mist back into himself and fell. He was shaking all over, grey-faced.

"Marcel. No ... please, no." Fenris crawled over to his friend and pulled Marcel into his arms. "You shouldn't have done that. You should have—why can't you ever do what I say?"

"I wasn't going to let you die," Marcel muttered. "I'll be okay."

Fenris hugged him close. The rooftop battle had grown quiet. He swore when he realized Josephine had disappeared once more. A new sound caught his attention. "Can you get up? Because I don't think I can, if you aren't able to help me."

"Hold on." Marcel stood, wobbling. Once he became steady, he helped Fenris to his feet. He chuckled when Fenris staggered against him. "We're a mess."

"Yeah." Fenris looked over Marcel's shoulder. Now, the sound was recognizable. Helicopters were approaching.

"Where's Laurel?" Marcel asked.

Fenris stiffened and looked around. The door to the stairs was open, creaking on its hinges as it swayed in the wind. "Downstairs. Come on."

They raced as fast as they could, but even in his weakened state, Marcel soon outpaced the limping Fenris.

"Fen, can you—"

"I can't. Go on, I'll catch up."

"I don't know if—"

"Go! She might need you."

Marcel shot down the stairs. Fenris hobbled as fast as he could, the pain in his leg increasing. He did his best to ignore the blood he left dripping along the stairs. With a cry of relief, he burst through the last door into sunlight. The helicopters they had seen from a distance on the roof were closer.

He tracked around the building, sliding to a stop when he saw Marcel kneeling before Durgan's broken body. Laurel was holding her father in her arms. Reaching them, Fenris sank down to his knees. Durgan was alive, but barely. Clenching his jaw, Fenris took hold of one of his hands.

"Marcel?"

"I'm not sure ..." Marcel's eyes had filled with tears. "Fen, I don't think I can—after using that other Gift ..."

"Try!" Fenris snapped. Durgan moaned and stirred, his eyelids fluttering. Laurel's arms tightened around him. "Hold on, Henry, please ..."

Durgan's mouth twitched with a ghost of a smile. "It ... must be ... bad. Using my first ... name."

Fenris choked out a laugh, tears falling down his face. "You're banged up, but Marcel will put you to rights. Hang on until he can."

"Fen?" Marcel whispered from behind. Fenris ignored him.

"Laurel ... you here?"

"I'm here, Daddy."

"Tell your mother ... Sorry for everything over the years. She was right ... to leave. Fen? You promised ... to watch out for her ..."

"You know I will—"

Durgan interrupted with a ragged breath, and a vague smile passed over his face. "I'm sorry. For everything."

"I know. Marcel! Do something!"

"He can't. I'm ... too far gone. Isn't that right, Marcel?"

"Don't say that."

"Leave me and get back to the others. You'll be taking over for good now. They'll be ... in the best of hands."

Fenris's heart clenched to the point of physical pain. "Don't ... we're going to fix you up and get back home. Take care of them all. The whole team. Both of us, like it's always been."

"I'm sorry, Fen. You were a son to me, and I—"

"And I forgive you, you idiot! Don't you know that? Marcel, please." Fenris was crying in earnest now, barely holding himself together. Laurel wept at his side.

"Fen, he's past my ability."

"What is the point of being a Healer—if you can't—?"

"I can't reverse this," Marcel said, wiping his eyes. "Even with my Gift, this would take a far greater Power than myself."

"It's okay," Durgan whispered. "I'm ready. My daughter's safe. Laurel ..."

A long silence followed as Durgan's body relaxed. Marcel held his hands out over him and shook his head. "He's gone."

Fenris sat back, stunned. Laurel wept harder, holding on to her father's body. The helicopters were closer. One landed on the roof of the building, while the other settled itself in the parking lot with a surging whoosh of dust and crunch of asphalt.

"I sure hope those are the good guys," Marcel muttered.

Several people jumped out, including Dellaney. His footsteps slowed as he took in the scene. "Durgan?"

Fenris nodded.

"Is this—are you Laurel?"

"Yes."

"Your father was very brave and did a great service for us. I'm sorry."

Laurel bowed her head and continued to hold her father.

"How are the two of you?"

Fenris and Marcel glanced at each other. There was the hint of shadow in his friend's brown eyes now; Fenris knew it would never completely disappear. Otherwise, his gaze was clear and serene.

Marcel. His port through many storms over the years, a little battered but steadfast as always.

"We're fine. Or will be, anyway." Fenris tried to stand, and Dellaney had to reach out to steady him.

"Shot?"

Fenris grunted in response. Marcel hauled himself up and held Fenris by his other arm. "Do you have a medic? I can't help him until I regather my strength."

"On it. And then you'll be home soon."

"Has anyone checked in on them recently?" asked Marcel.

"Your house? Not in a day or two. Things in Sacramento have calmed down."

Fenris regarded the helicopter. "Any chance we can get a ride on that thing?"

"I don't see why not."

"Great." Fenris turned to Laurel and placed a hand on her shoulder. "Laurel, let's get you home to your mother."

"I don't want to leave him," she said.

"If anyone knows how you feel, I do. But this isn't over yet, and it would be better if you were with her."

"I'll make sure she gets home safely," offered Dellaney.

"Thank you."

⌒⋇⌒

"Bad idea. Bad idea. *Very* bad idea."

Marcel forced a laugh. "I always forget you're afraid of flying."

"I'm not!" snapped Fenris. "But I do prefer doors when I'm a few thousand feet in the air."

Marcel grimaced, uncomfortable himself. The helicopter was a military design and definitely lacked doors. Fenris had checked his safety belt half a dozen times before takeoff, while Marcel had buckled his, said a feverish prayer, and gave in to his fate.

It had taken longer than they had hoped to get away. Marcel had no strength to perform any healing, which meant a medic had to stitch up Fenris's injured leg. Fenris wasn't used to the delay of conventional medical care and glared at Marcel through the whole process.

"I told you not to use that Gift!" he snapped. "I always knew it would drain you, which is one of the reasons I forbid it! Your Healing is far more important."

"Okay. Fine. Next time I see a man about to kill you, I will do nothing and let you die. It would serve you right."

"I have to hobble about on one good leg until you can manage to work your magic. That's fantastic. If there's fighting going on back home, how am I supposed to—WHAT THE—" Fenris interrupted himself with a yelp as the medic jabbed a needle into his leg. Marcel cackled.

"A shot for the pain," the medic explained, humor leaking out of his voice. "It will help, I promise."

Fenris leaned forward, and the ground trembled beneath him. "Get. Away."

The medic's grin faded. Ever so slowly, he backed away.

Now they were shooting south as fast the helicopter could take them. They both had to yell to be heard over the noise, and Fenris kept fussing with his phone that Dellaney had returned.

The co-pilot called back to them. "Dellaney said he's called their people in the city, and they'll be on their way, as well. They have a few Gifted with them to help, but want to wait until you get there. They don't want to get hit by friendly fire."

"Yeah, yeah ..." Fenris said, trying his phone again. "Pick up, please pick up ..."

There was no answer, and Fenris slammed the phone in frustration.

"They aren't expecting us to call though," Marcel said. "We told them we wouldn't."

"I know," Fenris muttered before raising his voice again. "Hey, how do you think Dellaney even know where we were?"

"Oh, I had a tracker."

Fenris gaped. "What?"

"You aren't the only one with a secret or two." Marcel winked as he twitched a necklace from under his shirt. An ordinary-looking saint medallion hung from the chain. "Dellaney gave it to me the morning we picked up that rental car. They most likely they had our location pinned down the day after we disappeared. They didn't know we were in trouble though. We just happened to escape a short time before they got here."

"Did it never cross your mind to tell me this?" huffed Fenris.

"Well, I didn't want get your hopes up. It was never a foolproof plan."

"Great." Fenris groaned. "Typical incompetent Feds, taking their sweet time."

"How much longer?" Marcel yelled at the co-pilot, daring to peer out at the landscape before them.

"Almost there, get ready. Remember, you need to clear the way and give the signal for us to send help."

"Got it."

The helicopter took a pass over the house before landing. Smoke rose into the sky, and Marcel's hands clenched. "Why is the Shield down?" he said, looking at Fenris. "Frances ..."

Fenris tried to think of another reason the house's protection had failed that didn't mean death. The helicopter set down, and they hopped off. With the painkiller, Fenris had forgotten about his leg, and he fell hard onto his knees, ripping the stitches the medic had hastily sewn. He swore, and Marcel helped him up. "Got it?"

"Yeah. Come on."

Marcel jogged alongside Fenris, who grabbed him by the arm. "Don't get ahead of me. You have no Shield. I can't protect you from behind."

"I'm still here, aren't I?" Marcel snapped.

They dashed up the lawn to the yard gate. There was a zapping sound, and Fenris jumped on Marcel, tumbling down with him before a stream of acid shot where he had been standing. As it was, drops fell on them, burning through their clothes and hitting their skin.

"Where did that come from?"

Another barrage of acid flew at them, breaking Marcel and Fenris apart on either side of the spill. At the same time, an unnatural wind kicked up as it swirled around both men.

"Watch out!" cried a voice, and a massive fireball was launched from the patio, scattering several enemy Gifted. Streams of electricity followed, throwing one of them to the ground, screaming in pain. Fenris's eyes stayed on the fireball, which expertly pinballed several of the enemy at once.

"Toby?" he whispered in awe.

"You're alive!"

Fenris and Marcel whirled around to see Toby and Erin, looking battered but rather pleased with themselves. Marcel rushed to them with Fenris following at a slower pace, his leg aching and bleeding. Toby had lost control of the fireball, and it careened into a lawn chair, bursting into flames. Fenris had to smile, it was so ridiculous.

"Nice fireball."

"Thanks! Erin's been helping me. They told us you were dead."

"Back at you. Where's everyone else?"

"Most everyone who isn't a fighter is down below. Sophie. Frances. The Aguilars—they're all down there. Sara ..."

Fenris stilled, wanting to sink into the ground.

"Where is she?" asked Marcel.

"We don't know," said Erin. "Earlier, several of us were running interference, trying to keep the enemy occupied while everyone else could get downstairs."

"Where's the other fighters? We were told you were all dead."

Erin scoffed. "No way. They're scattered, dealing with skirmishes. At this point, we have everything more or less under control."

Marcel looked at Fenris. "She's here. Somewhere. We'll find her." He returned his attention to Toby. "You said Frances is down below?"

"Yes, she's been having labor pains."

"What? It's too early!"

Erin snorted. "Tell that to the baby."

Wild-eyed, Marcel spun around, and Fenris pushed him. "Go to her."

"Are you—"

"Go! I'll find Sara."

Marcel dashed away. Fenris turned back to the others. "What's out there, past the patio?"

"No telling."

"Okay. Stay here and keep guard on the house. Listen, the Feds will be here with their own Gifted—"

"The Feds have Gifted on their side?"

"Yes, and I don't have time to—listen, don't blow them away, okay?"

Toby grinned. "Got it, boss!"

Fenris squared his shoulders, cursed his wounded leg, and shot off into the smoke to find his wife.

ONE LAST FIGHT

S ara pushed herself up from the ground. The light had changed, and she wondered how long she had been out. She pressed her hand to her abdomen, praying she hadn't landed too hard when she had been thrown back.

Prickles danced up the back of her neck. It was too quiet. Except—there was the sound of fighting in the distance. It was hard to see anything with the smoke drifting in and out. The smell of burnt wood flared in her nostrils, and she wondered if Toby had let loose another fireball.

Her gaze caught movement, and she ducked behind the wall of the bathhouse. A tall, lean figure limped toward her, drifting in and out of the smoke like a ghost not quite materialized. Sara tried to breathe, but the fumes sent her into a wracking cough. The figure stopped moving, and a strange sensation washed over her. Like someone was using a Gift to sense her out ... a nudge.

She *knew* that nudge.

"Fenris!" she screamed. The figure cried out and began hobbling in her direction. Sara staggered a few steps before falling into his embrace. His strong arms crushed her, lifting her off her feet. Kisses rough and tender all at once.

"I thought you were dead!" he sobbed while her fingers brushed away his tears. His shaking hands held her face.

"You're alive? They told me—"

"I know. Sara, sweetheart, I'm so sorry."

"Don't leave me again," she whispered against his lips. Their foreheads tipped into each other, breathing each other in, eyes locked.

"I won't. I promise," he said hoarsely. "I thought you would be safe, I swear—"

She shushed him with another kiss before jumping back. "Sophie!"

"She's down below. I saw Toby and Erin on my way in."

"Did Marcel and Durgan come back?"

"Marcel is already down with Frances," Fenris hesitated. "We got Laurel out. Durgan ..."

Seeing her husband's face go pale and tears well back up in his eyes, Sara moaned. She brought his head to her shoulder and held him while running her hands through his sweaty hair, trying to soothe his hurt.

When he pulled away, a shaky smile tipped at one corner of his mouth. "You're not hurt, are you? Do we need Marcel?"

"No, but I want to find Sophie—Wait! There's something I need to tell you."

"Now?"

"Yes, I should have told you before you left—"

"Well," dripped a voice from behind Fenris. "Isn't this a charming reunion?"

Sara felt Fenris stiffen, and her knees went weak. It had been months since she last heard that voice, but it had come up in her nightmares often enough to recognize it.

"How many?" he muttered, not moving.

Sara peered over his shoulder. "Josephine. A guard on either side. They have those weapons."

Fenris took a deep breath. "Okay," he whispered. He whipped around, throwing pure power at the three. It collided with the electricity shooting out of the guns, and the resulting explosion threw them all to the ground. Fenris struggled to his feet, hooking his arm around Sara, and raced to the bathhouse. As soon as they reached cover, he groaned and fell to one knee.

"What happened?" Sara cried out at the sight of blood soaking through his pants.

"I'll—be okay. I think."

"Why didn't Marcel—"

"Long story. I need ... we need to figure this out." He risked a look around the bathhouse and saw Josephine and her minions recovering. "Well, you've always wanted to see me fight. You're about to get a close-up view. You ready for this?"

"I'm ready for anything now that you're here."

Fenris kissed her and whispered, "You're amazing."

"How do we do this?"

"Let me think."

"We don't have time."

"My Shield won't hold against those guns, but yours does, right?"

"Yes."

"You can't cover me, or my Gifts won't work against them. This is going to take precise timing."

"Mine is offensive, too, don't forget."

"Oh, I haven't. I've used it. You need to—"

Sara shoved his shoulder. "You stole my Gift!"

"Ow! Of course, I did. It's incredible. You think I'm going to let that go—"

"How dare you, without even asking!"

"Focus, Sara! You're going to need to bring your Gift in and out to work with me, or we won't get far."

"Fine. What's the code?"

"The co—what?"

"The thing you and Hugo say to each other. Released?"

This teased a grin from him. "Unleashed. But that works, too. You ready?"

They both jumped from behind the building. Josephine and her men were closing in. The men raised their guns to fire. Fenris distracted them with a blast he knew they would see coming, but they weren't prepared for Sara's massive bubble of light that emerged around her and Fenris. The blue, electric crackle of the guns bounced off her Shield and ricocheted around them.

With a smirk, Josephine waved her hand, that diabolical whip emerging. She cracked it against the Shield. Sara gasped, but the Shield held. After two more snaps in succession, she was pale and sweaty. Fenris could see her strength waning.

"Sara!"

She shook her head. "I can't fight that whip! If she snaps at me again—"

Fenris dashed forward as Josephine was bringing her whip back again. It slapped against the golden bubble. Sara shrieked, and the bubble collapsed. Fenris crouched as a gun crackled overhead, his arms crossing as he threw an ice dagger from one hand and a fireball from the other. Both struck the guards on either side, sending them to the ground. The whip slashed across his chest, and he fell back with a scream.

Sara cried out and her bubble was back, covering him. Fenris clutched at his chest, his heart speeding, stopping, speeding again. A great ball of light separated from the Shield and sped to Josephine, but a flick of the whip dissipated it easily.

Fenris rolled over with a groan, not sure he wasn't dying. "Keep throwing those things. Let me out."

"She'll kill you!"

"Keep distracting her."

In a flash, the bubble fell back, exposing him, then pushed out again, with fat, golden drops falling like rain upon Josephine. With the Shield gone, Fenris was ready, throwing both hands out at Josephine with the full force of his remaining power. The whip blew into bits of light, scattered around them.

Josephine laughed. With a dramatic sweep, she unsheathed out her sword. It glowed with a silver beam of light.

"Did you think that was my only Gift?" she sneered.

Sara pushed the bubble back over Fenris. One swipe of the sword cut through it, and Sara collapsed with a cry to the ground, unmoving.

Rage shot through Fenris, and he lunged at the woman. The silver sword flashed at him, but he ducked under. He shot a fireball at her, yet she batted it away, sending it speeding away into the pool. "You can't beat me, Fenrir. You should have learned by now."

His hands tingled, and a secret awareness lit up the neurons in his overactive brain.

"You sure about that?" With a casual wave of his hand, a golden whip of his own emerged.

Josephine's eyes went wide in surprise. "You can't!"

"Oh, but I think I can." Fenris snapped it at her, getting tangled up with the sword. Sparks flew all around them. For a second, Fenris feared he would lose control. He jerked, and the sword was torn from her hands and went clattering across the courtyard tiles, its light fading.

"You see," he said, pacing around her. "You're not so special after all."

With another crack of his whip, he struck her down. Josephine lay there, eyes wild with terror. Fenris stood over her, the end of the whip undulating in the air, a golden tendril of potential death.

"No," he muttered. "I'm not going to kill you. Not because you don't deserve it, but because I don't deserve to carry another death on my conscience."

Fenris paused, considered all he had been through, and shrugged. "Then again, I'm no saint." He cracked the whip once more, leaving her unconscious. The whip's color turned soft green, and he roped it around her body.

At the sound of a small whimper, he spun to see Sara trying to sit up. He rushed to her. "Sweetheart, tell me where you hurt."

"I don't—know—" Without hesitating, he scooped her up into his arms and started limping to the house. She protested weakly.

"You don't need to—shouldn't we do something about them back there?"

"The guards will be out a while."

"Josephine?"

"She's not going to bother us again."

Once inside the house, he set Sara down on a sofa and knelt in front of her. She bent to kiss him as he began searching her for injuries. "I'm all right, Fen."

"You sure?" He sighed with relief and pulled her down onto the floor and into his arms. "I love you so much," he mumbled into her hair. Strawberries. How he had missed that scent.

Mid-kiss, she stopped him, her eyes sparkling. "Fen—you need to know—"

"In a minute ..." He kissed her again.

"I'm sorry to interrupt—" came a voice out of nowhere. Fenris yelped and blasted into the wall, missing the suited man by inches.

"Careful."

"Never sneak up on a fighter." Fenris rose to his feet, swaying until Sara helped steady him.

"Rough day?"

"Rough year."

Senator Jacobs gave him a rueful smile before turning his attention to Sara. With a courteous incline of his head, he murmured, "At your service, ma'am."

"Senator, my wife, Sara. This is Senator Jacobs. Josephine is tied up out there, near the pool. Not sure how long she'll be out. I might have ... er ... inflicted some permanent damage."

"No harm, no foul. We have some backup ideas if she does come to." Jacobs snapped his fingers, and several black clad figures rushed past him toward the courtyard. "Thanks for what you've done, Trygg. I'll be seeing you."

"That's it?" Sara demanded. Both men stared at her, taken aback. "That's all you have to say? 'Thanks for what you've done?' You take my husband, almost kill him. Leave the rest of us to deal with all this—"

"Your wife has some sass," murmured Jacobs.

"You have no idea," said Fenris with a proud grin.

Jacobs sighed. "Tell you what. When all this is cleaned up, and you've had a chance to rest, come see me at my office. My real office. Let's talk and figure out what we can do for your—for *our* people. Together."

He held out his hand to Fenris. After a momentary hesitation, Fenris took it. "Deal."

Jacobs raised an eyebrow to Sara, questioning. She gave him a pert nod and muttered, "That's a start."

"I can see I'm going to have to work hard for her vote. Later, Trygg." With those words, Senator Jacobs snapped his fingers again and disappeared. Fenris swore.

"I didn't know he could do that, too! How many Gifts does he have? I need to—" Sara's lips were on his again, and he fell silent. One long kiss later, he whispered, "Let's go find the others. I want to see my girl."

⁓✳︎⁓

Sara knew she would never forget the look on his face when Sophie cried out "Daddy!" and rushed toward Fenris.

Startled, he froze until Sophie had her arms around his neck. He squeezed his eyes shut and held her, murmuring all the while, "Soph ... My sweet girl ..." They remained that way a long time, and more than a few pairs of eyes were wet afterward.

Marcel's safe return had been effective at easing the labor pains Frances was experiencing. After a rather excitable argument in Spanish between the two of them, it concluded with Frances weeping in her husband's arms, and him cracking jokes to cover up his own relief at being with her once again.

It was fortunate Mrs. Aguilar had recovered by the time her two boys returned, or they might have gone on a rampage of vengeance. As it was, she hugged them both and set about rummaging up a meal in the kitchen. Like magic, delicious smells began to float across the ruined courtyard.

Fenris and Marcel surveyed the property, taking notes on the damage.

"What a mess," said Marcel.

"Let's be thankful the property is all that was damaged. I can't believe we didn't lose anyone."

"Yeah."

It would take weeks to repair, but Fenris found himself excited for the challenge. Sometimes to work with one's hands and not think about the simmering powers always lurking beneath the surface was a healing unto itself. They stood in silence until Fenris cleared his throat. "I'm—sorry about what I did to you back there. You have no idea—"

"It's okay." said Marcel. "Durgan told me what you said."

"No. It's not okay. Look. I've lost a lot of people over the years. You and Sara—you are the ones that would break me. I wanted to protect you, but you're right. I'm not the boss of you or your life."

"You were right, too." Marcel rubbed the back of his neck. "What it does to ... it changes you. I don't regret it. It felt good to fight for once. That said, I think I'll stick with healing from now on."

"Speaking of which ... think you could manage this gunshot? I'm not going to lie. It really hurts."

"Maybe. If you ask me nicely."

"Please," growled Fenris.

They began laughing but then fell silent. Fenris shuffled his feet and muttered, "Come here, you idiot," before pulling Marcel in for a hug.

"I always knew I was your one true love," cracked Marcel.

"Shut up."

WINTERPAST

They couldn't leave as quickly as Fenris wanted. There were things to be done around the house. Marcel had poured out healing powers to everyone who needed it. They all sat down to eat, with Mrs. Aguilar fussing over Tudor, shoving food at him, signaling he was now the newest adopted member of the Aguilar family. While they ate, Marcel and Fenris told everyone about their adventures.

"I have a question for you both," interrupted Sara at one point. "Marcel's other Gift. If he never used it, how did you even know it was even there? After the Changing?"

Marcel and his mother exchanged glances, and Fenris fixed his gaze upon his plate of food. Frances was the one who spoke up.

"It was Fen. He was picking up Gifts from everyone and had no idea what they all did. On one of his first encounters with Hunters, he shot out this black smoke and—"

Fenris stiffened and gripped Sara's hand. "Don't tell her the whole story."

"Well," Frances faltered. "He found out what it did, and we traced it back to Marcel."

"You had never used it?" Sara asked Marcel.

"Hmm, I hadn't yet. I didn't even know I had that potential until Fen told me. After that I practiced it when I knew no one was around, to understand how to control it in case I never needed to use it."

"I thought Fen had to see a Gift in action or something to pick one up?"

Fenris shrugged. "I don't know. Maybe I was around Marcel enough to pick it up."

"You've never tried it since that one time?"

"No. It terrified me. Plus, it drained my powers for days afterward. Even if it didn't do that—I never wanted to use it again."

Sara had more questions, but let the topic drop.

The hardest moment for Fenris was telling the group what had become of Durgan. Even though he made it clear Durgan was with them in the end, the hurt and confusion would take a long time to heal. There was a long silence after telling of his death.

"Do you think Laurel will be okay?" asked Marcel.

"She has her mother, and she's smart," said Fenris. "Tough. I'll keep an eye on her."

"*We'll* keep an eye on her."

"Yes, okay. We." Fenris smiled through the ache in his heart.

After all, there was always a reason for why things happened the way they did. That was enough. He didn't feel the need to understand it anymore.

⁓✳⁓

Fighters and office people began heading home, eager to sleep in their own beds. They all agreed to meet the next day to regroup and figure out what to do next. Toby and Erin disappeared together. Tudor volunteered to ensure that Laurel had made it home to her mother. Hugo fell asleep on the sofa, snoring.

The sun was low in the sky when Fenris felt free to gather his little family and go home. He wanted his books. And his piano. Most of all, he wanted to be alone with his wife.

"Right. Let's go." Fenris smiled. "I can't wait to be back home. Nice and quiet, with just the three of us."

"You mean the four of us," said Sara, mischief lighting up her eyes.

"Four?" Fenris arched an eyebrow, concern passing over his face. "You okay, Red? You sure you didn't hit your head or anything?"

Sara giggled. His bafflement increased, and he let out an uneasy chuckle. "I know you love Marcel and missed him too, but we can't take him home with us. He's not a stray dog you can load up into the car. He already has an owner, and I don't think Frances would—"

"Oh, Fen ..." whispered Sara.

Frances laughed out loud.

"What?" Exasperated, Fenris spun around and saw realization beginning to dawn on Marcel's face. In fact, Marcel was *beaming*. "What is going on?"

Everyone burst out laughing, and Fenris stood there glaring, thinking over Sara's words. What had she said ...? With a gasp, he whirled to face Sara again and stared at her, white-faced and stunned.

"Fen, are you okay?" Sara asked, disturbed by his absolute silence. "Marcel, is he—?"

"I don't know, Sara. You might have made him finally crack."

"Fen ..." Sara reached up and put her hand on his cheek. He blinked at her touch.

"You—you—you're not—" He choked on his words.

Sara smiled, her eyes shining. Fenris inhaled and launched himself at her, catching her in his arms. A muffled sob came from him as he buried his face into the crook of her neck. "You—you—how long?"

"More than three months."

His face fell as he did the math. "You knew before I left?"

She hung her head, embarrassed.

"Oh, sweetheart. You should have told me. I never, *never* would have left ..." He kissed her—and kissed her—until a cough from Marcel interrupted them. He pulled away, his eyes searching hers. "I should be furious with you—"

"I'm sorry."

"It's okay, I guess." He took a step back and laughed. "We need to get you home! You need rest. And we need to do ... things. I don't know. What do we need to do?"

"My stars," said Frances with a roll of her eyes. "We won't be able to live with the man, he'll be crazy."

"He's perfect," Sara said, bringing him close.

He rested his forehead on hers. "I'm not, and I don't deserve you. Or any of this," he whispered fervently. "But I'll take it."

"Hey," Marcel piped up. "Before you go, question. What does *winterpast* mean? You never said."

Sara glared at Fenris. "You *told* him?"

"Not exactly. It's a long story, but he knows now. Do you want to tell him?"

"Oh, go on if he knows already. We're all family here."

Fenris gave her another long kiss, then looked over her head at Marcel. His deep voice was quiet as he said, "'My beloved spake, and said unto me, rise up, my love, my fair one, and come away. For, lo, the winter is past, the rain is over and gone; The flowers appear on the earth; the time of the singing of birds is come.'"

There was a long silence following the words. Marcel affirmed them with a vehement, "Amen."

෴

Sophie raced up the walk to the front door, but Fenris stayed near Sara, taking her arm when they reached that tricky step. "Watch out for the—"

"Step. I know, Fen. You are *not* going to be hovering around me the next six months."

"Yes, I am and—six months! That's it? Sara, I don't know—" All his anxieties began to overtake his joy, and he looked at her in a panic.

She took his hand and squeezed it. "The fridge is desolate, and we have nothing fresh in the house. Why don't you take care of that and make us some dinner. I'm desperate for a shower and then I'll unpack. Yes?"

Thankful to be told what to do for once, Fenris bobbed his head obediently. Sara chuckled as he dashed off. It was going to be a *very* long six months.

෴

Fenris chattered with Sophie while putting away groceries and orchestrating their meal, hearing all about the time he was away and telling her some of the funnier parts of his own story. She giggled hard over the bowling.

"Will you take me bowling someday?"

"Absolutely. We can even go with Uncle Marcel when Teresa is a tiny bit older."

"Teresa is getting a baby."

"That's what I hear."

"You and Mommy are getting a baby."

"Yes!" he said, happiness filling his heart.

"Will I have to leave?"

Fenris stopped grating cheese and studied the child. Her little face was pinched with worry. He leaned over the counter. "Why would you ask that?"

"Because I'm not really yours."

Fenris set the cheese down. "You are absolutely ours. Hey, did you know I was there when you were born? I've been right here with you all along. So when you think about it, all this time I've just been waiting for my turn. And you know what?"

"What?"

"You were worth the wait." He tweaked her nose, and she laughed. Taking a deep sigh of relief, he went back to grating cheese. "Good. That's settled."

"Can I have an olive?"

"Sure. Watch out for pits."

"There's never any pits."

"Life *is* the pits, kiddo."

Sophie giggled.

⟡

Dinner was nothing more than frozen lasagna and a salad, but it was the most delicious meal they could recall eating, cozied up at home and together. At bedtime, Fenris insisted on putting Sophie to bed.

"I'll sit with her a while," Fenris said, cuddling up next to her. Sara kissed Sophie and Fenris both on their foreheads and left the two of them, smiling.

"Are you happy to be back home, Soph?"

"Yes! And I want stories!"

"Whoa, okay. Not tonight, but yes, we will do stories again. Will you want something new or something we've read before? I think I have a children's edition of Dante—"

"I want *Frog and Toad*!"

"An excellent choice." Fenris chuckled. So much for Dante. "We'll start tomorrow."

Sophie bounced up and down in her bed. He handed her Bun and tried to tuck her in.

"Settle down now, you need to go to sleep."

Sophie giggled and bounced all the harder. "I See something and I want to show you."

Fenris froze. He'd had quite enough of that for the moment. "I don't know, Soph. Maybe another time."

"It's a hap-hap-happy thing," she sang.

"Well, if that's the case ..." He remained tense as closed his eyes and reached out to her, waiting to See with her.

Colored mist swirled around him before settling on the edges of his vision. Through Sophie's eyes, he saw them both decorating a Christmas tree. He laughed with Sara, bending to kiss her blossoming belly. Sugarplum fairies danced across the stage of a ballet. The colors bled through the image and rearranged themselves to show the house, full of children. Laughing, happy children. Redheads and some with black curls. Messy house. Fenris laughed, already knowing Sara wasn't the best housekeeper.

His heart thudded with a painful joy as the colors came and went, showing the passing of the years. A black-haired boy swinging a baseball bat. Sophie in a white dress, beautiful. Sara snuggled against him on the sofa while they watched a ball game. The feel of her hand in his.

The mist swirled over his vision, and he was back in Sophie's room. Fenris took a deep breath, awestruck, tears stinging his eyes. It wasn't a settled future. Things, so many things, could alter everything. But it was a path that led to joy, and he was willing to step out and walk that path, grabbing what happiness he could out of this life he had been given.

This wild, crazy, amazing life.

He smiled down at his little girl. "That—that was nice, Soph. Time to go to sleep, okay?"

She curled up in the blankets as he kissed her forehead.

"Night-night, Daddy."

Fenris swallowed hard. He hoped Ted would approve of the title. "Nighty-night. Love you."

In a happy daze, he walked down the hallway. A soft voice lured him like a siren's call, and he paused at the studio doorway. Sara hummed as she unpacked her art. Fenris watched her for a moment before moving on to the library. The aching happiness in his heart was almost too much.

It would be nice to settle down with a good book, but as he searched the shelves, he couldn't decide what he wanted to read. Nothing fit his mood. His thoughts wandered, and he jumped when Sara's voice cut into his reverie.

"I'm sorry, what did you say?"

"Not often I startle you. Everything okay?"

"No, it's not okay." He dragged Sara over, trapping her between his arms that held on to a bookshelf on either side of her. "Everything is perfect."

He kissed her, lightly at first, with a slow heat building. How long had it been since they could take their time, breathe each other in, holding each other's hearts?

"I want you," he mumbled between kisses.

"I'm right here."

Happiness bubbling up, he kissed her longer, deeper. He pressed her against the bookshelf. Her arms were around him, tugging him closer. Still closer. His breath came short, and his heart thumped so hard he was sure she must hear it.

"Sara ... I *need* you."

"I am yours."

He had his hands on her then, around her waist and almost lifting her up. A few books tumbled down, and one fell on his head. He yelped and pulled her away from the bookshelves. After contemplating various furniture pieces, he opted to move to the bedroom.

They made their way down the hallway almost dancing—always kissing, their hands caressing. They crashed into a wall on their way to the bedroom, fell through the bathroom door, tripped over a laundry basket—her giggles and his deep, throaty laugh echoing through the house.

As they tumbled into the moonlit bed, Fenris paused, taking her in. She brushed her hand over his cheek, and he thought his heart would explode. The vision had not shown him everything; there were things even Sophie would never guess. Only he would know of these quiet hours, these nights of laughter and love. This woman—this woman!—who had torn down his walls and fears, who had healed him with her love, changing and rearranging the map of his heart. A lifetime with her would never be enough, but he would treasure every second he was given. Sunshine-filled mornings, firelit evenings, and these long, slow, delicious hours holding her in his arms.

"Where are you, Fen?" Sara whispered. "You're far away again."

"Sorry. I was thinking."

"That much I gathered. You going to tell me?"

"All the love stories I've read over the years, even the truly great ones. You know, they all got one thing wrong."

"What was that?"

"None of them had you."

BACK TO THE BEGINNING

F enris neither noticed nor cared that it was a beautiful spring morning. All he wanted was a cup of coffee.

He walked with a determination that was, if not cheerful, at least came close enough. Passing by a parked stroller, he took a quick peek inside. Fenris couldn't quite prevent the smile that lit up his face when he glimpsed the chubby cheeks of a baby. Shaking his head in amusement, he crossed the street.

As he pulled a key from his pocket, his attention was arrested by a sign at the door of the nearby coffee house. *Change in management. Gifted welcome.* Fenris stared, scenes of the past flooding through him.

"It's fantastic coffee. But I can't. They won't let us ... well, me ..."

"They don't allow Gifted? That's preposterous!"

Exploding coffee mugs burst into his memory, and he outright chuckled. Maybe later he would get a coffee here and see if it was as good as he remembered. For now, it was time to work.

He unlocked the gate and trotted down the stairs. Several passcodes later, he entered the familiar basement office. There had been a few changes implemented since they had returned to this location, with all the security details revised and updated. The glass-enclosed office no longer existed. It had been emptied and dismantled, and the new open space filled with comfortable chairs.

His own desk remained in the same location as before, a little larger than its predecessor. He was the boss, after all, and he needed room for the photos. The one with him and his dad was still there, but there were new additions. A wedding photo. A family photo of him, Sara, and Sophie hiking near Mt. Shasta. His favorite was a single shot of his wife he had captured one day, with her familiar, sweet smile that always sent a happy jolt to his heart no matter how many times he saw it. Fenris reached out and brushed a finger over it and sighed, looking at the empty desk next to his.

Even some of the best changes in life could hold a bittersweet edge.

He smiled at the sight of Marcel, bouncing in late as usual, calling out his greetings to all. Some things never changed, and for that, Fenris was grateful.

"Hey buddy, how you holding up?" Marcel asked as he arrived with two cups of coffee, handing one over.

"I'm fine. Everything is fine."

"Liar. You look like you haven't slept in a week. You know it's only going to get worse."

"Thanks. Hey, be sure and tell Hugo he's in charge of the fighters for the next few weeks. I don't care if the whole world is burning."

"I will, but I don't think you'll have anything to worry about. Those new proposals by Senator Jacobs have done a good job shutting down the Hunters for the time being."

"Never mind that I wrote them. I do all the work and he gets all the credit."

"Maybe you should think about running for office someday."

"There's an idea."

"They wouldn't know what hit them."

Fenris paused sipping his coffee and barked out a laugh at the idea. Marcel chuckled as he settled at his own desk. Sharp words came from across the office as Erin bickered with one of her brothers, whom Fenris had recruited into the Guild based on Sara's recommendation. He laughed softly. Everything was back to normal.

Well, almost.

With an exasperated huff, Fenris pulled out his new reading glasses and got to work.

⁂

Fenris was pouring a fresh cup of coffee and stifling a yawn when Marcel yelled out for him. "Fen! It's Mama on the phone!"

He rolled his eyes. "Tell her I had to skip church because Sara—"

"She's calling *about* Sara! It's baby time!"

Fenris froze and stood there, never noticing the coffee overflowing the cup and spilling onto the floor.

"Fen? You okay?" Marcel smacked his arm. "Snap out of it!"

Fenris exploded, slamming the coffee pot down. "Blasted woman! Why did she call you and not me?"

"I can't imagine. You always handle everything so calmly, too."

But Fenris had blown past him, yelling some nonsense. Erin darted out of his way as she approached Marcel. "What's with him?"

"Sara."

"Everything okay?"

"Fine as far as I know but, well. You know him."

Erin rolled her eyes.

Fenris spluttered curses from his desk. "I can't find my keys, Marcel!"

"They're probably in your—"

"Marcel!" Light shot through the office, bouncing off the walls.

"Okay, okay. You know, you might be overreacting a little ..."

The lights and computer screens flickered.

"How dare you steal my Gift!" Erin snapped.

The building trembled. Marcel held up a hand. "Yeah, whoa. How about I drive you? Erin, can you—"

"Got it. Get him out of here before he brings the office down on us."

Marcel grabbed Fenris by the arm and hustled him out. "Sheesh, Fen. It's just a baby. Frances has had two, and I never—"

Fenris came to a dead stop, a frantic expression on his face.

"What if I can't do this?"

"What are you talking about?"

"This. All of this."

"Fen." Marcel edged closer. "You're going to be a great dad. Look how you are with Sophie."

"She wasn't a baby ..."

"Trust me, this baby is going to be a lot easier to handle than your pint-sized prophet." Marcel chuckled. Even Fenris cracked a smile. "You okay? Let's at least get you to the car first. Baby steps."

"Very funny."

"I thought so. Let's go."

⁂

Sophie was waiting at the door and flew into Fenris's arms as he ran up the walk. She was all smiles and light. He hugged her, needing it more than he could say. "How's my girl?"

"*Abuela* says the baby is coming."

"Yes, she called us." He smiled at Sophie referring to Mama as her grandmother. At this point, he guessed she knew Spanish as well as he did. "How is Mommy?"

"She's yelling a lot. Laughing, too. She's wanting you, Daddy."

A woman's cry rang out as they entered the house. Fenris let Sophie slide down and staggered against the wall. Marcel patted him on the back. "Better get in there, buddy."

"Marcel ..."

"It will be fine. I'll be right here if you need me."

Fenris looked at his friend, his eyes stinging. "You always have been." He cleared his throat. "Right. Here we go."

With that, he walked to the bedroom, to a new world waiting for him.

༄⁂༄

"Never in my life ..." Frances exclaimed. "You okay, Fen?"

"Yeah. Sorry about that."

Sara laughed. "Poor Fen. Our mighty hero felled at last by a tiny baby."

Frances stood over Fenris, glaring. "Never mind the hours of labor your wife put in, you have to go and faint the moment things get—"

"I didn't *faint*. I just got a little woozy," he insisted, but his heart was anxious. "Sara? Are you really okay? That was horrible."

"It was the easiest labor I've ever seen," Mrs. Aguilar chuckled as she approached Fenris with a small bundle. "Now, are you ready to hold this baby or not?"

Eyes wide, Fenris could only nod as the bundle was placed into his arms. "Wow," he whispered, his heart beating wildly. He had thought he learned a thing or two about love over the past two years, but this was a love like he had never imagined.

"Come here, Fen." Sara patted the bed beside where she lay, propped up by pillows.

Fenris stood, testing his feet before walking, snuggling the baby. He eased onto the bed and kissed Sara's head. "You're amazing. I can't believe you did this."

"*We* did it."

"Well, you did the all work."

"But all the midnight diaper changes are yours."

His throat closed in a hot knot that he struggled to swallow down. He looked at his wife and blurted, "You're so beautiful."

"Oh, Fen." Sara reached her hand to his cheek and brought him down for a light kiss. "I love you."

"I love you more," he said. He kissed the fuzzy baby head. "You too."

Marcel poked his head into the room. "Can we come in? Got a little girl ready to meet her brother."

Fenris waved them in. Sophie approached shyly and took a quick peek. Smiling with sisterly satisfaction, she crawled into the bed and snuggled down next to Sara. Marcel caught his friend's eyes and grinned. "Made it through, buddy?"

"Barely. Thanks for everything."

"Anytime. What's his name?"

"Robert Marcel."

Mrs. Aguilar nodded. "Thank heavens you chose a proper name. I was worried it might be Odin. Or—"

"Fafnir?" suggested Sara with a sly look at Fenris. He smiled, heart melting at the memory of the first day Sara arrived at the office.

The day he came back to life.

Fenris gazed again at his son, enraptured. He cocked his head, trying to determine who Robert took after. A thatch of black hair was the only obvious inheritance Fenris could see. "He looks awfully red and squished or something. That can't be normal."

Sara burst out laughing. "He's perfect. Calm down."

"That will be the day," Marcel muttered, rolling his eyes.

Frances had left the room and returned with her own baby, practically throwing her at Marcel. "Take this one! She needs a change."

"You should—"

"Are you arguing with me?"

Marcel sighed and called out, "Teresa, get sissy a diaper." Turning to Fenris he grumbled, "Why did you get a boy on the first shot?"

"Don't worry," murmured Fenris, never taking his eyes away from his son. "You have several coming."

"Uh, what?"

Fenris and Sophie looked at each other, and she giggled. Marcel groaned. "You guys have got to stop doing that. It's creeping me out."

A dark-haired toddler trotted in, dragging a heavy diaper bag behind her. Marcel winked at Fenris. "Watch and learn from the best, buddy!"

Sara looked at Mrs. Aguilar. "Mama, I remember a long time ago you told me something I've never forgotten. That for Fen and me, our story wasn't over yet. How's this for a happy ending?"

Alicia Aguilar didn't answer immediately. Instead, she scanned the room, seeing those she had loved and cared for all these the years. Frances, who was busy cleaning up the space with efficiency and thoroughness. With Teresa on his knee, Marcel made silly faces at his younger daughter, causing the baby to gurgle. Sara was snuggling Sophie.

As for Fenris—he sat with one arm around his wife, the other holding his son. His eyes were bright and clear, joy shining through.

There were no more shadows of darkness hiding away.

Even as the Changing had altered everything about his life, tearing it apart, love was now changing him into something new. Hero, husband, father ... the world lay at his feet once more.

She shook her head at the wonder of it all.

"Oh *mija*, you are so young," said Mrs. Aguilar, smiling. "No, Sara, this isn't the end for you and Fenris. Your story is just beginning."

As I sit at my desk with the February sun streaming in through the window, my publisher is tsking at me (very nicely), because I've taken far too long to write these acknowledgments. I'm normally good about deadlines, but for weeks I've put this off, although I wasn't quite sure why until now.

It's because I don't want to say goodbye.

I have so much love for this world and all the characters that inhabit it. Mrs. Aguilar with her loving wisdom (can we just all agree that we want to be like her when we grow up?); Marcel's funny cackle and loyal friendship; Sara's quiet bravery and affectionate tolerance of Fen's eccentricities—they've all been such a joy to write.

And then there's Fenris. How can I possibly say goodbye to my sweet, overly-caffeinated, emotionally messy Fen? From the moment he appeared in my head—angry, confused, always stressed, and so very sad—I knew deep down there was a heart of gold that only needed a little nudge to reveal itself.

In book trope parlance, I fell first, and I fell hard.

Fen was so easy to work with, so earnest. We understood each other, and his emotional growth over these two books has been such a satisfying thing to unwrap. I also grew as an author while writing these books, and for that I am eternally grateful.

But I remind myself, I don't have to say goodbye, not really. His story will live on in my head and maybe in yours too. But it is time for me to let go and move on to other things. Perhaps someday I'll revisit this world but, for now, let's leave Fenris & Co. in the best possible place—happy and safe, looking to the future with hope and not despair.

And with that, some thanks to those who gave me hope while writing this book.

For my FFM crew—as usual, thank you for the chaos, the cheese toast, and the laughter. And for the memes. All the memes. I wish every writer had the community we have.

Thank you, Cathy McCrumb and Brigitte Cromey, for your extra eyes, and Katie Fitzgerald for ensuring I got certain Catholic minutia correct. And all my beta readers! Some of you have been around for all three of my books, and I appreciate each and every one of you!

There's not enough words to thank my Sola Sisters—Emily Barnett, Andrea Renae, Katee Stein, and Rachel Lawrence. Especially Katee, who was crucial in helping me flesh out the characters and some key moments. And always a big thanks to Rachel, who loves Fen almost as much as I do and has been his #1 fan since the beginning. You're all the butter to my toast.

A shout out is due to Emilie Haney for the gorgeous covers on both Unleashed and Released. I can't believe I lucked out to have you as the cover designer for my books. I will also be forever grateful to Magnus Carlssen for bringing my characters to life in the audiobooks.

Thank you to everyone on the Quill & Flame team but most of all Anna Augustine, Crystal Grant, and Vanessa Burton ("why is it always you three?"); Brittany Eden and her never-ending font of marketing strategy (see what I did there, Brittany?); my editors Meghan Kleinschmidt, Jessica Gwyn, and Ava Lauren Grayson; and of course, many thanks to AJ Skelly for her unceasing enthusiasm for this story.

To my husband Mitchell and my girls, thank you for your patience and putting up with me when my brain wanders off into another world now and then.

And last (but definitely most important), a huge thank you to everyone who read *Unleashed* and cared enough about the characters to pick up the sequel. Thank you for all the frantic/angry/upset messages you sent me, they give me such joy. Your love and support keeps my creative engine running better than chocolate.

And now it really is time to go.

But in truth, the story is only just beginning.

Soli Deo Gloria

Milton Keynes UK
Ingram Content Group UK Ltd.
UKHW010833230424
441593UK00018B/400/J